From HELL to

the Middle of

HEAVEN

One man's story about pain and torture, to his peace with life.

D.T. SHANNON

From Hell to the Middle of Heaven

One man's story about pain and torture, to his peace with life.

D.T. Shannon

From Hell to the Middle of Heaven

To Yakima

Thank you so much
for the love and the support

D. T. Shannon

[signature]

From Hell to the Middle of Heaven

Copyright © 2016 D.T. Shannon

Acknowledgements

First and foremost I would like to thank God for giving me the strength and the ability to tap into the most creative parts of my mind to be able to finish this book. It has been a long time coming, but it was all worth it at the end. I've spent three years of my life working, and creating this book, which I call my first masterpiece. This book is a testament to the amount of love, and support I had all along the way. Thank you to those who show love and support, those who hate, the ones who won't support, and most of all to all of you that read.

A special thanks to my parents Larry and Tonya who have never stopped supporting me in all that I do, I have been blessed to have both of them in my life and continue to give me guidance through my ups and downs. Growing up I was taught by both of them the value of hard work, but most importantly I was shown by their example.

A Big thanks is needed to my many aunts and uncles on both sides of the family, though they may not see it, they have all influenced me in life and the directions I chose to follow.

I want to thank my Spanish teachers who have kept me on the right path more than once Mrs. Tanika Vincent, Mrs. Elisa Ware, and Miss. Vildalici Paredes. Time after time they have humbled me and showed me different ways to captivate on my creative side; never giving up on me. And I can't forget the ones who are really responsible for me taking this risk, Mrs. Vanitrice Sagoes, who called my mother to let her know I wasn't doing my homework, but I was selling cakes. By the way, she was the only one who extorted me and I couldn't do anything about it. And last but not least Ms. Kanisha Carter, who exposed me to a new world through reading.

Thank you to my best friends Brasheia Shepherd, Charlie Parks, Rudy Simpson, and Contrell Sims. No matter what I do they have always had my back. Love you all!!!

And to my brother for life Tevin "Scooter" Graham dog words cannot explain how much I love you and how much you mean to me, you will always be my right hand man. We have been through so much together and will go through much more, but either way I'm blessed as long as I have you by my side.

And finally to my heart, Bernee "Brooklyn" Jackson-Shannon, my biggest supporter, my best friend for life, and my Buddy!! God really surprised me with this one and I am truly thankful. Without your support, and belief in me I don't think this book would be complete.

Mind Up!

Chocolate Superman

Daniel Tariq, Shannon

Dedication

I would like to dedicate my first published novel to my late grandmother's Cynthia Taylor & Juana Shannon, without them playing an active role in my life then I would not have had the drive to finish this book. I would also like to make a reference to my siblings Alex, Kyle aka Elmo, Justin, and Domonique. They have always pushed me to be the leader and have been my motivation to strive for Greatness since day one. Love you all.

Chapter 1

ᗞECON RICE

I broke into the office with my .38 pulled and ready to unload on Kane. The room was empty and no one seen or heard. His computer was still on and there was coffee inside that ugly yellow and brown mug sitting on the table to the left; it was still hot. Flashbacks of my sister ran through my head. I couldn't take it anymore the pain that the memories gave me were becoming too much to hold on to. As soon as I opened my eyes again I saw the Taser coming my way; to slow to dodge it "**zap**" the surge of electricity screamed through my body locking my muscles to a complete halt. I hit the ground with a thump!! As I lay on the ground still and motionless that feeling came over me again; that warm, embracing feeling. A flash of yellowish golden light blinded me. Let me go back to as far as I can remember on how I even got to this point.

To me my life started when I was seven years old, young Decon Christian Rice, in the back of my grandmother's house in Winter Haven Florida, blowing up toads and lizards with cherry bombs. I was born and raised here, your typical country boy who loved to have fun with nature. My mother was a crack fiend who to this day I've hated with a passion; one for giving me this fucked up name "Decon" and two for not loving me the way a mother should; well that's how I felt at least. That's enough about my mother for right now, I'll get back to her soon. Deloris Rice my grandmother the sweetest woman on Earth, and that's not just because she was the local pastry chef in town. "Hmm the thoughts of her are enough to put a smile on my face every time." Everyone called her "*Mama D*". She was like a mother to everyone in the whole town. Yea sweet Mama D, she's always a good memory. She raised me along with my older sister Mary and two twin cousins: Luke and Lemon. They weren't my real cousins; they were two children that my grandmother adopted. I don't know much about their family except that their mother was a lady of the night if you will. She died one night from what the authorities reported was an accidental overdose, no one knows for sure, and their father was a pimp somewhere in Brooklyn, New York. The twins hated that their father was alive, but didn't want anything to do with them. I ran into him when I got older, but that's a story in its self. The twins are three years older than me. We all caused trouble but they stayed in trouble with Mama D, and the police, especially Luke.

Luke was the youngest of the twins by six minutes; they both were short but he was short and fat with a lazy left eye. He had a hard time breathing and always took a breath after every sentence he spoke, and to top it off he had a strong stuttering problem. People would tease him about that; which was one of the reasons he was always getting in trouble. People would talk about him one second, and the next second they were catching a strong right jab to the face. Luke would bully me and Mary, but let someone else try that and he would set them straight. Lemon on the other hand was the bulky quiet twin. People in the neighborhood would call him straight crazy. He never started trouble but trouble kept ending up in his hand. He stayed to himself a lot and always had to watch his brothers back and get him out of the trouble he was getting into. He was smart both in the streets and in school; I gained my love for working out from Lemon who would help me lift weights. My sister Mary was a year older than me. We were close and from time to time we would hear how much we look alike. Of course we looked alike we had the same parents; but she was the optimistic type. She was also my best friend who understood me and held me when I would cry late at night from missing my mother. As much as I hated my mother, Mary would always defend her, saying stuff like "You know mama loves us right?" I saw the truth, but she couldn't see past the fact that my mother loved the pipe more than her own kids. Mary was tall and light honey-brown like my mother. She had long curly brown hair and soft slim lips I like to think that she got that from Mama D. Her eyes were hazel brown with spots of green, very exotic. She had this crazy birthmark on the corner of her left eye that looked like she had one cat's eye. I love that girl to death, and I would die for her at no cost. **"Bang!"** I was into death at a young age. It brought a smile on my face, and the sight of seeing a huge toad splatter from the cherry bombs I attached to its back was my main source of entertainment. As I looked in the bushes for another toad or even a lizard, Mama D came outside and called my name.

"Decon!!! Come inside Decon time for suppa!" Mama D loved yelling from the kitchen window, "I hate my name" is what I would say to myself every time I heard my name being called out, "comin Mama D." Running into the house I remember her telling me, "Go wash your dirty hands from playin with those toads. GOD's gonna get-cha for killin' his creations!" Mama D was big on the whole church and GOD thing, and every night for dinner she would pray and sing before we could eat. "Oooooh magnify the Looorrrddd for heeee is worthy to be praised!!" Mama D's voice was beautiful, and I loved listening to her sing. But it was something about "GOD" that I didn't trust even as a little kid. As my grandmother would pray over the food, my eyes would peak open; and on one particular Sunday dinner I remember gazing at the gooey macaroni and cheese, hot buttery biscuits, sweet and savory glazed ham, garlic mashed potatoes, and grilled corn on the cob, Mhmmm those Sunday dinners were the best. At the end of all her prayers she would throw in an "And please Lord take care of my daughter and all my grandchildren." Once amen was said it was like a race to the feast. Luke was always the first to put his fork on the meat, "ha-ha fat ass Luke." The house we stayed in was built by my grandfather who was killed at his construction job a few years back, God bless the dead. The house was pretty big, I shared a room with Luke in the basement, Lemon slept in the guest room across the hall, and Mary had a room upstairs next to

Mama D. I hated sleeping with Luke in the same twin sized bed; he pissed the bed till he turned thirteen. Waking up every morning smelling like urine and wet used to piss me off. Lemon would always tell me, "Don't tell no one that Luke pees the bed. He can't help it." I never told anyone about that until this day. I looked up to Lemon. He stood up for us: me, Mary, and Luke, he was a big brother to all of us. Going to school for me was different I wasn't dumb, but I wasn't super genius either. Now Luke, well that's another story. He was held back twice in the 7th grade. Me and him were in the same grade and went to the same school, *Saint Mark's*. Mary skipped a grade and was in the same grade as Lemon at Fair View High School. Me and Luke went to this crazy Christian school full of most of the kids in the town. I hated that school with a passion. We would get taught about Jesus this and Jesus that. The teachers would beat us with paddles if we were caught doing wrong, but I think they used to get off on that shit. It was a Friday and everyone was ready for the weekend, we just got finish with our end of the year test to move on to high school. My math teacher, Mrs. Chavez was also excited ready to never see us again I guess. This was my last class and me and Luke were in it together. "Okay y'all!!" in her country accent "who's ready for the summer break?"

Everyone was excited and ready to have fun, that was everyone except Bobby Walker; this chubby kid who was Black and Asian and had this serious look on his face.

I will never forget his name or face. This motherfucker is one of the reasons I am the way I am to this day. As we were leaving the classroom, I guess I made him upset for stepping on his shoes, "HEY BITCH!!!" that stopped everyone, and Bobby walked up to me and pushed me into the wall. You could tell he was angry. His light skin complexion started to turn red and the hallway shortly became crowded with a mass group of kids who wanted to see a donnybrook. "GET THE FUCK UP!!" He yelled out at me as I picked myself up off the floor, *"POW!"* His fist smashed into my nose causing me to drop to my knees quickly and blood began to flow. Out of nowhere a familiar voice came from behind the crowd, "You fucked with the wrong cousin!" It was Luke rushing through the crowd and punching Bobby in the back of the head, causing him to drop forward. He smashed his face into the floor. *"CRACK"* Everyone heard that sound and we all wondered what happened. But we all knew once we heard the whimpers coming from Bobby. He got up with blood running from his mouth like it's cool. Luke looked at the ground where Bobby was and shouted "I knocked out his tooth!" Everyone busted out with laughter and as always the school's security wrapped Luke up and escorted him out the building; I got up and took off behind the crowd. The walk home was the worst, Luke told me that it was time that I learned how to defend myself and that I should be taking care of my own because he wasn't going to always be there for me. I told myself never again, and that summer I started my love for Martial Arts.

I got into Aikido and GoJu-Ryu that summer and quickly advanced. Bodybuilding was also a major thing in my life at that time, my biggest influence at the time was Dexter Jackson, he is the man. Lemon helped me a lot and I quickly through on some weight going from 140lbs to 174lbs over the summer. This was a major transformation for not only my body, but for my mind and soul. Besides my Martial Arts training I can't hardly remember the 9th and 10th grade, but by this time it was graduation time for my sister. Lemon dropped out, don't know why and he never told us either. All I know is that him and Mama D got into a big fight when it happened. My sister on the other hand was gifted very smart and graduated as the schools Valedictorian, and President of too many clubs and organizations for me to remember. She got numerous awards and scholarship money. She was Mama D's perfect child so to say. At the graduation party Mama D invited everyone to come out and celebrate.

"Come see my baby. She done made it y'all!" Mama D had the biggest smile on her face that day. I had never seen her this happy before. Mary was also excited. It was a great day for everyone and the day ended with nothing going wrong.

That summer I became a black belt in both styles I was taking and crushing competitions left and right. I was labeled as one of the deadliest fighters in Florida. I went on to practice Jujutsu, Wing Chun Kung Fu; a style Bruce Lee was famous for being a practitioner of. This was my get away from the world; this was my serenity. I never stopped practicing the other styles. I just advanced and added more techniques to my tool box. A few weeks after the party, early one Friday morning *"ding dong"* Luke went to go answer the door. I was up meditating when I heard the doorbell. I went to go see who it was at the door from the basement window, but I couldn't make out a face. "Is Deloris home?" I heard the voice say. "Who Mama D? Yea she ho... ho... home wait one minute," Luke replied with excitement. "No, no I'm her daughter I want to surprise her I'm Decon, and Mary's mother." When I heard this my heart stopped, my knees got weak quick and as if I was pregnant, I got sick to my stomach. I couldn't believe my own ears. I went from shocked and sick to straight irate. I locked my door and sat in my anger hoping and wishing that what I heard was a lie. This day was the start of the pain from the memories, the day my mother came home to get me back. "Decon come upstairs!" Mama D yelled for me from the top of the basement stair case. I didn't move, tried my best to ignore her but she kept calling 'till finally I heard a knock on the other side of the door. "Boy we don't lock doors around here!" I opened the door to see Mama D and standing next to her was who I knew as Kimberly Ann Rice, my mother.

"Hey Decon, can I get a hug?" Her arms fully extended and a yellow tented smile across her face. I looked at her with slight disgust and without thinking I said, "Why is she here?" I asked Mama D. I could see my mother getting a little uneasy and uncomfortable with the way I was acting. "Decon it's me your mother." I faced her and said, "My mother never left me. You're a stranger, and I was taught not to speak to them." Mama D grabbed my arm and slapped me across the face. The tone of my voice and what I said made her angry. "Boy don't you ever disrespect your mother like that, now apologize." I turned to my mother and moved closer for a hug, just being around her made me sick and touching her again all these years it hurt harder than any other pain I felt before. My mother stood about five eight and she was wearing this ugly brown and green sweater with a few bleach stains on the collar. She had on these brown sweat pants that she kept pulling up on her and these house slippers that you could tell she wore everywhere but the house. Her honey brown hair was pulled back still curly, but needed to be done a few weeks ago. She had a red bandanna wrapped around it to hold it down. "Listen Decon, you and Mary are going to come home with me." All I could think was *what kind of shit was this? She comes to Florida after all these years. I'm sixteen now living a good life where I was.* "What you mean home, I am home" I told my mother. Mama D grabbed me and looked me in the eyes, "I told your mother that it was ok to take you all back with her to the big city, New York!!" Mama D tried to make it sound nice to me, but this wasn't what I was expecting to hear from her. What did we do for her to just give us up like that? Why did she want to just let us leave out of her life? Well it was simple my mother convinced Mama D that she was clean and ready to take care of me and my sister. This was the start of one of the worst summers of my life, sixteen years old and relocating with a once crackhead mother, that was the worst feeling I had in a long time. I tried to hold back the tears building up in the corner of my eyes, but the pain was too much to bear and I finally allowed them to fall. Mama D hugged me and kissed my forehead telling me that everything will be okay. I wiped my eyes and started to pack my clothes. My mother and grandmother walked upstairs to talk with Mary. Luke helped me pack, "So this is it huh? Y'all lea...lea...leaving us now going to New York?" I tried to explain to him that I will never forget him, and that we are still family no matter how far, but he was angry and kept saying that I was going to forget about him just like his father. This added to the hatred I had built up towards my mother. At the time I was six foot two inches, and sitting on two hundred and fifteen pounds, all muscle, rounded chin, and these whiskers that hated to grow all the way so I stayed with a smooth face. I had this teacher named Mr. Scott who used to tell me in front of all the girls, "Hey Decon you better be-careful those green eyes are going to be trouble for you." He always laughed every time he said it to me. That thought ran across my mind as I looked into the small bathroom mirror one last time. Being sixteen years old and looking cut up like Michael Jai White, the Martial Arts training and weight lifting with Lemon really helped me out a lot. Speaking of Lemon, he was hurt. I could tell from the look in his eyes that he didn't want us to leave. When we made eye contact he turned his back towards me and walked downstairs; damn that hurts. Mama D came out of the room with my mother and hugged and kissed me and my sister. I knew this wasn't the end, but I would be lying if I said it didn't feel like it.

As me and Mary walked to the same beat down purple Honda civic, with duct tape on the passenger side window and the paint chipped from years of mishandling, I looked at Mama D and from that moment seeing her cry on that porch killed a part of me that I would never get back.

Chapter 2

𝔚ELCOME TO NEW YORK CITY

As we drove off I sat in the back of the car and closed my eyes. The trip to New York was a blur nothing special, just a long hot eighteen-hour drive from small town Winter Heaven to Flat Bush Brooklyn.

"These great minds comprehend addiction. The pain that flows through my veins is non-fiction.
There's no amount of pills that could erase the thoughts in my head. My spirit is contempt my body is dead.
This anger which lives deep inside of my heart

detonates, ripping my chest apart.

I turn to sin considering some answers,

the devil is my pimp and I'm his dancer.

The resentment grows in me like a cancer

filling my soul like blight.

My face hardened, fist ready to fight.

Looking for a cure, misery Loves Company,

so I sing the melody of a dead man's

symphony.

I could go to God and cherish what I have left,

no FUCK THAT!!! I'm following Satan and battling

to the death. "

What I remember was waking up from that angry dream sweating and mad at my mother. I couldn't tell you why I was even upset. Coming across the Jersey turnpike the big city, as Mama D put it, was off in the distance. There was a large body of water that I just kept staring at, trying my best to remain still acting as if I was still sleep. We came up on heavy traffic as we drove across a huge bridge that read *George Washington Bridge,* it went straight into Manhattan. I was excited at the change of scenery that I only saw on the travel channel or music videos, but I masked it still being upset about leaving

Florida.

My mother took the long way through the giant city so that we could get a look at our new environment. I could tell I was going to hate this city. Well that's what I thought when I first arrived. "Wake up y'all we're here, your new home!" My mother said proudly to me and Mary. "Decon look, LOOK!!!" Mary was excited looking at all the different sites and lights all around us. I had to admit the city was one to marvel over and I was in a state of shock. It took us about three hours to get through the traffic and stops to look at some of New York's famous landmarks. I remember driving over the Brooklyn Bridge and Mary's excited face as we crossed over into Brooklyn. As we drove past Brooklyn Heights I started to remember Lemon playing a track called *Bonnie-n-Shyne* from his favorite rapper Shyne, he would always say that when he gets paid he's gonna find him a gangsta chick from Brooklyn. I remember us pulling up to this busted ass apartment projects, it was a cinderblock gray building with a large courtyard, and a kid's playground in the middle. There were kids playing in the street and a few people standing all over the area, this place was screaming with life, but it didn't feel like home. "This is where we live?" I asked my mother in a sick and disgusted tone. "Yes it's not much but, it's all I have for right now. Come on it's much nicer on the inside."

"Yea right," I said under my breath. I got this chill as soon as I walked into the project gates. Going through the front door, instantly a rush of fresh urine and weed smoke hit our noses harder than a left hook from Mike Tyson. The sounds of baby cries and domestic violence ran into my ears adding to the already festering anger, I could tell that I was going to hate this place. "What's good Ma?"

Yo shorty was gud wit-chu!"

Yo come here ma!!" Cat-calls from the three dudes standing on the corner of the stairwell came at my sister and mother; yea I was going to hate living in New York. We lived in apartment 15D in a building of 23 floors and the elevator as a doormat to all sorts of debris and liquids I couldn't make out. I learned quickly what city life was all about. The inside of the apartment wasn't all that bad like my mother said. She was right about something for once but it was aight, it will do. As you walk in there was this coat hanger with a *"Welcome Home!"* plaque above it and to the left was a closet door. Down the short hallway ahead was the living room, it had a small bunny eared television set that sat on top of an old wooden entertainment system that looked like it was picked up from the side of the road. There was a dusty green and beige couch that sat in front of it with a black coffee table that had a few JET magazines on the top of it. Around the corner to the right was the kitchen. It was small with this floral design on the floor. I thought it looked nice, nothing much to it except for an empty fridge and a microwave that looked like someone left their Chef Boyardee in there for too long. The little antique clock stood to the left against the wall, and this rusty red chair sat off in the corner. "OH CRAP!!" Mary screamed as a giant cockroach ran across the room from under the couch. I laughed and watched her jump around. To the right was a hallway with four doors. The first door on the right was the bathroom; the room across from it was my room and next to me was Mary's. My mother had the big room in the middle. There wasn't much in the rooms. As you walked into mine there was a window that faced the back of the complex and the courtyard, a twin sized bed with purple beddings. I had a tan colored dresser against the wall, and there was a rusty ass pipe that went from the ceiling to the bottom of the floor. Mary's room was the same except, there was no pipe in there. "This is going to suck," I said to no one in particular.

"Decon, come here please." My mother called me into the hallway, "How do you like your room?"

"It's whatever."

"Oh well, I will let you get settled in and I'm going to order us some pizza. New York has the best pizza in the world." My mother said exactly, "Oh and before I forget, if you and Mary want to go downstairs and check out the area, just be careful this is a pretty rough neighborhood and you can also go to the rooftop and get a great view of the city." She explained, I could tell she was trying to be a good mother, but that didn't make up for the nine years she wasn't in my life. Later that night I went into Mary's room after we ate our pizza, once again good ole Kimberly was right again about this place. I wanted to see if she was sleep. Marry was up gazing out towards the neighborhood with tears in her eyes. "Mary what's wrong?" I asked as I sat next to her on the bed. She was a little upset that we had to leave Florida in the beginning of the summer, and she was missing Mama D and I was to, "yea, I wonder what the twins are doing? I bet they are all at the pool with everyone."

"Yea, I bet." I didn't want Mary to feel the way she was, but I was feeling that way to. I just tried my best to hide my true feelings, she didn't need to see me in that state, I had to be strong for her. We talked for a few more hours on past memories of us when we were younger and all of our friends we left in the south. I started to get sleepy and Mary was already nodding off but as I listen to the sounds coming from the other side of the window, my mind slowly began to drift to a state of meditation. The next day I woke up next to Mary, I must of fell asleep in her room. It was a Saturday and on Saturdays Mama D would always have something good cooking in the kitchen, and boy I was in need of some good ole country grits and cheese eggs. I stretched out my arms and walked towards the kitchen, my mother was sitting on the couch eating a bowl of flakes cereal, and watching soul train reruns. "You not gonna cook?" I asked my mother in a confused, yet disgusted tone. "Oh I'm sorry, I forgot to go shopping. All I have is cereal and toast. I will go shopping in a few minutes ok." My mother responded, as she tried to cheer me up with this smile on her face. Pain and anger rose day by day the more I spent in that damn apartment. I didn't leave the apartment the first two weeks we were in New York, except to the store and outside in the courtyard with either my mother or Mary.

I finally gave up and went for a walk with Mary around the neighborhood. "So how are you doing?" Mary asked me; seeing that we've been distant since we moved. "It's a change. I'll get used to it soon," I responded back in a monotone voice. "Let's go watch the game." Mary was making reference to the basketball game going on in the park not too far away from the projects. As we got closer to the gate to enter the park, a few girls were staring at me and smiling; a couple were whispering to each other and giggling from time to time. Some even waved at me, that made me blush a little "I love your hair sexy." One of the girls shouted out making a reference to my wild curly head of hair. I grew up shy around girls, didn't really have much to say, more like didn't know what to say. I always got nervous, insecure you know? But this was different. It was summer time, around 90 degrees, and the ladies were looking HOT!!! Short shorts, miniskirts, low cut tees, hair down, it was a great feeling and a beautiful sight to see. These girls made Mary look overdressed. Come to think about it, she was overdressed; being that we didn't get any new clothes since we've been in New York, and our grandmother didn't allow certain things for us to wear like short shorts, and miniskirts. We were like outsiders to these "city folk." Mary was wearing this long jean skirt, a plan white tee shirt, a gold cross, and fourteen karat gold hoop earrings; Mary loved gold. Despite the clothing being a little country, she was still fly and the looks from the eyes around us made my deliberations a reality. Mary had this artistic flow when it came to her makeup, it never looked sloppy, it was always on point. She had did her eyes in a yellow and white formation, with black lip liner that brought attention to her from all angles "What's good thun?" This short chubby kid, wearing blue jean shorts and a white tee said to me. "huh? What is thun?" I asked properly. The kid laughed hysterically and said, "OH SHIT! You not from here huh? I can tell with your country ass accent ha-ha check it out FAM, thun means you; it's how we speak in the QB. Instead of saying sun like most of these New York niggas we made our own slang, hence the word Thun." I was looking dumb as shit at what he was telling me. I didn't understand him, and what the fuck is QB? Was all I could think, "What is QB?" I asked him. "Oh my bad thun QB is short for Queens Bridge."

"Is that here in Brooklyn?" I asked him "No nigga it's in Queens. We in Brooklyn, Flat Bush, the hood." He was talking to me like I was dumb but I didn't blame him, I was lost as hell that day. He sorta reminded me of Luke, but without the stuttering and the southern accent. "I'm a Queens' nigga, I just like kickin it here in BK" as he pointed to a group of females, who walked past us. "I see."

"Yo, thun I'm Nate." I would later learn that Nate was short for Nathaniel; ha-ha I thought I had a funny name. I extended my hand and told him my name, "I'm Decon." Nate looked at my hand like it had an STD, "Nigga you's corny ha-ha" Nate said as he slapped my hand. Mary walked over and smiled. Nate quickly licked his lips and looked hard at Mary. "Hey ma, I know this is a little forward but it has to be said, your ass is too damn fat for it to be hidden in that long ass skirt. Let me get your number so I can show you how real New Yorkers get down." Before I could even do anything, Mary hit him with the "DON'T play with me little boy" Mary said with a strong attitude and her hand on her hip. It was too funny, Mary didn't play those games, well she didn't but I'll get to that story later. "Yea that's my sister Mary" as I smirked just a little. Nate bounced back from the little embarrassment and was like "It's all good my bad shorty. So, where y'all from anyway?"

"Flordia"

"Oh word, Miami?"

"Naw Winter Haven, it's in Orlando." Nate was looking at me like I was speaking a foreign language. "Whatever man, ha-ha check it, I'm like the ambassador of New York, I know just about everyone, but let me fill you in on a little sum,sum. Here in Brooklyn, these niggas play by a whole different set of rules, see them over there?" He said pointing over to a group of people wearing black and white, "That's the Black Knights, if I was you I would stay clear away from them if you don't want any problems. That group of niggas wearing all red, well their Bloodz. Stay away from them too, they are quick to leave you with a buck-fifty, ya heard."

"A buck what?"

'Don't worry about it, thun just don't mess with them. The only reason them and the Black Knights are even in the same eye shot of each other, is because money is on the game and one of the two are gonna leave with a big payout." 'What about them over there?" I said pointing to a group of people sitting on the bleachers together. "Oh them? Ha-ha, those are my niggas, come on I'll introduce you."

Chapter 3

THE CREW

Nate introduced use to a few of his friends, there was Peter a dark bronze slim medium sized cat who was wearing these thick ass glasses, a navy-blue Yankee fitted covered his bald head, with a sleeveless camouflage vest that was opened exposing his skinny frame. He kept mixing patwa and English together as he spoke; it took me a minute to understand him or even make out what he was saying. Then there's Mark who kept his hair in tight box braids that dangled along his shoulder; he was the shortest one in the group. His skin complexion was close to the color of cheerios, and stood about five, five with a high pitched voice. One thing I noticed about him was that he was always singing some song or tune; that's mostly how he got girls, he reminded me of the main singer from the group *"112"*. After I gave Mark a head nod, Mary's Green and spotted brown eyes got caught up in the sight of this tall dark-skinned brother who looked like he should be drafted to play for the Harlem Globe Trotters.

"Who, is, that?" Mary asked lustfully at the dark-skin brother with the tight fade. He was rocking a blue and silver jump man shorts and T' set with matching Air Jordan Retro XII's. "Who Claxton, that's my cousin." Claxton was busy looking at the game that was going on, until he heard his name being said by Nate. "Dog, how tall are you?" I asked out of curiosity, "Six, eleven." His sensual deep based voice damn near stopped Mary's heart; she was hooked. He was cut like me with short curly hair on the top of his head, but without the build. He was two years older than Mary, but she cared about at that time was his deep brown eyes locked into hers and from the way he was looking Mary had him open as well. For as deep as his voice was he was very soft spoken and hated raising it more than he needed to. Well that's what Nate said, speaking of Nate. He saw the looks both of them were giving each other and had the urge to say something, but was quickly distracted when these two gorgeous girls came walking over from the other side of the crowded courts. "Yo Decon, these young gangsta bitches are Empress and Diamond. "But everyone calls me S-Dot." Diamond said in her strong Brooklyn accent.

Empress was as short as Mark and didn't say much at first, she was a light caramel colored goddess who was slim yet slight curvaceous with light baby brown eyes on a face that screamed "Vogue cover model", the eye on the left was a little lazy but it was cute and gave her this innocent look about her. Her hair was in a funky eighties style afro that was blonde and purple, I had to say she had a catching style about her. S-Dot was the total opposite; she was around five, ten with silver eyes. Her jet black hair was braided into micro braids that kissed the top of her plump ass. She was high yellow and turning rose pink from the heat, and her facial features were perfect. She had this look about her that was quirky, yet very cute. Both girls wore matching beige short shorts that showed off their assets and pink crop tops, and all white Nike Dunks. "Damn easy god, you gonna burn a hole through them the way you beamin." I shook my head low in embarrassment, and turned around to see who it was with the scratchy deep voice. "My nigga, wat up G"

"Not much god, you know how it is." The scratchy voiced kid said giving Nate dap, "Yo who's the lame?"

"Oh, him ha-ha just some southern nigga I found walkin the park." The two of them broke out into laughter at Nate's joke. He must've seen me looking like I was about to go berserk at the sight of being made fun of, "chill god we only playin wit cha, my name's Lord Solomon 7, but just stick to calling me Solomon 7." He said extending his fist towards me, I bumped his fist and changed my demeanor. "Solomon7?" I said in complete confusion "Yea my peoples are god body, five percenters, so that's how I got my government." I still didn't know what he was talking about but I just went along with it. Solomon 7 was an even six feet sporting a brown and black camo fit with a thick gold rope chain around his neck and blacked out Timberland boots. Everything he talked about was tied to his way of life. He had a crazy attitude, but if he liked you then you were ok. Skinny to the bone and wasn't afraid of shit. He kept looking around like someone was after him and he spoke about his recent fight on the train in the Bronx with his cousin. This was Nate's group of friends; they called themselves the West Indian connection. Being that all of them were tied to the West Indian Islands of the Caribbean. Mark's parents were from Tobago, and Claxton's mother was Jamaican and his father is a Cuban drug lord in Cuba, from time to time you would catch Claxton speaking Spanish. Peter was born in Jamaica and his family moved to New York when he was eight years old. Solomon7 was from Trinidad along with Empress's father, who I would find out later on that he was a big time hustler around New York. S-Dot was Jamaican and Cree Indian, and Nate was a pure bread Jamaican, and he let everyone know it. I guess you could say myself and Mary were the only ones who stood out.

The final game was about to begin and we all sat down to watch. The game was down to this team from the South Bronx called the originals, and the East Flatbush Dawgz. It was getting intense, the crowd was going crazy, and both teams were good. During the half time break a slight commotion broke out between this big swole guy and a member of the Black Knights. "Yo chill the fuck out nigga! Nobody wants a problem with you."

"You got a motherfuckin problem already, so you either tell me where that nigga at or your problem will turn into drama." By the way the big dude was yelling, you could feel his anger with every syllable, "Hey who is that?" I asked Nat as we ran over to get a closer look. "That six, five ape looking beast is Luther. He's basically the uncrowned king of Brooklyn and he roll's with some dangerous niggas." Nate spoke about Luther like he was some type of legend from Greek mythology. He had to be sitting at around two fifty and looked like he did a few bids upstate. That day he wore his thick dreads that he wrapped up to the top of his head with the tips hanging bellow the knot that held them together. He had on these red shorts construction Timbs, and no shirt on. I saw a huge tattoo across his chest that read: *"**KILL THE WEAK AND STOMP THE DEAD.**" No homo this dude was buff* *and kind of made me look small compared to him. But back to the story;* he came out the crowd which parted like the red sea, and interrupted the basketball game yelling, asking for a guy named Larry. I don't know what Larry did or what he didn't do, but whatever it was Luther was pissed and wanted revenge. Luther came out of the crowd calling for Larry and pushing people out of his way. As he made it to the front of the crowd, dude stood there and looked around at all the faces starring back at him. It was crazy, the whole area got quite and no one said a word. I was confused and wondered why everyone got all scared, but this wasn't the time or place to ask any questions. Luther meant business, and I wasn't about to give him any. "Aight ill find you!" Luther said with a nasty smile that let you know he wasn't going to forget. He pushed his way out of the crowd, before he could make it back to his black SUV this dark skin kid who was with the Bloodz shouted out "MAN FUCK THAT NIGGA!" Luther stopped short after hearing that and the laughter coming from the crowd "WHO SAID THAT?" Luther said hurrying back over to the courts holding in both hands this gigantic gun that looked like it was from the military, no one said anything; it was silent again "Okay so nobody spoke huh? Cool, keep trying me and watch me turn this motherfucker into a murder scene. Luther said turning and walking back to his SUV and drove off.

About fifteen minutes later the game went on and back to the enjoyment. "Damn that shit was intense." I said to Nate in awe of the situation. "Yea trust me, you don't want to be on his bad side at all, last week that Nigga killed some dude up in Harlem over a missed phone call." I thought Nate was hyping up the story but later on in life I would find out that the incident was true and he did it during broad daylight. After the game we went to the hand ball court to chill and as we sat and cracked jokes with each other, this group of girls walked up to us all wearing these short shorts in all different colors with these sexy tops to match. I couldn't help but stair. "MmmHmm! Look at this shit right here!" S-Dot said aloud "Good Gawd!" Empress chimed in. I didn't know any of them, but I saw a few of them at the game when I was walking up with Mary. But there was this one who stood out. She was leading the group and had this look on her face that spoke true beauty and a walk so mean you would think she was on the catwalk, but even then I caught this feeling of danger. Something wasn't right about this girl and how she carried herself amongst the others, but lust was controlling me and took over any other thought that was in my head. They walked right towards us and stopped. I stepped closer to her and gazed at the beauty upon me. She had a slim curvaceous frame with these nice size breast and beautiful brown eyes, her hair was blond and dark brown that was wavy and rested on the middle of her back. She was wearing these orange shorts and a pink tank top with pink and orange Nike Uptowns. She was fresh and smelled like sweet strawberry nectar and honey baked softly together in a coat of sugar. There was something about this dark brown cutie that told me not to trust her, but damn the girl was fine. "Hey sexy," she said as she placed her hand on my right arm and smiled at me.

I was looking around like I was stupid looking for the right words to say, or even words at all. Mary and Claxton were talking and giggling in the far corner of the court, Mark was busy singing to these two Spanish twins, and the rest of the crew were wrapped up with the other girls. "Uh humm!! Are you ok?" she asked me again, this time with an attitude. "Yea I'm good sorry about that. I'm Decon, what's your name?" I bounced back quickly from what could have been a very embracing moment. I could tell she was stunned by my voice; a lot of people were especially females. *My voice is a mix between Barry White and Isaac Hayes, very smooth if I might say so myself, but what was so shocking was that such a strong voice came from a young face.* In her Brooklyn attitude she responded, "Well damn took you long enough ha-ha I'm Leandra, but everybody calls me Lele." As she shook my hand and smiled that was the day I knew my life was in for a twist. She was soft as velvet and had a smile of pearly whites that could brighten a dark room. "Where you from? I've never seen you around here before."

"I just moved here from Florida."

"Word? I've been to Florida before, but only to Miami and Orlando."

'I'm from Orlando, I lived in Winter Haven."

"Yea I never heard of that place, ha-ha. So by the look on your face when I walked up I could tell you feelin me huh?" I was shocked by her straight forwardness, but I guess she could read right through me, "Yea, you're gorgeous. I never seen a girl like you before." I said a little nervously, Lele just laughed and played with her hair twirling it around her small finger. After about three hours of just talking, laughing, and talking shit to each other the street lights were starting to come on and Mary was ready to go. "Decon let's go it's getting late, and I'm tired." Lele looked at me and smiled "It's ok, here get my number." She took my phone and put in her number. "Call me anytime" she said giving me a playful wink as she walked away with the other girls that were with her. Nate and the rest of the crew took off after we all exchanged numbers, S-Dot and Empress went off with a girl for each of them from Lele's group and were giggling the whole time. Mary was smiling the whole way home talking about how cute Claxton was and how he was being so sweet. "I saw you Decon, Lele is cute and she had her eyes all on your body." Mary said jokingly punching me in the arm. I couldn't help but smile and laugh, "She was huh?" I responded back and thought to myself, *"Man I might like it here after all."*

As we were walking the four blocks back to our project building, three guys wearing all black walked up to us. "Yo ma run yo chain!" This one guy with the gold teeth said to Mary as he eye balled her gold cross. "What?" Mary said obviously confused about what the guy was saying to her. "Give me your chain! You understand now?" He said this time no longer smiling. Mary looked at me with this face of confusion and annoyance, "NO!" She said with an attitude. The other two guys looked at each other and the one on the left side tapped the other in the chest pointing to Mary. The guy with the gold teeth stepped closer to Mary and before he could fully extend his hand to grab her chain I grabbed his hand and threw it away. He looked at me and right away from the look in his eyes I could tell shit was about to go down. He reached into his waist band and pulled out this black gun and pointed it to my face. "Maybe you ain't hear me right, "Give me the fuckin' chain!" he pushed the gun harder into my forehead and tightened up his grip on the gun as he twisted it to the side. My face was hard as stone, but on the inside I was scared not just for my life but for my sister's. Mary jumped when he pulled out the gun and started panting. "Here just take it," Mary said as she took the cross off and held it out towards the guy.

He looked at it and told one of his friends to grab it and he pointed the gun towards Mary and told her "Now wasn't that easy?" He lowered the gun and took off running in the opposite direction.

After they left I begin to tense up so hard that my eyes begin to water and my face turned red. We walked the rest of the way home, and Mary kept telling me that it was ok, and not to worry about it. But that was beside the fact; they embarrassed me and took what was mine in front of my face. Once again I felt low, and my mind went back to Bobby Walker and the anger began to surface. I pushed open the gate to our building and pushed the front door open to the complex so hard that it slammed into the back wall causing the glass to the door to crack. Like always the stale piss and the domestic sounds were in the air. The elevator was broken and the walk up the fifteen flights made matters even worst then what they were. We got to our floor and went inside the apartment. My mother was in the living room laughing and joking around with this guy named Price that she was dating at the time. *He didn't mean anything to me at the time, but later on in life he would be known as a notorious figure all over New York.* "Decon what's wrong?" My mother asked me as she noticed that I was angry. I didn't respond to her, I simply walked to my room and closed the door behind me. I sat in that dark room in silence, closing my eyes and allowing the darkness to control my thoughts. The anger that was inside me slowly left as I thought of memories of Mama D and the good times I had had with my cousins Luke and Lemon.

Chapter 4

ℭHE DREAM

She held my hand when I cried, kissed my
cheek when I slept.

She caressed my body when I was hurt and
led me to the light when I was lost.

She gave me the truth when the obvious
wasn't present,

Taught me how to survive when life wasn't
pleasant,

My dreams are now more than just dreams,

But hurt when they never become reality.

Sometimes I ask GOD for help, but he denies
me an ear,

I get angry and un-patient, and then the
devil gives me a peer,

Plays with my emotions and fears.

I can't see my future getting any brighter, I smell my soul engulfed in fire.

Heaven seems so far and non-existent,

Then I think back to my grandmother praying whisperin

"Lord save his soul, forgive him for his sins, bless his heart, and remove him from the situation that he's in.

I pray for my daughter, she's done him wrong.

Lord I ask that you save her, and keep him strong.

Watch over my family were all we got,

Lord thank you for this one, I know it was a long shot.

In these we ask from heaven above, amen."

The prayers of someone who cared carried me far beyond reason, life dancing in front of me teasin.

I woke up with my heart pounding and out of

control, looking out the window I could see the beauty of the universe, a full moon tonight, and below its amazing glow I see the horror of the streets drug dealers and fiends, crawling the streets like cockroaches. I closed my eyes, took a deep breath and feel back asleep thinking about the dream I just awoken from.

Chapter 5

$\mathfrak{L}$OOK BEFORE YOU CROSS ME

About two weeks after meeting the crew and Lele, it became routine to hang out together. We did everything from Coney Island, to house parties in Jersey, and roof tops in Crown Heights. There was this one day though, I was with Nate, and Mark in Queens, just chilling outside of Lindens super store when a black truck pulled up and this big dark skinned guy stepped out of it. He was huge had to be about three hundred or sum, but something about this guy gave me an uneasy feeling. He walked into the store and shortly after, this girl by the name of "BG" one of them boyish types walked up to us "Hey, y'all might want to get out of here, Lace and his boys bout to spray this joint." She said with her raspy voice as she kept looking behind herself and at us as if they were coming anytime soon. "Where they at?" Mark asked looking around the corner to see if he could see them coming. Now I didn't know Lace but something about this whole situation was telling me that I was about to find out. Not even five minutes later this dark green Jeep pulled up right behind the truck in front of the corner store. BG, Mark, and Nate took off running in the opposite direction, but I was frozen I couldn't move. Three guys hopped out wearing black and white bandanas over their faces, all of them had these sub-machine guns in hand. As soon as big man walked out of the store, his face dropped instantly and the bag that was holding his bottle of Old English hit the floor, his eyes got big and from where I was standing I could damn near smell the fear coming off of his V-neck.

About seven to twelve rounds apiece were let out after they pulled the trigger; they went quick and ate up the front of the store. I snapped out of my daze from the sound of the rapid gun fire and took off running towards Nate and Mark, with a quick glance backwards I saw the rounds rip through big man and saw his body falling backwards; Lace and his people jumped into the Jeep and sped off as fast as they could. We all ran into BG's block and waited out for a minute to let things cool down. BG was this low level drug dealer and knew a little bit of everything that was going on in the streets. "Yo dog you straight crazy, or just stupid as hell" BG said to me as she lit a blunt, "Yea thun you could've gotten your ass blasted" Nate said to me as he took a pull from the blunt that was being passed around. He coughed and let out a cloud of smoke from his mouth "What were you thinking?" he asked me looking at me with a confused look on his face. I thought about it and I couldn't come up with a reason of why I was standing there while they ran. "I don't know, just wanted to see if they hit him." I responded back to him, Nate shook his head and passed the blunt to me; I inhaled deeply and pushed out a deep part of my stress with the exhale as the weed started to calm my nerves and relax my body. That wasn't the first time I smoked weed, it was something that Luke was into after he dropped out, and I had my first experience with him one day in the basement. I don't remember much, but I do know that I liked the after effects. We had to be there for about an hour or so until this big nosed kid named Biz ran up to BG and told her that this girl named Taquana who worked for BG from time to time, was stealing from the place where they hid the weed. The "stash spot" and she was reselling it to get more money for herself. BG wasn't playin that one because that wasn't her weed to steal she just sold it and if she came up short then that would be her ass. These types of actions couldn't just keep going on, and BG needed to put an end to it sooner than later. We followed Biz to Ajax Park where Taquana was getting high at with a few catz from the neighborhood. "HEY BITCH!! Who the fuck you think you stealing from?" She said in her raspy voice. Taquana jumped up and dropped the bag of weed that was in her hand, "what? naw BG I aint steal from you, I swear" Taquana was real jumpy and kept playing with her hands. "BULL SHIT! She tryin to play you B!" Biz said full of rage "I say you fuck her up." BG had to grab onto Biz and tell him to chill out who was now in Taquana's face with a twisted scowl. "You know Luther would kill you if he caught you stealin, now WHY THE FUCK YOU DO IT BITCH!!" BG was heated and I could feel the tension rising. Before Taquana could give another excuse BG punched her dead in the face splitting her bottom lip, Taquana dropped to the ground and put her hand up begging BG not to hit her again. BG slapped her hand out the way and punched her again with a two punch combo, dropping her on her back. "Don't you ever steal from me again BITCH!" BG searched the crying Taquana and took all of her money, and the rest of her weed. From that point on, I learned that the streets could be your friend or your grave.

After the fight I was feeling lightheaded and hungry, I told everyone that I was leaving and took off to the train heading back to Brooklyn. When I was waiting for the G-Train I got a call from Lele. She asked me to meet up with her at the park when I touched down. I agreed and hung up the phone. The train rolled up and I boarded, it took me about an hour and thirty minutes to get there and I saw her as I walked up the block, wow she was shining I'm talking about straight beauty oozing from her wide hips and thick thighs to her exquisite face. She was wearing this yellow sun dress with her hair braided up in one single braid going from her left shoulder to her chest. I step to her and gave her a hug, oh my God she smelled lovely too. I was in love ha-ha, "Hey sexy" she said to me smiling as we hugged "Wat up, shawty?" I said in my southern accent "Let's go for a walk" She said grabbing my hand and pulling me with her. We walked the streets talking, flirting; you know all that mushy stuff. "You know you gotta pay for all the freebees, right?" Lele said pulling away playfully, "What you mean by dat?"

"You know, all those free looks at me you be getting."

"Oh I gotta pay, but everyone else can get free

glances whenever they want?" I asked smiling from ear to ear. "That's just it, they get glances. You on the other hand be taking snapshots with them sexy green eyes of yours." Lele responded this time looking me directly in my eyes. I didn't know how to respond to her quick comeback right away, so I just smiled until the right words came to me. I returned her glare just as deeply as she was doing to me, "Well if you stopped grabbing my attention then I wouldn't have to savior the memory." She smiled at my smooth comeback and the sight of seeing her like that, made me want her that much more. We walked to her house about seven blocks past the park and the sun started to go down, she was looking me deep in my eyes. "You really do have beautiful eyes" she said smiling and rubbing my face, I started blushing and walked over to the fire hydrogenate right in front of her house, I was looking at this girl who was all of heaven and the stars above, *"dog she was amazing."* She walked up to me as the sky turned raspberry red and the air began to cool, she hugged me and kissed me on the lips. I was hesitant and a little scared, mainly because I didn't want to fuck this up. As I relaxed and kissed her back passion flowed and moved us both and the sheer bliss was beginning to rage. My hands moved south from her lower back to her butt, she smiled and continued to kiss me as I squeezed that soft fat ass. All I could say to myself was *"DAMN!!!"* It was great, "So I guess you're not seeing anyone huh?" I asked her looking into her eyes with a smiling face. "No but I have a special someone in mind" she said as she pushed away from me and ran up the short stairway, "I'll call you later." Lele said as she sauntered into the house.

I watched her go inside and couldn't help but to smile. I walked to the bus stop so that I could get back to the projects, my stomach was yelling at me from the hours of neglect. The excitement from meeting up with Lele made me forget all about food, so now I was starting to pay for it. On the way there I was just thinking of how great my evening was going, I couldn't wait to get back home and talk to Lele. I was about a block away from the bus stop and these guys dressed in all black were walking towards me, *"Shit!"* I thought to myself when I knew exactly who they were. It was the same niggas who robbed me and Mary a while back and I knew I had to do something this time. "Hey what up sun run them pockets" the one with the gold teeth said to me as he walked up, thinking emotionally and slightly nervous I swung wildly at him, he dodged my punch and came back with a strong left hook into my ribs that caused me to wrench in pain. I pushed him away and the guy on the left came at me with a two-punch combo, I dodged the first punch but got hit with the other blow square on the side of my face, from there on I lost balance and begin to trip. I haven't worked out in so long, nor worked on my martial art skill set, *"Was I beginning to lose it? Let's find out from the rest of the story."* I fell to the ground and covered my face instantly as they punched and kicked me over and over. My body was starting to go numb and the pain was almost unbearable. *"Now this was some superhero movie shit that happened next"*, this guy came out of the shadows almost as if he was a ghost, he had to be about the same height as me or more with dreads hanging down to the middle of his chest. Out of nowhere he grabbed one of them by the neck and picked him up in the air,and slammed him to the ground on some *WWE* shit. The one with the gold teeth looked at him and backed off as if he knew the guy who came to save me, and he took off running in the opposite direction. Leaving the other guy on the floor in pain and the other stuck to defend himself. The guy reached into his pocket to draw his switch blade and when it was exposed, the guy quickly grabbed his arm, twisted it and disarming him. With the knife in his hand he grabbed the attacker from behind and pressed the knife to his cheek, "Say cheese." He said swiftly riding the blade down through his cheek to his mouth. The kid let out a loud scream of pain and dropped to the floor holding on to his face.

The guy who saved me helped me up to my feet, "You alright, you took some beating kid" he said as he started laughing. " Wait a minute, I've seen you somewhere before" he said as he looked me in my face from left and right, and said "you're Decon Rice! Yea that's you!" My face dropped in confusion as if it was saying how did this guy know my name? He saw the look on my face and fished his pocket for a business card," Hey, if you want, I'll love to sit down with you a chat. Here give me a call I have to go." as he handed me a business card and picked up his bag and left walking back into the shadows. The front of the card was black with a red dragon and the ying yang symbol in each corner; he owned a dojo not too far from where I was. I continued walking the rest of the block to the bus stop, about two minutes later I got on the bus and rode the few blocks back to my neighborhood. Walking into the front gate my face was tight and sore, my body ached, and there was a knot on the side of my head that came with an angry headache. My left side began to swell a little bit and it hurt to walk, cough, or anything at that. I walked into my building and embraced the natural smells and sounds. The elevator was broken, again, so I had to take the stairs, as painful as it was I made it to the apartment and walked in. To my surprise all I heard was silence, it was only eleven and the whole house was quite. I went straight to the bathroom and shed my clothes. I ran the hot water to the shower, and looked in the mirror to see my wounds. My lip was bruised and my side was bright red, I was lucky my ribs weren't broken, but they were sore. I allowed the water to run down my hair and body, the soothing sensation allowed me to relax and brought me to a slight state of peace. After the shower I made my way to my room and laid down in the darkness. Thoughts of Lele helped me sleep, and before I knew it I was knocked out.

Chapter 6

COME WINTER

The summer was coming to a cool end, and school was going to be starting soon. Timberland boots and Northface jackets were soon going to be the best couple for the season. The leaves were changing their form and the winds picked up a bit giving that nasty chill early in the morning. Me and Lele started dating not to long before the summer ended, actually it was the day after I had gotten jumped. She hit me up asked if I could meet her in the park at our spot. I agreed and into the bathroom to wash up. My face was still a little tight and the swelling on my lip went down a bit, but my ribs were still sore and tender. I was dressed in a gray sweat suit and some black Nikes and dashed out the house as quickly as I could. I made it to the park and Lele was standing by the handball court as always. She was wearing tight blue denim Prada jeans with these honey brown leather knee high boots. Her huge breast were trying to burst free from the small purple top she was wearing, and the honey brown jacket she had on over the top matched her boots perfectly. I was amazed how her hair was now twisted into two different pony tails that danced playfully over her chest. She had on pink lip gloss that made me desire those juicy lips of hers that much more. Her dark brown features were being blessed by the rays from the sun, man I was hooked, today was the day I made her mine. "What happened to you?" Lele said looking at my swollen face and lip, "I got into a fight last night."

"Oh My God!! Are you ok?" Lele said running over to me and caressing my face. "Yea I'm good shawty, I'm doing really well now that I'm around you." I responded in a way that I can change the subject. To be honest I was embarrassed about the whole thing. "Aww you're so sweet" Lele was smiling hard and I knew this was my chance to take full advantage of the situation. "So let me show you how sweet I can really be."

"How so?" She replied, I looked her deep in her lustful brown eyes and spoke from my heart. "From the moment I saw you I had to have all of that chocolate to myself. I mean let's be real you are more than a beautiful face and a gorgeous smile. Your mind is a canvas of true artwork, similar to a painting portrayed by Van Gogh. Your style is pure and original, like no other you can be compared. The closer I get to you I feel like there is no one else around. Your smell, your touch, your very being is heavenly. I am enticed by your being and moved by your very nature. To be completely honest I want you and no one else." Lele's face dropped from my words. She hung on to each syllable as if they were coming from Jesus Christ himself. As I finished speaking she adjusted herself, cleared her throat, and licked her lips. "Well damn daddy, who knew Florida had so much game. Boy I'm yours." She leapt into my arms and kissed me passionately. We lost each other in the passion of our lips pressed against each other, and our bodies touching. The hairs on the back of my neck were starting to stand up, as well as other parts of my body as well. We laughed together and made a few laps around the park talking and enjoying our moment. I found out we were going to the same school, so that made it easy on both of us. High school in New York was going to be different then back home in Florida, all new people and a new set of friends.

One morning I called Lele and asked her if she wanted to go school shopping, she was excited and told me she was on her way. I waited outside for her as she pulled up to the corner where I was standing. She was in this black SUV and instantly my mind traveled to when I first seen Luther at the basketball game. I will admit my body clenched a little when this huge gorilla looking beast of a man stepped out of the driver's seat. He stared at me long and hard as if he could see my thoughts. The long scare across his right cheek looked like someone was trying to give him a permanent smile. He spat on the ground and opened the back-passenger door. Lele stepped out wearing a pair of black leggings that had symmetric slits on the sides. Dark brown beef and broccolis hugged onto her feet. She wore this Burberry short dress that brought together her whole look. Her hair was wavy and free flowing around her shoulders. She ran into my arms and gave me a hug and a kiss; I was dumbfounded, completely lost for words on this situation. "Who is that?" I asked her pointing to the black SUV, "oh that's Elroy my brother's driver" as soon as she said that the passenger door opened, and Luther stepped out of the car and walked up to me. "This is my brother Luther," as she said that I could feel this dark presence all around me, it felt like Satan himself was trying to tell me something. He was sizing me up as if I was his next opponent. "You're Decon huh? My sister talks about you a lot, I'm watching you nigga remember that" I just stood there and watched as he walked back to his car with no fear. Elroy got into the car after him and drove off with Luther. "Don't worry about him, he is a sweet guy when he wants to be." Me and Lele walked off towards the train station and got off on 42nd street. We must have walked all over the place and she wanted to shop everywhere. "So are you ready for school on Monday?"

"Yea I'm ready, I guess."

"Ha-ha, trust me you will be fine, niggas are mostly talk, but you can handle yourself." Lele said feeling me up. "So what's the deal with your brother?" I asked, but Lele just stood there in brief silence, being careful of her words. "Look D, he's in an organization that makes him notorious in the streets of New York. The way he conducts business is deadly, but he's really a good guy at heart."

"So what is it that he does for a living?"

"I can't say right now, but in time you will know. For right now, how about you focus your attention on me, as well as those juicy ass lips." I was curious about Luther but really I was worried about what it meant for me, especially since I was dating his sister. What got me was that Lele had a lot of money for a chick with no job and I mean A LOT of money, she was buying me things. Everything from clothes to jewelry, my mother only gave me two hundred dollars so everything else that I got came from Leandra. As the night came into view, we grabbed a bite to eat from this Greek spot on the pier, and watched as the sun went into resting. The moon shined over the Hudson and made the evening even more romantic. After dinner, we took the train back to Brooklyn, a little tired from the day I rested my head against the window and Lele wrapped her arm around mine, I was starting to feel some type of emotion for this girl, I never had a girlfriend before so this was new to me. Maybe this is what Carl Thomas was talking about. I started to have visions of Luke and Lemon, thinking about how they were doing, wondering if everything was going well back home in Winter Haven.

It was late when we got back to Brooklyn, and Lele was ready to go home. By the time we made it back to my projects the SUV was waiting outside for her, with Elroy standing outside of the door. Lele leaned into my right side of my face and whispered in my ear, "goodnight sexy" as she kissed me on the cheek and ran to her brother. I watched as they drove off and walked into the house with a huge smile on my face; my mother and Mary were standing in the kitchen when I walked in talking about where Mary wanted to start school. Mary saw me first with a huge smile still scratched across my face and both hands full of bags, "Why are you so happy?" Mary asked and my mother chiming in "Yea Decon what's going on with you?" I told them about my day and Mary started laughing adding red to my light complexion. I was having a great night and couldn't stop thinking about my day. I went inside my room, and put my new gear up. I called Mama D to check up on her to see how things were going on down south. 'You know me baby, if God is by myside then I'ma be alright." Mama D didn't sound like she was doing well and when I asked about her health she just kept on telling me that it was nothing, and I shouldn't worry. Hearing her sound like that made me feel a little sick, I didn't want anything to happen to my grandmother and the thought of her being sick was killing me. I ended the phone call with Mama D, and fell asleep texting Lele.

School started and I was looking in the mirror adjusting my wavy hair that grew over the summer, it was hanging down to my shoulders. Mary braided it up right before I left the house. I made it to the corner of the neighborhood where I spotted Empress, and S-Dot. They were fresh wearing matching pink bomber jackets with black leggings, pink and white Retro 6's and a white crop top that hugged both of their bodies. "What's up ladies?"

"What up nigga." S-Dot said looking me up and down, "You fresh as fuck!" Empress said. I was wearing these Black Levi jeans with butter Timbs, I had a long sleeve black cotton shirt that fit my body well enough to show my build. "Yea I try" I said smiling a little, we started our walk to school instead of taking the bus, "So you and Lele huh? You hit that yet?" Empress asked with a smile, "Naw I didn't hit yet,"

"Damn nigga what you waiting on marriage?" We all broke out in laughter from S-Dot's comment. *In my mind I wanted to have sex with Lele, but to be truthful I was a virgin and I was nervous.* We continued to joke and laugh as we made it to Erasmus High school or E-Hall for short. It was different then the high school I went to in Winter Haven, way different. Everything had its own life from the groups of friends, the cliques, the gangs, everything. It was like I stepped into a whole new world; Solomon 7 was outside talking with some people rocking a heavy leather jacket with this crazy symbol of a star and the number 7 stitched on the back of it. I originally thought it was custom because of his name, but I found out later that it was the five percenters symbol. On his feet were these crazy looking Adidas and he stayed with a thick gold chain around his neck. Lele was just being dropped off by her brother. She looked amazing as always, she showed up to school like she was trying to prove a point. She had on the dark purple Sarah Burton mini dress I picked out for her the day we went shopping. She complimented the dress well, with her make-up done in different shades of purple and even her six-inch lavender Gessippie heels married well. You would think she was going to Prom and not just the first day of school. As we all showed each other love and acknowledged each other's fresh gear, the truancy officer was starting to hurry the students into the building.

Nate, Mark, and Peter all went to school in Queens, and Mary used her scholarship to get into NYU as a full-time student studying pre-law. Claxton went to Saint John's playing ball and studying accounting. We all had our plans and everything was starting off on the right foot. The first day of school was crazy I met different people I've never seen before and a few faces I recognized from around the way. I had home room with S-Dot; we had a teacher by the name of Mr. Wilson. He was a short black man holding on to his balding hair, he started out the class talking about how he doesn't play that bullshit. The first week of school went well, got a chance to meet new people, but for the most part I stayed with my crew. One day we were in home room taking attendance, when this girl named Rosetta Gómez started talking shit to S-Dot. Rosetta was a pretty dark skinned Panamanian chick with nice sized breast and long black hair with red highlights. "Stupid bitch ass hoe!"

"Who the fuck you think you talkin to?"

"You bitch!"

"Don't make me get up out this seat; I'm trying to be civilized."

"Naw you just scared nigga!" Rosetta shouted from across the room, the class erupted in Oooo's and Awww's. Someone shouted out "World Star," while another shouted out "Hit that hoe!" Mr. Wilson slammed down his clip board and silenced the whole room, "Didn't I tell y'all that I don't play that shit! Now shut the hell up for I get to fighten!" S-Dot sucked her teeth and just stared at Rosetta with murderous eyes. The bell rang and it was time for the next class, S-Dot stayed seated and waited for Rosetta to walk out of the room with two of her friends. I waited with her and it was as if her sliver eyes were turning blood red at how mad she was. When she finally got up out of her seat, we walked into the hallway together; she sped up her walk through the busy hall pushing past people in her way. I could smell the violence in her system; "I'm gonna wash that stupid bitch, she think cause she light skin with silver eyes she running shit, I can't wait to get my hands on her." Rosetta was saying loudly opening up her locker, as soon as it was opened S-Dot wasted no time in her attack. "Bitch!" S-Dot yelled has she pushed Rosetta's head into the metal locker, her head snapped back and S-Dot turned her around and slammed her fist into her face splitting her lip. Once blood was drawn S-Dot grabbed a fist full of hair and pulled her in for another meet and greet with her fist, this time landing a few serious uppercuts. Rosetta's body tried to fall, but S-Dot held on strong and slammed her head again into the locker over and over. The crowds of students were all around and were capturing the whole fight on their phones. Rosetta's friends tried to break up the fight, seeing that their friend was getting beat badly, but sadly failed with one even taking an elbow strike to her face. By the time school security showed up and pushed past the students, Rosetta was bleeding from her nose and lips, with a few knots on her head. It was a bad turnout for her, and all S-Dot did was smile, pick up her bookbag and walked towards her next class like nothing ever happened. Later that day the videos were all over the school and S-Dot was suspended from school for about ten days for that event.

The rest of High School went by quick, I barely made it seeing that I was never in class I was either ditching with Lele or with Empress and S-Dot. Sometimes I would just not want to go to a certain class. For the most part I stayed out of trouble and just did what I had to do to get by. Me and Lele became closer to each other and this chick had the whole school wrapped around her finger. I got a bad vibe at times when I was around her, it felt dark but I ignored it and acted as if everything was normal. It wasn't that long ago from when I got jumped but I found the card that the guy had given me. The name on the card read *Kane,* I called him when I got out of school one day just to check out his spot. "Wow! I was starting to think you forgot about me kid." He was surprised that I called, and invited me to come to his dojo so we can talk. I got on the bus and rode till I got to his dojo; it was this building with a giant glass window that you could see into. There was a class going on, and right away I felt like I was home. Being here brought back memories from when I used to compete, the floor was fitted with mats and punching bags, striking bags, wooden dummies, just about everything a fighter would need to train. In the middle of the mat was a red dragon, the same as the one on the card. I walked inside and took off my boots and placed them at the doorway, that's when Kane saw me and greeted me with a bow "Decon would you like to join me in a little demonstration of a proper jumping spinning kick?" I couldn't resist and I took off my jacket and made my way to the middle of the mat where Kane was standing. He stared at me and grunted I lifted my jeans and let out a war cry, jumping in the air and executing a spinning kick and landing perfectly, I still had it in me, as I gathered myself and bowed towards Kane and then to his students. "Wow, you're even better in person." Kane said, "Thank you, I try."

"Do you have some time to spar?" Kane asked, "Yea I have sometime"

"Cool, I have a black belt who would love to spar with a legend." Kane walked over to his students and talked to a tall kid with a funky high top haircut. As he talked I prepped myself to fight, putting my mind at ease and trying to focus, I felt at home standing in the mist of the dojo. "Decon this is Joe, he will be the one sparing with you when you're ready. I told him to take it easy on you, being that you haven't been on the mats in quite some time ha-ha." I laughed at Kane's joke but in my mind I was all business. I met Joe in the middle of the mat and bowed he got into his stance as I took off my shirt and lifted up my heavy jeans. This kid showed no fear and was ready to attack, Kane shouted out "FIGHT!" and like a bomb Joe exploded towards me with a fury of punches left and right I dodged them and spent around and hit him with a kick to his stomach. He flinched and moved to a low kick at my shins. I jumped and dodged his kick, I moved back and got myself together pulling up my pants to stop them from getting in my way. Joe ran towards me and I shifted to the left and hit him with a strong knee to his chest dropping him to the ground and winning the fight. I bowed towards Joe and helped him up from the floor. Kane started clapping and congratulated me and brought me into his office. "Hey Decon I'm so glad you stopped by, I know you're wondering how I know you. Well I was at one of your fights in Florida, you know the one you won with the triple kick, and from then on I was amazed. You have this fighting style that is unorthodox, and your composer, everything about you reminded me of myself, and I was hoping to get a chance to speak to you and here you are in my dojo." Everything Kane said made me think hard, this was crazy I was known further then I thought. Kane started to tell me that he could see I was a little off; he offered to train me and help improve my skills if I wanted. With an offer like this how could I decline, I told him that it would be an honor, but in my head I could hear Mama D saying that nothing comes for free. "So how much is this going to cost me?" I asked Kane, he told me that he would charge me $75 a month, that's not a bad deal from what he normally charges, so I accepted but there was one problem, I didn't have any money.

I spent the rest of the night raking my brain thinking about how I was going to come up with the money. I had options, I could've worked with BG, or asked to get put on with some of the kids around the school, but that was risky. I just feel asleep praying for an answer.

Chapter 7

A DEAL WITH THE

DEVIL

The next day at school I couldn't stop thinking about getting the $75 for the classes, I thought about robbing people but what I saw in Queens and from what I've been hearing around the projects I didn't want to mess with the wrong person. The bell rang and I went to go meet Lele in the lunch room, I sat down next to her and told her about the offer from Kane. "So you couldn't come up with anything huh?"

"No, I could get a part time job, but I need the money now na mean."

"Yea I feel you." She smiled and had this crazy look in her eyes, "look don't worry about anything, I might be able to help you out." I didn't know why, but I knew she had money I just didn't know how it was going to affect me. I didn't dwell too much on it, I just agreed and finished my lunch. *"But remember what I said nothing comes for free, NOTHING!"* The next day Lele met up with me outside after school let out and handed me a large envelope "Take this."

"What? Naw I can't—"

"It's not up for discussion." Lele said seriously cutting me off. I accepted the money and met up with Kane. He opened the envelope and looked at the money inside, "Yo you do know that this is enough for the rest of the year right?" I shrugged my shoulders and just stood dumb-founded "So when do we start?"

"Today." The months went by and the training was crazy and intense. This was my main focus, I ate slept, and dreamt training. Kane didn't let up either he would push me to new limits; I didn't have time to hang out, party, or even chill with Lele. She understood and she stood by my side the whole way, she was happy for me more than anyone really. My mother would ask from time to time but she was mostly wrapped up with work or doing her own thing. The school year ended and I graduated, that same year my body transformed into a new machine unlocked and ready to destroy anything in my path.

"Hey Decon, get dressed." My mother yelled out from her bedroom. I didn't know why, I just got dressed in a blue button up, and dark blue jeans. My mother came out of the room with a beautiful blue dress that hugged her body showing off her curves, she had on yellow open toe stilettos with a yellow scarf that wrapped around her curly brown hair that was slightly wild. She smelled amazing wearing this new perfume from Victoria Secrets. Her nails were freshly done painted steel blue with the middle finger in silver glitter; she even had on make-up that made her look a decade younger. I was lost for words, literally and if you didn't know we were mother and son, you would think we were dating by the way she looked. "Wow! Look at you sexy!" I said flirtatiously "Thank you baby! I said we were going out for your graduation and I had to take care of my baby boy." I was in real shock, this was a real turn of events for our relationship and I had to admit I was living in the moment.

We caught a cab to the Barclays center to catch a Brooklyn Nets game versus the Hawks, Brooklyn won the game and I was able to see my mother in a different light. No matter what our past had been, this was starting to be the start of a better future. "So are you hungry?"

"Yea I can eat."

'Yea I know I saw how you killed those two hot dogs ha-ha." She said busting out in a laugh. We went to Junior's and ate dinner. "So how are you and Leandra doing?"

"We are doing well; we haven't spent much time together since I've been training." I said filling my face with shrimp pasta, "Oh yea, I see that you put on some weight, I like it." She said smiling, we finished our meals and she treated me to my favorite dessert Red Velvet Cheese Cake. We walked the city night laughing and getting to know each other better. She had just got a promotion at her job at the bank and she was smiling from ear to ear. I was excited for her and the fact that she stayed clean for over three years made me even happier. We ended the night on a good note and headed home to sleep.

It was hot July morning I woke up to the sun beaming straight into my face; I rubbed my eyes and looked out my bedroom window. It was a normal summer morning in the courtyard, elderly people were sitting on the benches and there were birds singing in the trees, it's crazy how this place looked like a normal world during the day, and at night it turns into the slums of New York. I went to the bathroom scratching my crotch and yarning, looked at myself in the mirror and my curly hair was all over the place and I still had sleep in my eyes. Shit even my facial hair was starting to come out, but I liked the baby-faced look so I constantly shaved. Since I've been in New York I grew to about six feet four inches, and weighted about two hundred and twenty-five pounds all muscle. My chin was more defined and thick; my chest had gotten wide and compact. I noticed that my neck and traps were thick and full. I started to flex my arms, displaying the layer of muscle that formed into the peak of a mountain. I've always had abs but thanks to the strict diet that I've been on they were more defined and solid as an ice tray. I looked down at my legs and saw that the muscle formation that developed was more complex then Chinese arithmetic. I was huge but still flexible and fast, and solid as cold steel. I was getting more attention from more than just the ladies, people were starting to call me little Luther, not quite sure what that meant; but by this time the whole hood knew I was dating his sister. After I got out of the shower I noticed that my mother was watching TV in the living room, and I asked her if she needed anything from the store, she wanted me to pick up a pack of Newport's and a Vanilla Dutch. I stepped out and told her that I would return in about thirty minutes; making it about a block down the street Luther pulled up and rolled down the window "Yo

D come here nigga." I walked up to the SUV "What's up son" I said to Luther, ever since I found out that Lele confided in her brother, to get him to pay for my martial arts classes he made it his business to check up on me regularly. He told me that he was just checking on me and asked if I wanted to make some runs with him in the neighborhood, I told him I couldn't and that I had some other business to get too, he smiled took a pull from the joint in his hand, "I don't think he understood me Elroy. Decon get the fuck in the car." I reluctantly got into the back of the SUV with Luther. There was nothing but silence as we drove down Church Avenue. We pulled up Prospect Park and Elroy double parked on the side of the road. A large man wearing all blue was standing over by a tree. He was average height but wide and had a large brown paper bag in his hands. "Stay here with Elroy; I'll be back in a sec." Luther stepped out of the car and walked up to the man and started talking. The two of them started what seemed to be a civil conversation, but quickly turned out to be an angry dispute. I couldn't hear what was being said, but from inside the car I could tell that the two large men were not seeing eye to eye. Big blue said something foul and all I could make out was the words FUCK YOU being yelled out towards Luther. Luther cold cocked the guy with a surprised right hook to the side of his jaw, and pulled out a giant gun from the back of his waistbands. In broad daylight Luther placed the gun to the guy's temple and squeezed the trigger putting his face and brains all over the park floor. I jumped at the loud roar of the giant pistol and was in aww, as I watched people running all over the place screaming, Luther just simply bent down unmoved grabbed the paper bag and walked back into the SUV, he ordered Elroy to drive and head back to my neighborhood to drop me off.

Luther grabbed an old shirt from the back of the car and wiped off his hands and face of blood from his recent victim. "Hear you go D, a lil sum to hold you down for a while."

"I can't accept that dog." I said to Luther gently pushing the bloody paper bag from in front of me. "Look nigga, I'm trying to be nice to you, fool. I'm not asking anything from you, in fact I'm trying to give you a gift and this is how you show your respect? You can't be dating my sister and you're fucking broke! Nigga take this shit and shut the fuck up about it." I felt like accepting his money was like making a deal with the devil, he was right though, I was broke. I thought about how she took me shopping and it would be nice if I could return the favor. So, left with little choice and nowhere to run to I took the bag. "I don't have to tell you to keep your mouth shut about today do I?"

"Naw dog, I ain't saying shit."

"Yea I know, now go about your day lil nigga, I'ma get at you later."

Yea it definitely felt like I made a deal with the devil.

I got out of the SUV and watched them drive off; I exhaled deeply and had a slight moment relief. My heart danced in my chest going a million miles per hour from the fear of being killed just as easily as the guy in blue at the park. I went off to the corner store, grabbed the stuff for my mother and headed back home to rest my head.

***

The next day I got a call from Lele telling me that her brother wanted me to meet him in queens, I didn't know why he wanted me but I learned when dealing with Luther, I learned not to ask. I made it to Queens about an hour later and was approached by Elroy, Luther's driver who told me to follow him behind the interstate wall where there was a crowd of people and two dogs fighting in the middle of this makeshift ring. Luther was standing with this gray tank top and blue shorts with a pair of dark blue Jordan's, he had these two fine ass females standing next to him on either side of him. I was looking around at the scene to get adjusted to the atmosphere; "HEY D!! COME OVA HERE!" Luther shouted out from the crowd. The walk from one side of the arena to the next felt like a mile, eyes from all over were staring at me, it felt like a movie walking through a cloud of weed, and cigarette smoke finally making my way through the crowd to Luther. He was happy from all the money he just made betting on the Rottweiler who just won the fight, Luther put his huge arms around me and spoke loudly to over talk the crowd. "My nigga, I'm happy to see you here, you know paying for all those classes and watching you grow has given me an idea. I want to see you in action, TODAY!" the sinister grin he gave me after he spoke sent a bone chilling vibe through my body that made me go numb.

I looked into his eyes and could tell that he wasn't joking, nor was he going to take no for an answer, "OK who do I get to beat first?" I said to him in a very cocky tone in my voice. Luther pointed across the way on the other side of the arena, and standing there was this big chunky guy they called Buda, he was hopping up and down on his toes and smacking himself in the face, I guess to show some type of toughness. I took off my white tee shirt and entered the ring with a bare chest and green basketball shorts, Buda stepped in and smiled "ALL THEM MUSCLES AINT SHIT ONCE I LAY YA ASS OUT!" He was serious and looked like he was used to this type of environment, I looked back at Luther and saw him nodding his head up and down as if he knew I was about to fuck this dude up. I looked back at Buda, smiled and walked up to the middle of the ring motioned my hand for him to come get me. Buda didn't like that, and ran towards me with his arms spread out wide as if he wanted a hug, I jumped up and went into a round house kick causing Buda's head to snap violently, and his body to fall right and landing face first into the ground. He was knocked out cold and motionless, the crowd shut up quick and for a second you could hear a rat pissing on cotton it was so quiet. Luther let out a loud roar, causing the crowd to go bonkers. I walked over to Luther and put my shirt back on; the crowd was still going retarded, cheering and patting me on my back and all I could see was Luther's smile and feeling his arms around me squeezing me close to him as he cheered me on. "I told y'all my nigga was gonna do it, I told y'all. Yo where's my money?" Luther released me and started to collect his money and told Elroy to get the car. I could tell there were a lot of people betting against me from the sour faces and mugs I got as I walked out of the crowd, I got into the car with Luther and his two groupies.

"That shit was fire my nigga, I mean FUCK!! You destroyed that fat motherfucker with one kick I love that shit!" Luther was hype and kissing the girls next to him, I felt good after fighting outside of a controlled environment like the Martial arts tournaments. On the ride back to Brooklyn we listened to music and talked about how much money he just made. Before he let me out Luther looked me in the eyes and said if I needed anything to make sure I called him and let him know. "We will be in touch my dude. I have some plans for sun, I have some plans." Luther flashed me a smile and had Elroy pull off and like that they were gone.

***

My phone started to buzz-off from Nate who was calling me, "What's good?"

"Yo Thun, you need to get over to Empress and dem spot ASAP kid, she trying to fight that chick DeAndrea from 94th."

"What? Aight, say no more, I'm on the way now." I said taking off quickly to where Empress lived. She didn't live far from my projects but it was still a journey. I made it just in time to see Empress going one on one with DeAndrea. DeAndrea was getting her ass whooped and her friends weren't happy about that. Nate was holding back Deandrea's boyfriend who was starting to get fed up with Nate, 'Nigga if you don't take your hands off of me we gonna have a problem!" DeAndrea's boyfriend said pushing Nate's hand away. Out of nowhere S-Dot came from behind the crowd and punched one of DeAndrea's friends who had a thick stick. The girl crashed into the floor from the punch and was bleeding from her nose, S-Dot sparred no mercy in giving ole girl the beating of her lifetime. This sparked a chain reaction and the angry crowd became an angry brawl. There were more of them then it was us, and I jumped in just in time to save Empress from getting a brick smashed into her skull. I pushed kicked the girl who was trying to bash Empress's head in, she flew back about fifteen feet and smacked the back of her head onto the concrete floor. Another girl had a broom stick and was coming after S-Dot who was still busy with ole girl. The girl with the stick took a baseball stance and swing towards S-Dot. I blocked the blow with my forearms causing the stick to crack in half upon contact. The fight felt like it was going on for hours given that it was only five minutes; Empress's sister came outside with a gun and let off shoots in the air. The whole mob stopped fighting at the sound of gun shots and ran off in all directions. "Oh Shit! My nigga came in on some X-Man, Luke Cage shit. Breaking brooms with your forearms what the fuck!" Nate said, still hyped over the fight, "Thanks y'all, that shit was crazy." Said Empress trying to catch her breath, "Empress get ya ass in this house now!" Ruby, Empress big sister barked from the top of the staircase. Empress and S-Dot walked inside and I left with Nate back to my projects, "I' ma split kid gotta make some runs tomorrow with Mark, we bout to be about our music in a minute."

"Word? I feel ya, you know ima be down no matter what."

"Cool my nigga, one!"

"One"

Chapter 8

𝔉EAR NO MAN

When I came back home that day Frank, my mother's current boyfriend at the time was in the kitchen drinking milk from the carton. This nigga didn't even live here and he was walkin around topless and in his boxers drinking out of the carton and shit, this was starting to piss me off beyond my limit. Frank had the funkiest breath I ever smelled, he didn't last too long, then my mother got involved with this guy named Jonathan who worked for the cable company. He used to hook her up with weed and free cable, but two weeks into them dating he was arrested for violating his parole. About a week before the month was over my mother's new boo moved in with us Keith. This big black motherfucker about Six feet ten inches with a black and gray goat-tee, and a shiny bald head. He was moving in with us because she said she wanted her man to be closer to her. They were dating for about two months, and if you asked me the nigga was a bum. He was locked up on a drug charge and was out for about a year, but something about the nigga just didn't sit right with me. I didn't like Keith and I could tell he wasn't too fond of me either. Keith weighed about three hundred pounds and kept his P.O. off his back by working as a bouncer at a few clubs, but from time to time I saw him selling drugs on the corner around the parks and store fronts. My mother met Keith through his cousin who worked in the hair salon, talking about how he was a nice guy and needs a nice lady to settle down with. With a few sweet words and a couple of dinners he and my mother were an item.

***

It was a windy, rainy September morning Mary had come home to see how mommy was doing and I was sitting on the couch watching TV and eating a fried bologna sandwich, when Keith walked over to me and told me to go make him a sandwich. *"This nigga gotta be out of his mind"* I thought to myself, who the fuck he thought I was his servant. I guess being in Brooklyn for a while changed the way I spoke, the way I thought, the way I walked, just my whole personality succumbed to the New York lifestyle, I even lost my southern accent. I gave Keith the craziest look and I presumed that pissed him off, and this was when he made it his job to teach me that he was the new man in the house. Keith walked over to me and knocked my plate on the floor, I stood up and looked up to his face staring him straight in the eyes showing him that I had no fear of him at all. "Look here boy you going to respect me" he got a little closer and said in my ear "them pretty eyes would get you in trouble in prison nigga, I would've made you my little bitch!" His hot breath gave me an uncomfortable feeling I pushed him away forcibly and within seconds his giant bear hands grasped my neck. He was chocking the shit outta me and I felt helpless, I tried to break his grip but it felt almost impossible. I heard my mother and Mary laughing walking from the back rooms, Keith let me go as he pushed me down on the couch and smirked. I held onto my neck trying to regain my breath and control my emotions; Keith walked to the kitchen hugged my mother and the way he looked at Mary was the way a rapist looks at his pray. Mary looked at me and asked if I was ok seeing that I was turning red on the face, I nodded yes and picked up my sandwich from the floor walked to the kitchen threw it in the trash and walked to my room.

I sat in my room going over in my head what just happened, over and over the scene of Keith grabbing my neck and chocking me made me furious. It felt like his grip became tighter and tighter, I fell out of my trance when my phone vibrated from a text from Lele asking me if I could meet her at the bodega, I replied yes and grabbed my coat and walked out of my room. The laughter from Keith, my mother and Mary was making me sick, walking past the kitchen my mother asked me where I was going "out" I replied as I walked out of the house and headed down the stairwell. Claxton was walking up as I was going down "What up D, haven't seen you in a while son how you been?" I told Claxton that I've been good just real busy at the dojo, he told me that he was taking Mary to a museum in Harlem. We dapped up and went our separate ways.

Walking down the street that feeling of being weak, being exposed, used just like that time with Bobby Walker came all over me and all I could see was a dark spirit circling around me. I made it about two blocks down the street and a feeling of danger; something wasn't right about the air. It was a cool mist that blew around me and the streets were empty except a group of three dudes standing on the corner wearing black hoodies. "Yo what's good sun, come ova here." One of the three shouted out, I recognized that voice as soon as he spoke. It was the guys who had jumped me before and I knew what they were capable of. I tried to avoid them by walking to the other side of the street "This nigga deaf?" one asked the other as he pointed to me, I knew what was next I seen them eagerly walking towards me. So I took off running and like clockwork they were in pursuit, I made a left about a block away from the bodega and I was stuck in this ally with a giant cement wall blocking me from going to the other side. I was stuck and out of breath and these three goons walked around the corner laughing once they noticed that they had me cornered. "You aint hear me calling you, pussy ass nigga?" one of them shouted at me as they slowly moved towards me. I saw the one with the gold teeth smiling at me as he removed his hoodie from his head, and then I saw Mary's cross around his neck. I couldn't just back down, I couldn't just be a bitch, this was going on for way too long, and now It was time for it to end.

The painful memory of Bobby Walker and Keith took over my body making me angry and fueling my body with this crazy energy: power. I walked up to them and took off my coat and dropped it to the floor and prepared myself for a fight I knew in the back of my head I may not win. The first guy pointed at me and looked at his friends laughing and stepped up to me and threw a left straight punch towards my face, I quickly dodged it and kicked in his right knee cap dropping him to the ground as he let out the loudest cry I ever heard from a man in my life. You could tell that the other two weren't ready for what I just did, as their jaws dropped and eyes widen. The one with the gold teeth put his hands up but waited for me to make my move which I didn't hesitate to make. I threw a fake left, as he attempted to dodge I hit him with a sweet three punch combo that split his lip and caused him to start bleeding from his mouth. He staggered backwards as his friend thinking he was slick came up behind me and wrapped his arm around my neck. I grabbed his arm and twisted it around my head to where his palm was facing the sky and his elbow was on top of my shoulder. I bent his arm down with crazy force causing the bone to rip right threw his Adidas sweat jacket, and him screaming to the top of his lungs.

The one with the gold teeth looked around at his friends, one may never walk the same and the other in so much pain he didn't care about the fact that he won't be able to use his arm for a long time. The same guy who had so much to say, so much shit to talk, robbing me every chance he got, was now speechless and had a mouth full of blood. I walked up to him, he threw a right and left punch that I dodged and I leg swept him causing him to hit the floor with a hard thump. I grabbed Mary's cross and snatched it off his neck and put it in my pocket. "You fucked with the wrong nigga." I told him as he lay on the floor squirming to his feet. He slowly backed away wiping the blood from his mouth "yea kid my bad, it's all love fam" he said as I could tell he was ready to take off, at this point I was too heated and feelin myself to let him get away this easy.

Chapter 9

𝔍NITIATION!!!

Gold teeth took off in the opposite direction with me right behind him, surprisingly he ran right into Luther who happened to be walking with Lele trying to figure out what all the screams were about. "Yo Luther, dog my bad man I didn't mean to run into you like this, but look I was just coming to see you about the money, I swear but this nigga tried to rob me." I couldn't believe this bitch as he turned to face me and lie on me like that. Luther looked very angry and his chest started to puff out, Luther asked him what happened when he came around the corner and saw the other two guys lying on the floor in pain. I knew it was serious when Luther's eyes got blood shot red and the veins in his body began to grow right out of his arm and neck. "See Luther I told you he did this." The guy with the gold teeth was looking at me and pointing trying to explain himself to Luther. I looked at Luther and stared into his eyes and shaking my head at the lies this guy was telling.

"Hey Decon what the fuck is going on, you tried to rob my man Larry over here?" Luther asked me, "Naw, this nigga has been fuckin with me since I moved here. I was trying to avoid them but they just had to follow me."

"Is that right?"

"Word to everything" Luther turned to Larry and smiled, "So you just couldn't help ya self huh?" I could see Larry's face was filling of anger as he looked at me. " Man fuck this nigga, I should ju-" Luther pulled out his .375 magnum and shot Larry in the back of the neck cutting off his sentence, the powerful round roared out ripping a hole that stretched from his lower jaw to the top of his chest. His body dropped limb. I jumped from the sound of the loud gun, my heart racing ten thousand miles per second as Luther wiped the blood from his face and walked to the guy with the broken arm, and shot him twice in the body. In my mind, I saying *"what the fuck!"* repeatedly. Luther stepped on the guy with the fucked up leg right on his dislocated knee cap and told him "Listen to me very clearly, tell everyone that this is what happens when you fail to pay your debts or fuck with my main man Decon, can you feel me!" Luther said as he put more pressure on his leg before he walked away. Luther meant business and everyone in the neighborhood knew this, he had the city on lock. The whole time all this was going on Lele didn't lose her composer nor did she flinch just a little. She was standing there laughing like this was some type of Saturday morning cartoon.

"Let's go" Luther said as he walked around the corner towards his SUV, Lele looked at me "You okay?"

"Yea, I'm straight"

"Why you lookin like that?"

"Nothin, it's nothing" I was freaked out, totally confused on what the hell just happened, I mean pure blood being spilled right in front of me like I saw in movies but this wasn't no movie this was real life; just like that time I went for a ride with him to prospect park. I could honestly say that this was the beginning of my heart turning dark and cold. As we sat in the car Luther pulled out a towel poured water on it and wiped his face. The look on Luther's face was cold, he had no heart and something about the sight of death sorta gave me a happy feeling. I don't know what was going on with me, I tried to think about Mama D but it was as if the darkness was blocking any pure thoughts from entering my mind. Luther told Elroy to drive us to Queens.

***

We made it to Southside in front of this green and brown house that looked rundown. Elroy stepped out and went inside to collect the money; I didn't know what to think at this point or how to feel about sitting in a car with a killer and his crazy sister. *One would say that I was pure at this point but what will happen next was my journey to the dark side.* Luther instructed Lele to grab the black case from the back and give it to him; I watched as he opened the case and pulled out a silver Glock .45 and a full magazine clip that he inserted into the gun. He handed the gun to Lele and said "Remember what we talked about" she nodded and told me to get out of the car. *"I would admit at this point I was scared for my life and as I stepped out of the SUV I was convinced that this was going to be my last sight at life."* She led me to a side ally with stairs leading down to this red door, I looked around and saw no one outside, no birds, just the chilly air that blew around us and Lele with this gun in her hand.

"Open the door." Said Lele, as I went down the stairs I start feeling sick to my stomach, I thought I was about to lose the rest of my breakfast at the thought of being killed in a dark basement. "What's going on ma?

Why do you have that gun?" Lele didn't say a word she just kept motioning for me to move along into the room. "Come on Lele tell me something. Why are we down here?"

"Don't worry boo, you will find out soon enough, but for now, just keep going inside." I walked into the dark damp room, it was a little warm and it smelled of trash and a mix of spoiled feces. Lele turned on the lights and strapped to a chair on the far end of the wall was Taquana, the girl who got caught stealing from BG. The look on her face was of untainted fear and that was obvious from the stream of tears that were running down her face, she was stripped down to her bra and panties with blood running from her nose and lip. Her hair was shaved and thrown all over her, the scene was like a snuff film it was horrible, I never seen anything like this in my life. "What the hell is going on?" I asked Lele, she smiled "This little bitch was stealing from us and selling to the Black Knights for a personal profit. BG told me everything that went down the day she found out and gave her a pass." Lele took a pause to shake her head, "This bitch had the nerve to do it again after being given a second chance, so the price for stealing is death."

'okay, so why am I here?"

"Luther wanted you to be here and handle this; he wants you to be his personal hitman."

'So your brother wants me to do his dirty work, if he is capable to do it himself?"

"Look D, if you don't do this, you're gonna end up like Larry, and eventually her." Lele said pointing over to Taquana. I couldn't believe my ears; my own girlfriend was threatening me, I knew this bitch was evil, but this shit was on a whole new level. I grabbed the gun and cocked it back; I looked at Taquana and saw the fear in her eyes. Her life was in my hands and I was stuck between doing the right thing and end up dead, or take her life and survive to see another day. I pointed the gun at Taquana and thought about Keith, and how mad I got when he chocked me, and how pissed I was at this moment from being set up by this two faced bitch. The anger took over and I could hear the squeals coming from Taquana's gagged mouth, I closed my eyes and squeezed the trigger three times. The rounds were loud and echoed in the cramped basement. They went through her like a knife into warm butter, one round hitting her chin and the other two went through her chest. I saw this as I opened my eyes, the lifeless body of Taquana, her lower jaw was gone and blood pumping onto the floor. Pieces of flesh and blood splattered on the back of the wall. I just killed someone out of cold blood, I was one of them, no different than Luther and deep inside I enjoyed every minute of it.

Lele grabbed the gun from my hand and smiled, "Oh shit! Did you see how you tore her face apart? Damn that was crazy, serves you right you thievin ass bitch." Lele took the smoking gun from my hand and walked out towards the car; I stood there and looked at my work, messy and evil. I smiled and ran out of the basement behind Lele. Walking behind her I could see her smiling, she was sick and I knew she was going to be a problem, but at that moment I was a problem to myself. We got into the car and Elroy sped off, Luther started clapping his hands and was very excited when he heard about what I did. He took the gun from Lele and disarmed it and put it back in the case, he looked up at me and with that sinister grin "Welcome to the Kingdom."

Chapter 11

WELCOME TO THE KINGDOM

Luther leaned across the seat and slapped me on the shoulder and said welcome. I was confused and asked "What is the Kingdom?" Lele and Luther busted out in laughter; Luther lit a blunt and inhaled deeply letting out a storm of smoke as he explained the kingdom. "See blood the Kingdom is New York City, everything in it everything around it. It has only one ruler with twelve disciples, and no I'm not the ruler if that's what you were thinking. I'm just a disciple doing what the ruler tasks me to do." While Luther was talking I couldn't help but think back to Mama D talking about Jesus and his twelve disciples, and how similar Luther's story sounded just a like. Luther kept on explaining the natural order of things and who controlled what in the Kingdom.

"The ruler's name is Percy, he was a pimp from Georgia and he stays in Manhattan, but controls the streets of every borough. You work for me until told otherwise." Luther said as he handed me a stack of money and said that I was now set for life as long as I continued to pay my debts to the Kingdom, or tithes as he put it. I put two and two together and come to the conclusion that he was having me pay for the Martial arts classes. I counted the money, it was $100,000 dollars in brand new hundred dollar bills, I gotta admit this wasn't going to be something I could easily turn down. "So who are the disciples?" I asked being turned on by the stack of money in my hand that I stuffed in my coat pocket. Luther told me the breakdown in order from one to twelve, twelve being the highest. There was "Skinny Slim" a skinny black dude who shot first and asked questions later. He was in charge of the drug trade in Harlem, and then there was "Black King" a big fat motherfucker from West Africa who ran the drug trade in Queens. I saw him from time to time when I would visit Nate. I actually knew about him from S-Dot and Empress, they would get their hair braided by one of his daughters. *"Voodoo Child"* some believe she was a government assassin, others think she was just some crazy bitch. But she was this New Orleans chick who was in charge of moving weapons into New York anywhere Percy wanted them to go. I would later find out that working with her was no joy, and that she was more than one could handle. Next was *"Lord Shabazz"* a crazy dude from East Harlem with a scar running down his right eye from his bid in Attica. He ran the chop shops in Harlem, Staten Island, and the Bronx, and get this his cousin was *"Solomon 7"* who happened to be the fifth disciple, ain't that some shit? He ran chop shops in Queens, Brooklyn, and Long Island, no wonder he never had time to chill with us. *"Now get this"* the sixth disciple was my mother's boyfriend *"Keith"* he ran the drug trade in Brooklyn this shit was getting wild. The next one wasn't just one person it was these two Puerto Rican twins Rosa and Gloria also known as "Baby Doll" and "Spanish Fly", the two twins that were always around Lele I had a feeling that the two of them were trouble. They were the eyes and ears of the streets; they informed Percy on everything that went down in the city. They were also thieves who would rob you before you even noticed you had something to lose.

The eighth disciple was known as *"T.M.D."* which stood for Too Much Drama, this gay drag queen was as big as me who controlled and managed a lot of

Manhattans exotic clubs, the Kingdom washed a lot of their money through them. Then you have *"China"* this beautiful yet very deadly Taiwanese chick who often kills men after she slept with them, she started to gain the name the last kiss seeing that she was the last person you kissed before you died. She ran everything in Chinatown; she was that "Chinese connection". Then you have *"Luther"* well you already know about him, he was Percy's personal go to man to regulate everything on the ground. He was sort of a secretary force just don't call him that. *"Kartoon Killa"* a four hundred pound Puerto Rican and Jamaican killa who would stomp on anyone who fucked with him, he ran the drugs in the Bronx, Staten Island, and get this he was a policy director in Rikers Island where he also pushed a lot of the drugs and transport to upstate. The last disciple is the one and only *"King Jaffy Joker"* Percy's right hand man, he was about six feet five inches tall and had to be at least three hundred pounds, His ethnicity was Samoan, and he was tatted all the way up to his cheeks. People called him the face of death because anyone who ever tested him ended up dead and a new tattoo was inked on his body. He controlled the money; Percy's accountant. These were the leaders of the Kingdom and they were all dangerous. They had every gang in New York buying from them and selling through them, and if anyone ever tried to go around them, that's when they got dealt with personally.

***

After about an hour or so I was so wrapped up in what Luther telling me about the Kingdom, I didn't even notice that we were crossing over the bridge into Manhattan. We pulled up to this medium sized three story house in Manhattans Lower Eastside; it was in a quiet neighborhood and fit in perfectly. Lele escorted me inside, it was empty wasn't touched yet like they had just moved in. The first floor opened up into a large living room, a full sized kitchen was tucked off into the back, a door on the right led to the basement, with a stair case to the left that made its way upstairs. There were five rooms upstairs and three bathrooms, another stair case led to the attic serving as another room. Lele took me to a room in the back of the house on the second floor. There were guns and ammunition all over the place, "Go on grab what you want." She said throwing a small duffle bag at me. My face lit up like a little kid on Christmas morning, I grabbed a chrome .38 with this pearl grip, and then I saw an all-black 9mm in the corner that I threw into the bag. I grabbed two clips for both guns and a box of ammunition for both. "That's all you want?" Lele asked me looking very surprised at what all I grabbed. "Yea for now" I responded as I zipped up the bag I walked out of the room and headed towards the door. Lele grabbed my arm and spent me around kissing me on the lips and squeezing my back. I was shocked I wasn't expecting this, she looked up at me and said that we need alone time. I smiled and agreed, we walked out of the house and got inside the SUV, Luther was gone, and when Lele asked Elroy where he was he told her that Percy came and picked him up for a meeting. Lele told Elroy to drop us off at her house; I was a little excited all this time dating I've never seen the inside of her house nor seen her mother or father at that. At this time I totally forgot about what all happened today. We pulled up to the house and stepped out of the car, Elroy drove off and Lele held my hand and led me inside.

We walked inside, and I was shocked the inside was beautiful better then where I was living. "Stay here, I will be back" Lele told me while she fixed up her room. I didn't mind I was taking in this house little by little. In the living room there was a fire place that lit up by remote, a huge kitchen and another room full of pictures and a jet black piano with *"In Loving Memory Lisa P. King"* engraved in it. I looked around some more and noticed a picture of Luther, Lele and this beautiful black women with the most stunning smile I ever seen on a women. *"That must be her mother."* I said aloud to myself.

"Daddy come upstairs I miss you" the way she called for me was too sexy for me to resist. I walked up the stairs slowly and followed this wonderful scent, as I walked into the door the light from the evening sun sent a beautiful glow into the room through the violet and pink curtains on the window. There was Anthony Hamilton *[do you feel me]* playing and here comes this beautiful girl wearing this blue and silver corset with matching thong and baby oiled up to the point where my little man couldn't get much harder. She was wearing these silver heels that brought her up a few inches that added to her sexiness. I dropped the duffle bag to the floor and took off my coat, kicked off my boots and walked towards her, I took off my shirt that exposed my six pack and chiseled chest that she began to kiss and rub on. She looked at me and smiled when I bounced my pecks up and down, she slowly kissed me on the lips and her right hand reached into my jeans grabbing my dick, now hard as a rock.

The music was setting the mood right, she stopped kissing me and knelt down to undue my belt as my pants dropped to the floor, so did she started rubbing and licking me as I was already standing at attention. As she slowly moved her mouth on it my feet begin to get weak and I could hardly stand. I stopped her and picked her up carrying her to the king sized bed laying her down and began to kiss her very passionately. I undid her corset exposing her voluptuous D sized breast, I kissed the right one then the left, and I started to suck on them and rubbing on her clit through her panties which were quickly filling with moisture. She let out a soft moan when I squeezed on her right breast with my free hand.

I stopped sucking on her nipple and pulled her thong off, Lele lifted her hips just a little to help me get them off. I didn't have a condom and I wasn't thinking about one either, and neither was her as she pulled me in close to her and licked my ear lobe sending a chill down to my spine. I entered her slowly causing her to take a deep breath and relaxing again. It was warm and wet inside of her, and as we continued the noises she made became louder and louder, her nails gripped onto my back as I thrust a little harder. You could feel the excitement brewing in the room and the pressure started to build inside of me as I drove a little deeper. "Don't stop!" Lele yelled out, I couldn't hold out any longer and I could feel it coming. I grabbed hold of the mattress and leaned in a little closer exploding inside her, my eyes rolled to the back of my head and my body felt numb on top of her. The sweat on her body was like glue to her hair, I pulled out and rolled over to the other side breathing deeply, and it felt as if we ran for miles; my first time.

We laid in the bed as the sun went down sending in this dark amber color into the room talking about future plans for us and goals we wanted to reach. "Who is Lisa?" I asked her, Lele paused for a moment and sat up "Lisa is my mother, she was murdered when I was 14 years old" I didn't know what to say at hearing the horrible news, "I'm sorry"

"It's okay I've come to grips with the situation and it was so long ago."

"What was she like?"

"She was a wonderful spirit, she loved to sing and she would sing with this jazz band in the Bronx. Music was her life and if fate would have it she died from it as well." I lay quietly as Lele told the story of her mother, how she loved to sing and play the piano. "One night, she had just wrapped up at this club called Ray's in the Bronx. I guess she was craving a snack, so she had walked into a corner store; the stores camera's caught three guys rushing into the store. She was the only person in there besides the clerk, one of the men shot the clerk in the head and the other two found my mother trying to hide in the back of the store. The men took turns beating her and raping her one by one. The whole ordeal lasted for fifteen minutes, fifteen motherfuckin minutes with no signs of the police or any help from the outside world." Lele started to tear up at the recounts of the assault, "after they were done one of the men shot her four times and finished robbing the place."

"Damn, that's so messed up, ma... I'm speechless; did the police ever find them?"

"No, they never did, after three days of waiting Luther was fed-up and ready for war. He found the men with the help of the twins sitting outside at a park across the street from the Bronx Zoo, he was nineteen at the time when he stretched them all out in broad daylight, they didn't even have a chance to react." That's how he became so notorious in not only Brooklyn, but all over the city. He's been taking care of me ever since.

The sky was getting dark and the moon was brightly shinning, it was a beautiful night. I kissed Lele and got dressed grabbed my things and took off to my shit hole projects. I made it home a little after ten and I could see Keith in a dark hoodie talking to a few of the guys who lived in the apartments. "Hey little nigga where you been?" Keith shouted at me as I approached the front gate, thoughts of killing this nigga right here ran through my mind. I tried to walk past him without saying a word but he got close enough to grab my arm and squeeze tightly, "You didn't hear me talking to you?" Keith asked aggressively I stared at him still not saying a word; he smacked me across the head hard as hell "YO WHAT THE FUCK!" I screamed aloud, Keith started laughing and told me to get in the house. Deep down inside of me I knew I was going to have to kill this nigga. I shoved him off of me and went inside up to the apartment, I saw my mother sleep on the couch with a bottle in her hand and a burnt roach clip in the ash tray on the side. I just shook my head and walked into my room, closed the door and ripped off my clothes till I was naked and laid in the corner contemplating on how to kill Keith; I was death!!!

Chapter 12

$\mathfrak{I}$ AM DEATH!! AND I AM THE UNKNOWN

I fell asleep on the floor and I became victim to this evil dream that would forever change me from who I was to who I am today.

"My name is death and this is what I do.

I kill people sometimes out of the blue.

I take souls I end lives,

Rather it be by bullet, natural cause, or knife.

I need no reason I do what I will,

I told you my name was death I'll take you

out with a handful of pills.

You fear me when you're awake, you fear me

when you sleep,

You fear me when you pray, you fear me when eat.

I am death and this is what I do.

I leave no trace of my existence, I leave no clues. I am the unknown I make no sense

No one knows me, for I leave no finger prints.

I am the darkness I am the dark dream, I'm the crack rocks that turn a normal person into a crack fiend.

That irresistible attraction to methamphetamines,

Feelings of not being wanted pain and torment, that untold story of the forgotten

The eroded wood where the corps lay rotten.

I am the tears that rundown your face. That prisoner in the cell paying for a crime that he didn't want to affiliate.

I'm the mother who laid her son to rest, that father who killed his children and shot himself in the chest,

That grandmother who's thirty-five that eight year old involved in a rape crime,

No longer pure a defiled flower.
The more you fear me you give me more
power,
I am death and this is what I do, run, scream,
cry, bleed, I don't care you choose.
The grim reaper standing over your grave,
The undertaker prepping your body to this
day, you can't run from me when your time comes.
I am death time to have fun.

I woke up from my dream cold and sweating from head to toe, the sun was starting to rise and I reached up to the air to stretch the cold sleep away from me. I went into the bathroom, still naked I turned on the shower and allowed the hot water to engulf my body. I put my head into the stream and wet my hair making it curlier then it already was, the large fro I kept was sorta a hassle in the morning. As I pulled the curtains back shocking me was Keith standing in the doorway looking me up and down, *"I swear this nigga thought he was still in prison."* I stepped out of the shower and closed the door and wiped the fog from the mirror. I finished up in the bathroom and walked to my room, put on a pair of gray sweat pants and a white tee shirt. I looked down and noticed the duffle bag with the guns in it, I opened the vent that was behind my bed and placed the bag inside I also took the money out of my coat that I had on and placed it in there as well. My mother was still sleep in the bedroom and Keith was drinking some Kool-Aid in the kitchen. "Good morning to you to boy" I looked at Keith and shook my head as I walked out of the door heading towards the stairs to go sit on the roof and think about my life.

The view from up here was beautiful the ultraviolet light from the sun covered by a few clouds was my way of gaining peace and harmony. I started stretching and performing breathing techniques as well as a little Tai chi. about an hour into my workout I heard the door open and Nate walking out onto the roof. 'I knew that was you up here Thun. What's up kid haven't seen you in a minute" Nate was excited to see me and so was I "What up nigga" I greeted him and we sat up on the roof talking about what all we been into. Nate was up meeting this Ethiopian chick that lived about a block down the street and that's when he saw me on the roof. I told Nate what happened with Larry, and Taquana, everyone in Queens heard about Taquana. Nate looked at me and said that I was a different person; he said that I wasn't the same as I was when he first met me. I agreed and told him that I was now working for Luther, I didn't tell him exactly what I did, that would've sent some mixed signals.

Nate and Mark were talking about starting a rap group, and they were having a coming out party tonight that he wanted me to go too. I told him that I would be there and we dapped up and walked down from the roof together. As Nate walked down the stairs I went inside my apartment, my mother was cooking breakfast and Keith was in the back.

I walked to the back and noticed through the crack of the door that he was in there snorting cocaine, I couldn't believe this shit, my mother allowed this stuff back into her life. My mind went in circles and I grabbed my hoodie from my room and walked out the house. I called Mary and told her that I'll be coming to see her today. She was excited to hear that and told me that she would meet me when I get close. I got off the train in Manhattan and met Mary at this coffee shop near her school. "What's up big sis"

"Hey boo, how have you been?"

"I've been better, but im doing alright. How are you?"

"I'm good you know me, just working hard and taking it one day at a time." Mary said taking a sip of her ginger tea, "I spoke to Mama D yesterday."

"How is she doing?" I asked, Mary went into a long pause and her face turned sour. "She's not doing too well."

"Why what's going on with her?"

"They don't know, but I want to go see her soon."

"Yea me to." I missed my grandmother a lot and she was my heart, the only reason I stayed calm most of the time. "Look when I get some money together I'll get us some tickets to go down and see her." In my mind, I wanted to tell Mary what I just got myself into, but she was too pure. She was my only source of light and I didn't want to do anything to corrupt that.

Mary heard about the same party that Nate was talking about and asked me if I was going, I told her that I was and she said that Claxton was going to take her and told me to bring Lele. Thoughts of last night swarmed my brain and a huge smile swam across my face, of course I was going to invite my boo thang. We finished our drinks and Mary walked with me to the train station, we hugged and kissed and agreed to link up at the party before I made my way down the subway stairs. I got back on the train to Brooklyn, and Lele called me as soon as I left the tunnel, she wanted to see me and she asked me to swing by. *"How could I resist?"* I just knew I had to see my boo, I made it to her house about an hour later and she greeted me at the door wearing some blue jeans and this cut off white tee shirt that exposed the layout of a four perfectly cut abs on her stomach. I hugged and kissed her as I walked into the house, she had cooked breakfast and boy was I starving.

The food was what I needed and the sight of the beauty in front of me was an added bonus. "There's a party tonight that I want to go to" I said to her drinking what was left of my orange juice. "Yea Baby doll was just telling me about it, she said that Nate and Mark were going to be preforming." She was excited and said that we need to go shopping, because I needed to change my look. I guess I gave off this thug *"Ruff Ryder"* 90's looks and she thought that if I was going to be with her at a summer party that I needed to look more expensive and up to date. I wasn't about the flashy life, but I had to do what made her happy.

***

I kept having this feeling of darkness ever since my dream last night, I didn't let it affect me, I just kept pushing it to the back of my mind. After shopping with Lele I was in need of a shower and some more food, I jumped in the shower and as I came out Lele had ordered some Chinese food, what's New York without ghetto Chinese fried chicken wings and house special fried rice. Baby doll and Spanish fly came to pick us up me and Lele were matching all black everything, she had on this Prada spandex dress that hugged her body showing off her curves and leaving very little to the imagination. She paired the dress with a set of black red bottom stilettos and large gold earrings and bangle bracelets. I had on a crisp fitted Polo shirt, Levi jeans and Jordan sneakers, with a gold chain that had a gold cross with diamonds around the edges.

When we pulled up to the club there was a line reaching all the way around the corner. I worried that we were going to be there in that line for longer than I wanted too. Mary and Claxton were already inside and based off the heavy base flooding the streets on the outside, the party was poppin. "Come with me" said Lele as we walked up to the front of the line and greeted by this huge bouncer. "What's good Lele, how you been?"

"I'm good Tiger, how are you?"

"You know how it is, business as usual. Y'all trying to get in tonight?" Tiger asked "Yea, but we not waiting in this long ass line." Lele said jokingly, Tiger laughed and opened the club door, "You know damn well you don't have to wait in any line." Lele smiled and handed him a hundred dollar bill for good measure. Inside the club, the party was live, there were girls in miniskirts, short shorts, and small dresses, and the fellas were in their best. The club was pretty big, a large bar stretched across the left side of the building, a large dance floor held multiple people dancing along to the rhythms being put out by the speakers all over. There was a stag in the front of the dance floor that covered the back, with the dj and his systems. I spotted Mary on stage with Claxton dancing; she looked good too I must admit, she was wearing a blue full body romper and these silver six inch heels.

We grabbed some drinks from the bar and made our way to the dance floor, Nate was called on stage shortly after and started raping and out of nowhere Mark got on stage and began to sing the hook, the flow was hot and the crowd was feeling them. They performed five more tracks and the crowd was lit. Somewhere between three or four shots of 151 I ended up on the stage with my friends. About three hours into the party things started to slow down, I was getting tired and was ready to go, plus my world was spinning violently and I feared that I was gonna put all my consumed drinks all over the stage floor.

Mary and Claxton took off, while Lele and the twins dropped me off at the projects, walking inside the apartment I noticed that no one was home; I didn't mind, it was once peaceful in here, plus I wasn't in the position to deal with Keith and his bull shit. I went to my room stripped down and as I put my head on my pillow I got a call from Lemon. He sounded real weird on the phone and I asked him what was going on, he told me that Mama D, was in the hospital and the doctors said that there wasn't much more they could do, she was dying and I was stuck in New York separated from the rest of the world. I sobered up quickly, jumping up to the edge of my bed. "Let me talk to her" Lemon put the phone to Mama D's ear and allowed me to speak to her; she couldn't talk because she had a tubes down her throat keeping her alive.

I told Mama D that I loved her and that I'm so sorry for not being there for her, I cried on the phone and stayed on the line till she passed hearing the machines go off from a dead line made me cry even more. Whatever love or light was left in my heart was now stripped cold; I hung up the phone and cried myself to sleep.

***

I heard my mother and Keith fighting as I woke up with a headache from a mixed cocktail of crying all night, and the liquor. I walked into their room and saw Keith smack my mother across the face putting her on the floor. I looked at the dresser and saw the cocaine and weed all over, they must have been fighting over Keith's raging habit. My mother was half naked and Keith looked up at me standing in the doorway, "Yo what hell are you doin?"

"You want to be next lil nigga?" He said to me as he grabbed a handful of cocaine and shoved it into my mother's face pushing her back to the ground with her hair. I started getting pissed and I could tell he noticed from my chest and breathing starting to speed up, "She wanted to tell me what I can and can't do, I'm so tired of you niggas not showing me any respect." Keith Barked off as he took off his shirt already in his boxers "you can watch if you like" he said as he attempted to rape my mother in front of me. I looked over at my mother seeing blood and cocaine run from her face and the painful thoughts of Mama D, and what I was witnessing was too much to bare. It's been almost a month since I pulled a trigger and I was itching to do so right now. "It's time for you to leave" I said to Keith in a deep serious tone, Keith looked at me and laughed "Nigga I ain't going nowhere, so you can miss me with that tough guy shit. I got even louder this time as I barked "GET THE FUCK OUT NOW!"

His face was in a state of confusion as if I wasn't

talking to him, I could tell that this was going to be violent and I was ready for anything at this point. As he walked up to me, my mother stood up and grabbed him, Keith threw her towards the wall as she hit her head on the corner of the dresser to the right, I saw blood rushing out of her head and I blacked out. For someone I had hated so much and despised, I felt so much pain and sorrow for.

I ran up to Keith and punched him across the face, he was stunned and from the impact to his face my right hand became swollen. "SHIT!" Was all I could think to myself, I tried to strike again but Keith hit me with a hard head butt cutting my left eye and causing it to bleed out profusely. I stepped back and caught a strong left hook to my ribs dropping me to my knee. I grabbed onto Keith to try and pull myself up, he punched me across my head putting me on my stomach. *This next part that I'm about to share with you crushed my soul, and eternally changed my life forever.* What he did next I never saw coming, Keith got on top of me and the rays of the sun peering through the window were blinding my face. The strong stench of Hennessey were crawling out of his pores. He pulled my boxers down to expose my butt, as he pinned me down I tried my hardest to fight this dude off of me. "YO WHAT YOU DOIN MAN??" I screamed and struggled but nothing would throw him off of me. Keith punched me in my spine pinning me down damn near stunning me stiff as a shockwave of pain invaded my body.

Keith leaned in and said in my ear "this is how we treat bitches like you on the inside; I'M IN CHARGE NIGGA BELIEVE THAT!" Forcing himself inside of me, my eyes started tearing up and got wide, the pain was too great for me to handle. The tears started to fall, I clinched my fist trying to spread the pain, my jaw locked up grinding my teeth praying that the pain would go away. He continued over and over I couldn't hold on any longer the last feeling I felt was the sweat and saliva running from his mouth onto my neck and back. I closed my eyes and passed out. He took something from me that I would never be able to get back again. As I lay there this warm feeling came across my body, this flash of golden, yellowish light came across me, I thought it was the sun but my eyes were still closed and I kept hearing the voice of Mama D "Get up Decon, don't cry mama's here" my mind went back to the memories of Mama D helping me ride my bike for the first time. I saw Mary smiling at her graduation party and feeling the joy from everyone that was there. I saw Luke's smiling face on Christmas day eating a whole plate of ham to himself, all these feelings gave me strength but also hurt me being that these were the feelings that I missed the most.

I opened my eyes and saw the brightness of the sun going down and the twilight made it hard to see in the dark room. My boxers were still down to my ankles and my mother's lifeless body lay there in her own blood behind me. She died trying to protect me and all I felt was pain and anger. My ass was sore and I could barely move, my face and hand hurt and that warm feeling that woke me quickly went away as soon as I felt the malevolence of reality and the cold from my heart hit me harder than any other. I heard a loud evil voice in my head telling me to get up and grab my guns. There was a loud laugh coming from the front, the TV in the living room was up loud and saw Keith sitting there watching TV like nothing happened. I limped to my room careful not to make any loud noises, I removed the vent cover to where I hid the duffle bag and money. I pulled out the .38 and inserted a full clip. I cocked it back slowly and wrapped my pillow cover around my hand and the gun. Walking slowly to the living room I didn't want to put him out like a punk I wanted the bitch to see me, I wanted him to see the face of death. I wanted to be the last face he saw before his death. "HEY KEITH!" I yelled out as he turned around to see me pointing the gun wrapped in the pillow case towards him is eyes got wide "Go to hell" ***"BOOM"*** I pulled the trigger watching his face cave in blowing out the back of his head with his brains on the TV and wall behind him. The pillow case muffled the sound just a little bit, and caught on fire from the blast that quickly gave me an idea.

Chapter 13

ⓔVERYTHING THAT

IS BORN MUST DIE

I limped to my room and grabbed the duffle bag and put the money inside of it; I knew someone heard the gunshot and I had a feeling that the cops will be coming soon. I put on my sweats and a wrinkled gray t-shirt; I walked into my mother's room and stared at her body. I felt sorry for her and deep inside there was a love connection between me and her. I had the idea of burning the whole building down fuck these apartments and that's what I proceeded to do, I placed the duffle bag in a black book bag. I walked out the room and looked around; no one was in sight so I limped to the maintenance closet I found three large canisters of paint thinner and a jug of kerosene in the corner under a few painting supplies. I grabbed the paint thinner and the gasoline and headed back into my apartment. I nearly poured the whole thing of kerosene over Keith's body; I proceeded to dousing the whole house in paint thinner and the rest of the kerosene. Walking into my mother's room where she lay I picked her up and placed her on the bed and put a blanket over her body.

I kissed her on the cheek and drenched her room in paint thinner. As I walked out towards the door I poured some of the paint thinner on the stove and turned the gas switch to allow the gas to flow out of it. Walking out I had a trail of paint thinner going down the stairs behind me, striking a few matches I lit the paint thinner. A rush of blue flame screamed into the apartment, I walked as fast as I could out of the projects as the flames engulf the place I once called home. I caught the bus heading towards Corona Queens that just pulled up, as the bus hit the corner a huge blast shook the bus and the neighborhood scared damn near everyone on the bus. Finally making it to Queens I limped to Peter's house and as I arrived he come out of the house "Yo did you hear about your building?" Peter asked me shocked that I was even standing in front of him. I gave him a confused look, "Naw why what's up?"

"It's all on the news, but why are you limping? You look like you just got jumped, you good kid?" Peter said concerned, "Yea I'm good, this ain't shit."

We went into the living room to see the news, I saw that most of the complex was in flames, moments later I get a call from Mary, "Decon where are you?" Mary was frantic and I knew she saw the news and was worried. "I'm in Queens with Peter" I told her she told me that her and Claxton were on their way to come get me, shortly after that I got a barrage of calls and text messages from Lele, Luther, Empress, S-Dot, Natc, Mark, and even Solomon 7. They were all asking me where I was and if I was okay, I told everyone that I was fine and heading back to Brooklyn. About ten minutes later Mary and Claxton showed up and I got into the car with them heading back to Brooklyn. We arrived and the streets were packed like a block party on Labor Day.

"Where's mama? Have you seen her?" Mary kept asking question after question it hurt me to hold on to the secret that I held on too deep down inside of me. The flames were huge and half of the apartment complex was destroyed, and crumbling. Mary broke down and cried in my arms as I held her, my heart was so cold that I couldn't even began to cry, my body was sore and numb to the pain, but I was feeling dizzy and needed to lay down. Claxton took us to his home in Queens and I sat in the room with Mary till she fell asleep.

***

Later that night I took a bath and allowed the pain to leave my body into the hot water that I struggled to sit in. The bath water started to turn a brownish red from the blood coming from my rear end. I submerged myself deep in the water and started to shake at the very thought of me being raped. I got out of the water and put on a fresh pair of clothes and fell asleep next to Mary.

The next morning Mary tried calling Mama D to let her know what had happened to her daughter, *"its crazy how things happen in the worst times."* "She's not going to answer Mary"

"What are you talking about?" Mary asked with her eyes and face red from crying, "Mama D. Mama D died last night as well from lung failure." All this bad news hit Mary hard she looked at me with a sick look, this once beautiful angel was now gloomy and unlike herself, Mary broke down on the floor falling into her own vomit I couldn't bear to see my sister like this. My heart couldn't take any more pain and I became colder by the day, as a person, no longer looking to GOD for help, but now allowing this dark force to act inside of me. Claxton picked Mary up off the floor and took her into the bathroom to clean her up; I walked out of the house and walked to the park right down the street.

I looked to the sky and cursed out the Lord calling him a lie and I wished I was never born. The sky filled with darkness and lighting ripped through the heavens, at this point I smiled at the notion that he was actually responding to my plea for death. I sat as the rain poured down on top of me, the cold drops of rain hit my body with no effect at all giving me the pleasure I wanted. I didn't want to feel good I didn't want to be embraced, this was my walk down the dark path of hell and I wasn't going back; so I thought at the time. As I walked back into the house I went into the bedroom took off my wet clothes and went to sleep. The next day I received a call from Lemon telling me that Mama D's funeral was going to be Sunday which was two days from now I told him that me and Mary were coming down and we would see him soon. That same day we went to the morgue to identify my mother's body. She was badly damaged from the flames and the building falling down on her, we made arrangements to have the body shipped to Florida so that we could burry both my mother and grandmother on the same day at the same location. I bought the tickets with the money that Luther gave to me for killing Taquana and Mary and I were on the first flight to Winter Haven Florida.

***

Luke and Lemon came and picked us up from the airport, Mary had something of a smile on her face when she saw the twins. They were big, well bigger then when we last saw them Luke was bigger than usual and Lemon was buffer too. Arriving to Mama D's house wasn't the same, it didn't have that glow like it used to, it was dark and everything seemed dead, from the garden she loved so much to the little lime tree that was once full and healthy, was now dry and bare. I walked into her room and saw Mary sitting on the bed looking at a picture of her and Mama D on Mary's graduation. "You gonna be ok?" I asked Mary, she didn't respond just looked up at me and made a motion for me to sit down with her. I sat next to her and looked into her red eyes from crying and sore from wiping them countless times. She whispered in my ear "I can't be as strong as you D, I need you more than ever" I grabbed Mary and held her close to me as she cried. I left her in the room when she finally passed out, and walked downstairs to where Luke was cooking in the kitchen and Lemon was reading a FLEX magazine. "Hey Lemon can I talk to you?" I asked him, he got up and we headed down to the basement where we used to sleep, even after all these years it was still the same as when I left it. "What up D?" Lemon asked me looking concerned, "Look man I need you to keep a secret," Lemon looked at me looking confused and hesitant "What is it fam?" Lemon insisted. I told Lemon everything from Luther, to the death of Keith, and the truth behind my mother's death. Lemon was upset and tried to hide the tears that were beginning to breach the corner of his eyes. Lemon looked at me like he never did and asked me if Mary knew any of this. I told him that she doesn't need to know and I asked him not to tell anyone what I just told him, he agreed and we walked upstairs.

***

I remember the morning of the funeral a guy by the name of Jeff Milo came to the house and said that he wanted to go over a few things after the funeral if we had time. We agreed and proceeded to the graveyard, it was crazy for such a dark moment the sky was clear and the sun shined brightly, I figured that this was Gods' way of either taunting me or showing me how much of an angel Mama D was. After the funeral Milo came into the house and sat down with us, he opened up his briefcase and pulled out a thin red packet and opened it. He read off Mama D's will and told us each what Mama D wanted to give for each of us. She gave the house to Luke and Lemon, and a large savings bond to Mary worth two hundred and fifty thousand dollars, as well as some saving's that she had set up. To me Mama D gave me a key that opened a box with a bible inside, I was furious and wanted to toss the damn thing, but in respect to Mama D I kept my composer. After the meeting with Milo, Luke cooked dinner and we all sat at the table just how we did when we were kids. Luke told everyone to close their eyes as he prayed over the food, I kept my eyes open and looked at everyone praying, I couldn't help but think about death and how it made me feel. Luke said amen and we began to eat, the food was great and it almost tasted like Mama D's, "Ha-ha fat ass Luke can cook" I said to myself. We stayed in Flordia for another two days and caught a flight back to New York. On the flight back to New York I noticed a change in Mary, she drank herself to sleep on the flight that was out of her character because I never seen Mary drink so much.

Claxton picked us up from the airport and took us back to his place. Being back in New York felt weird but I was glad to be back. Arriving at Claxton's I got a text from Luther telling me that we needed to meet up ASAP. I kept thinking that maybe Luther knew it was me who killed Keith, or did he. I grabbed my book bag with the guns and ammo and headed out the door to go meet up with Luther in Brooklyn. Luther was standing in front of my burned down apartments looking up at the destruction I caused. "You know we had a Disciple living in this building with some bitch." Luther looked at me as I stood there looking shocked. I was thinking that maybe he did know, but I didn't say anything I just stood there and looked at him. "See you wouldn't know who he was because I didn't want you to know, no one needs to know about the disciples. I went to the morgue and viewed the body, he was badly burned and they say he was shot in the head before he was even set on fire." Luther looked away from me and looked back at the building, "we got some work to do" Luther snapped his fingers and Elroy walked up to me handing me a yellow packet. I opened it up and looked inside, there was a picture and a piece of paper explaining who the target was. Luther put on his shades and said "his name is Fredrick Starr but everyone call's him Black, he tried taking over Brooklyn a few times selling for the Panamanians, the Kingdom thinks Black is responsible for this. Decon we need you to handle this sooner than later." Luther got finished talking and him and Elroy walked to the SUV and drove off.

Chapter 14

GETTING CLOSE

I put the packet in my bag and called Nate to ask him about Black. If anyone knew about him, it would be Nate seeing that he was cool with everyone and knew a lot about the people in Brooklyn. Nate told me that Mark and him were throwing a party at this club called The Cave, and he said that The Cave was in blood territory and Black might be there tonight. I had to go just to scope out the area if anything, I got off the phone with Nate and called Lele and asked her to meet me in front of my building. About ten minutes later she arrived in this two-door blue Acura, it was clean the inside was black with white lining, I got in kissed her and told her to take me to the mall. We must have spent six grand on everything from clothes to jewelry. I had to look fresh to blend in and also not look like I was out to get someone.

On the ride back to Lele's house she told me that she heard her brother talking about my target, and she warned me about him saying that he was a little dangerous. At this point I didn't care if he had an army, I was set to do my job, that's all that was on my mind. We arrived at her house and sat around the couch in front of the fireplace, it was still early and the way this girl smelled put one thing on my mind. Lele put her legs around me and started giggling; I rubbed her smooth legs with my finger tips and started kissing on them. She pressed a button on the remote control and R&B started playing, I think it was Jon B or something like that. I got on my knees and grabbed her thighs bringing her closer to me, she was wearing this pink dress that I lifted up and started kissing on her inner thighs. There was pure ecstasy in the air and the feeling wrapped around me so tight that I could barely feel the pain in my ass. I used my tongue to rub against her thighs on up to these purple boy shorts that hugged her hips and thighs tightly. She let out a soft moan that made me pull them off smoothly, my tongue touched her clit and a slight shimmer went up her leg making her head fall back. I placed my mouth fully on her and moved to the motion of the music, she closed her eyes and lifted her hips a little bit grabbing my hair with her hands. She bit her lip and moaned a little louder as I licked and sucked on her. She tasted as sweet as peaches simmering in a pan full of brown sugar and vanilla topped with rich honey. The tension that I put on her body made her clinch up tightly, "Ba, baby please, give me a minute." She could barely utter a single word from the way I was going in on her. Her body began to shake from the excitement and bliss, she was so sensitive that every time I touched her made her climax that much more.

I pulled off my jeans and went inside of her pushing the elation even higher. She was wet and dripping from the spit that I left on her. I moved in a little more causing her hands with these blue and pink tips to dig deep into my brawny back. The pain she was giving me increased my desire to please her that much more. I was going in deeper and harder moving to the rhythm of her body until she screamed. Her legs wrapped around my waist and I picked her up in the air, my biceps were fully flexed and forearms looking unnatural. My mind went crazy; I was acting like I had a point to prove and I slammed her on me a little harder making her face riddle with expressions. Our sweat was coming through our clothing seeing that I still had on my shirt and she was still in her dress; as I placed her down on her feet she stumbled a little trying to regain her composer, it made me crack a smile a bit. I took off my shirt as she took off her dress and pushed me down on the couch and began to ride me. The feeling was so great that I couldn't hold on much longer, I squeezed her lower back tightly and released. With a winded smile on my face I asked her "Damn ma it's like that?" She smiled and hopped off of me, walked to the bathroom downstairs and I heard the shower running.

I sat there for a minute and closed my eyes; I could feel this presence of good around me that made me jump. I opened my eyes and walked into the shower with Lele; it was about nine when I started to get ready for the party. Lele laid out this black and silver vest with dark blue Levis, I bought these silver and black Nikes that went well with my outfit. Lele walked into the closet and came out with a black gun holster that held one gun and two magazines. I put it on and placed a clip inside of the 9mm and placed it in the holster with and extra clip just in case. The vest I had on covered the holster well; I kissed Lele and walked outside to the car. On the way to the club I called Empress to see if her and S-Dot were down to come with me to the spot. Empress agreed and she filled me in on S-Dot, while I was in Florida. She caught an accessory to arm robbery charge, and she was sitting in Rikers Island waiting on her trial. I picked up Empress from her spot, she was looking good, wearing these army fatigue pants that hugged her curves nicely, with black construction timberlands, and a black tank top. We pulled up to the club and it was packed, security was going hard searching everyone who went inside, I just knew that they would find this big ass gun. I texted Nate to see if he could get me in through the back, but no response. So, I texted Mark and still no response so right when I thought I had to leave this gun inside the car. Mark called me, telling me to come around back to where him and Nate were waiting for us. We came around and congratulated them on the success of the party; I asked them if they saw Black inside and Mark said that he saw him chilling inside with some of his friends and a few females. Nate asked me why I was looking for Black and I told him that I wanted to see who was running the neighborhood and was curious. Nate and Mark escorted us to the V.I.P. lounge on the upper deck, it was nice, bottles of hard liquor were everywhere and the room smelled of fresh weed and black and mild's. I sat down at a couch that was overlooking the bottom floor, the club was packed and trying to find one man was like looking for a needle in a haystack. "Hey fam anyone sitting here?" this tall skinny black dude asked me carrying a bottle of coconut Cîroc in his hand. "Naw" I told him as I continued looking for Black in the crowd. I kept getting this feeling from the guy sitting next to me and as he drank from the bottle I noticed the tattoo on his neck said *"Skinny Slim"* the 1st disciple was next to me and I didn't even know it. Skinny pulled out a blunt from the back of his ear and lit it up, the weed was strong and the aroma would not leave my nose.

He took in a long pull from the blunt and held it in his mouth for a while before he pushed it out. He then turned to me and took off his dark tented shades and looked straight at me. "Your either the "D's" or you really into people watching" Skinny said to me as he took another gulp from the bottle. "I'm looking for a guy name Fredrick Starr do you know him?" Skinny looked at me like I was crazy and then took another hit from his blunt that was starting to ash; "You lookin for Black ha-ha I hate that motherfucker, you don't look like the D's but if you were, fuck him he's over there in the corner with the rest of his bitch ass friends." I looked in the direction he was motioning towards and I spotted him dancing with two fine redbones and drinking from a bottle. Empress walked over to us with her favorite cocktail, a Cadillac margarita. "So what's good, you find Black?"

"Yea he's over there." I said nodding my head in his direction. We sat there in silence for a while, then the DJ announced Mark and Nate to the stage they were now known as the " WEST INDY CONNECTION" the crowd went crazy to see them on stage, they were becoming a huge success. It was like the perfect pair, Nate's strong lyrics and Mark's melodic tone with that Queens flavor hit all the spots. A few hours into the music the DJ called for last call, I stared at Black and wondered how I was going to get at him without being seen.

I stood up and walked toward the stairs, Skinny watched me as I moved across him; I walked outside to the car and waited for Black to come out of the club. Empress followed me and sat in the passenger seat, "How do you want to run this play?"

"I figure we just wait it out." I figured if I can't get to him inside I had to do it outside. About thirty minutes later people started to leave the club and walk to their cars, Empress saw Black with two other guys who were sporting all red sitting on top of this Oldsmobile that was vibrating from the music being pushed through giant speakers. "There he is" This was my chance I had to send a message from the Kingdom and I had to make it loud. I step out of the car and cocked back the 9mm, with Empress on my heels. I kept my nine in the holster till I got up close to Black and his boys. As we got closer to them one of them seen me coming and got the attention of the others, "Are you Black?" I asked as I stopped right in front of them, Empress was on my side smiling, Black stood up and asked me what I wanted. I looked at his friends who were ready to fight. "Luther said to give you this" as soon as I mentioned Luther's name their faces dropped as if they knew what was next. I pulled the 9 mil out of its holster and released two shots into Black's chest; I put one into the spine of the guy to the left, and out of nowhere Empress pulled out a small .38 and sent two shots to the guy on the right. One round went into his face while the other threw his throat; Black was still moving so I walked up to him and dropped two more rounds in him till he was dead.

Chapter 15

THE TURN OUT

The police sirens were getting closer and we had to get away before anyone saw us. I holstered the gun and took off to the car, "Nigga that shit was crazy." Empress said excitedly, "Where did you get the gun?"

"Nigga I stay strapped, I gotta hold it down no matter what."

"I feel you." I said taking the streets towards Empress's home. I pulled up to the curb and put the car into park, "Look stay low for a while, things are going to get hot."

"Bet I got you baby boy. Love you, hit my line when you get home." Empress jumped out of the car and ran inside. I drove the car back to Lele's house, the adrenaline was flowing and I was engaged. I couldn't get their faces out of my head as I pulled the gun on them, the fear, their shook faces, it was like pure energy to me. Luther's SUV was in the drive way when I arrived at the house; I walked inside and was greeted at the door by Elroy with another yellow packet and a white envelope bulging with money. Elroy walked out and into the car driving off down the street. I asked Lele what that was about and she said that Skinny Slim told Luther what happened so this was my reward.

I sat down in the kitchen as Lele ran my bath water, there was $15,000 in the envelope and I was ecstatic. Walking down to the basement I hid the money in a black duffle bag that I kept behind the water heater, I also kept my guns in this room that was tucked away in the corner of the basement, I sent a text to Empress and told her I would come see her later. I looked around the basement and decided to do all my planning and prepping for my next target. I opened the packet to see who I was going after next, it was this guy named Salis, some Puerto Rican cat who was starting to pull a lot of money in Queens selling drugs, now it wouldn't have been a problem, but the Kingdom wasn't seeing a cut and this was an issue. I had two days to get the job complete so this gave me some time to do some proper planning.

As I sat in the bath water I thought about my sister and wondered how she was doing. She was all I had left and if I lost her I wouldn't know what I would do. She stayed on my mind even as I laid down.

The next day I got up and drove to Queens to meet up with Claxton and Mary to see how things were going with her. Mary took a break from school when we came back from Florida; she wasn't the same anymore, when I arrived at the house I saw Claxton standing outside. He was holding on to his arm which was bleeding, I jumped out of the car and ran up to him to see what was going on. "Your sister man she is gone loca!" Claxton was upset and his arm was bleeding badly, I ran inside the house and saw Mary drinking a bottle of cheap vodka and welding a large kitchen knife. Mary was shocked to see me and got hostile, "Why are you here?" Mary asked me, I tried to get closer to her to take the knife away, but Mary ran up to me swinging the knife wildly. I moved to the side to dodge the swings grabbing on to her arm and the knife bringing her closer to me squeezing tightly. She started crying as we feel to the ground, the stress was starting to show through her body and I could tell that she was using drugs from the track marks in her arm. I held her until she fell asleep and walked up to Claxton, "Yo son she using?" I asked him as he washed his arm in the bathroom. "Yea she started two days ago, when I first saw her using I took it from her, today I tried to and she attacked me." I asked Claxton where she was getting the drugs from and he told me from this Puerto Rican that lived in the projects nine blocks away.

It had to be Salis he was talking about, now it was personal and I wanted to take him out for selling to my sister. I think about it now and I couldn't really be mad at Salis for selling, it was my sister's fault for going down that road, but the way I was thinking at the time you couldn't tell me anything different. I asked Claxton to continue to watch over my sister as I walked out of the house and drove to see where Salis did his business. The streets were busy with children running around outside, I seen a group of bloods also in the area and then I saw Salis. This guy was a joke, he wore this long powder blue robe, flip flops and long white socks that went to his knees, he was selling to little kids, pregnant women, and he had no code, no respect. I was disgusted and wanted to bust off a few shots at him right now but it was too bright and busy at the time for me to do anything. I wanted to do him dirty and I knew exactly how I was going to do it; I needed to go to the gun house in Manhattan to grab some supplies.

***

Luther was in the house organizing the layout, there were fine ass females all on the inside holding huge firearms and wearing lingerie or skimpy outfits. I never seen anything like it, they were the new security for the house, which was now furnished with wrap around couches, large flat screen T.V.'s and polished bedroom sets. I walked inside heading towards the room with the guns and got stopped by one of the guards as she cocked back this assault rifle and pointed it to my face "Don't move or I will blow your head clean off." Luther walked out and saw me with my hands up "Its ok ma, he's cleared." He said to her, she lowered her gun and I put my hands down. I walked inside with Luther as I told him what I wanted, he told to just grab all I needed. The back room where the guns were was now set up and organized neatly to where you could find all you wanted without looking too hard. I grabbed a sawn off shotgun and a box of shells, and a silencer for the 9mm. I walked back to the car and drove off headed back to Queens.

I went by to see Empress and give her a cut from the other night, I dropped off five stacks with her and told her that I would link up with her later. It was getting dark and the street lights were starting to come on around the projects where Salis was selling. He was still wearing his ridiculous outfit and I was ready to end this guy; I noticed that I didn't have my holster with me or the 9mm, "FUCK!" I said to myself I reached into the bag and pulled out the sawn off. I loaded the gun with two shells and shoved six more into my pocket, I was parked about a block away from where Salis was standing so when I got out of the car I knew he couldn't see me putting this sawn off in the back of my jeans. My shirt covered it up well enough for me to walk up to where he was.

Salis started to go upstairs and that's when I followed behind him trying not to expose myself, the streets were quite but the projects were full of kids, junkies, and a few of what looked like Salis's bodyguards, this was going to be crazy. It started to drizzle and I stepped on a piece of glass that caught Salis's attention, he turned around and noticed me behind him giving him this look of anger and I could tell he knew something was about to pop off. As our eyes met all I could think was that he was about to run, as soon as I had that thought Salis took off up the stairwell. I ruffled for the sawn off and I let off a shot as he slipped on the wet metal. The blast from the gun hit him in the ribs "DAMN!" was all I could yell when I noticed that he was still able to move up the stairs. The blast caught the attention of his guards and I knew I would have to deal with them; two of them came out of the apartment in front of me. I noticed that one had a .45 in his hand and I had one shot left in the sawn off before I had to reload, BOOM!! I split his chest wide open sending blood splattering all over the guy beside him.

I ran up on him and smacked him across the face using the gun like a club, I dropped the gun and grabbed his face pushing his eyes in with my thumbs causing him to scream out loud and being forever blind. There was another guy who was in the apartment shooting a small .357 at me, I dropped to the floor to grab the .45 and went around the door out of sight of the shooter. He came outside pointing the gun outside of the door first. I saw his hand and shoot it with the .45, he grabbed his hand in pain and I shot him in the face ending his life. I put the .45 in my jeans and picked up my shotgun that was next to the guy who was still squirming from me gouging out his eyes, following the blood trail up the stairs crawling on the floor was Salis in obvious pain, I could tell that he wasn't going to make it and I wanted to make sure. I reloaded the sawn off and pointed it to his back, BOOM... BOOM!! Both rounds went through his body shredding his robe and eating up his spine, he was dead and now I had to get away without anyone else seeing me.

I took off down the stairwell and ran into Peter knocking him down, he looked like one of those zombies who were lost, and I don't think he recognized me seeing that I was running so fast away from the scene. I made it to the car and drove off the opposite direction heading towards Brooklyn.

***

Lele was sleep as I walked in the house and I went down stairs to the basement to put the guns up and the money. It was time for a hot shower and some good sleep; as the water hit my body I kept seeing visions of blood. Not mine but the blood of others that I spilled, I closed my eyes hopping that they would go away but they just got more vivid than before. I stepped out of the shower and got into the bed closed my eyes and fell into a deep sleep. The streets were begging for answers as well as Johnny Law. Everyone wanted to know who was this mysterious person taking out big name criminals? One by one they were being taken out and no one had a clue on who it was behind the crimes. Luther called me asking me to lay low for a while before my next target, about an hour later Elroy came by the house and dropped off another envelope full of money.

The rest of the week in Queens was labeled as "hell week", horror struck hard in the streets when they found out about Salis. The Puerto Rican gang that he worked for started conducting a few drive-by shootings and gang style executions in the area looking for revenge. While the bloods started killing for the death of Black. I didn't know it at the time but the Kingdom had something big planned and they were going to use me to do it. Empress got arrested during hell week, she was followed home one day by a group of girls led by Deandrea. Empress made it to her house and locked the doors, Deandrea and her group were still outside cursing and going crazy when the top window opened up and a wave of boiling hot water and vegetable oil mixture came crashing into Deandrea and a few of her friends. Needless to say the water by itself wouldn't be as bad, but since it was mixed with oil, the pair acted as glue and Deandrea grabbed her face and pulled away flesh and leaving her with a world of pain, second degree burns, and Empress getting picked up on an assault charge. She was shipped to Rikers Island, ironically with her best friend and sister S-Dot.

About three months went by with no word on my next target, Empress and S-Dot were separated with S-

Dot in Bedford Hills, and Empress getting stuck on the Island. Mark and Nate were killin the music scene and making a name for themselves, Peter went underground and Solomon 7 was still ghost. The weather started to get a little colder and it was hoodie season all over again. Mary wasn't doing well; I would go by a few times and see that she was still using. Her beautiful green and brown eyes were now spoiled from stress, no sleep, and the drugs she pushed into her arms. I was working out in the park in Brooklyn when I saw this preacher talking about GOD; he was using all the recent deaths as his way to get his message passed. "It's hard enough to live a life of pure destruction, but to deal with the pain in life is even harder." Hearing this guy talk made me think hard about life and how mine was going in a downward spin. I kept thinking that GOD doesn't hear the reckless or those who embrace the darkness; but somewhere in my cold world there was that little feeling that tried to be felt.

I went home to take a shower and Lele handed me a yellow packet, I took the packet downstairs and opened it. The target was this white guy named J.R. who was snitching on a few of the Kingdom's dealers. This was a problem because he was causing us money. But get this he was addicted to porn and was always in Chinatown at this adult movie theater every Thursday around nine. You look at this guy and you see a normal citizen real business type, he worked for a real estate firm that ran a few major condominiums in the Manhattan area. This made me think that this was more than just some dealers going to jail. I didn't ask questions, that wasn't my job I just did the dirty work and I didn't have a problem with that.

I went into deep thoughts and plotted how I wanted to go after this guy, I heard Lele run into the bathroom throwing up in the toilet. "Hey ma you ok?" I asked her as she flushed the toilet and washed her face. She looked up to me and told me that she took a test a month ago and she took three this month. My eyes got wide as hell, and my mind went running in five different places at once. "What? When? How?" I didn't know what to say, I wasn't ready to be a father I didn't even know how a father act's. I guess that's what I was missing in my life, my father whom I never got a chance to meet, or know. I knew he was alive but that wasn't something my grandmother talked about or Mary, so I never asked nor cared especially at this point in my life. What was I to do at this point? Lele noticed that I was caught off guard and she told me not to worry too much about it, that everything would be ok. In my mind, I didn't want to be a father, but it wasn't my choice and I didn't let it show through my expressions either. I walked out of the hall way and gave Lele a kiss and got dressed, today was Wednesday and I was going to hit my target tomorrow, so I wanted to see how I was going to take him out. Lele needed the car, so I had her dropped me off at the subway station and headed into the city.

In Chinatown, it was like a normal day full of people and loaded with a lot of places to hide if I was going to take him out publicly. The movie theater was a little shady and it was in this back alley behind a fish market. This place was nasty but I guess there was a place for everyone. I knew where I needed to be, but I was ready to leave as quickly as I arrived. Mark hit me up saying that he was going to be in Harlem and I should come by and hang out for a while. I took a cab all the way to Harlem on west 145th to meet up with Mark who was chilling with the twins Gloria and Rosa. He had this thing for Gloria but I had a bad feeling about them both; Mark was sitting on the bench with them in the park when I arrived. "Wat up Thun"

"What's good son, hey ladies."

"Hey D" Rosa said "Hey pa" Gloria chimed in. The

streets were busy as usual and the sights of Harlem were busy with work. "So I hear you and Nate doing y'all thing out here man"

"No doubt the streets are loving our sound, B they keep begging for more." we sat and chatted for a while until I got this call from Claxton telling me that Mary was gone and he couldn't find her. My heart started racing and I took off to catch a cab all the way to Queens.

***

I got to Claxton's house and saw that no one was there, I called him up and this groggy voice answered the phone. "Stop calling this number blood, if you know what's good for you."

"What? Who is this?"

"Like I said don't call this phone no more motherfucker." The groggy voice said, "When I find you I will kill you believe that."

"If you want a problem, come get it nigga I'm on 87th with this bitch and her man." The groggy voice said, I was heated and wasted no time running the four blocks to this bordered up brownstone that was partially burnt up on one side. Claxton's car was outside, I had a bad feeling about this and knew that I was in for something that was over my head. I kicked in the door and saw a room full of spaced out fiends laying around and walking in circles, they looked like zombies and some of them smelled like it too. "Mary! Mary! Claxton!" I started yelling out Mary's and Claxton's name but I didn't get an answer, I walked past a few of the people lying on the floor and made my way upstairs to where it smelled like something died and more fiends were stumbling around. I saw Mary's necklace on one of the addicts and got furious, what I went through for that chain I was mad as hell. I snatched the chain off the girl who was wearing it, she tried to fight me for it but I punched her in the face and knocked her out. The rest of the addicts backed away and I saw a dark room in front of me with little sunlight coming through.

I ran to the room and broke inside to see Claxton lying on the floor with blood coming from his head; I looked up and saw Mary in the corner half naked and scared.

There was this old black guy whose dreads were falling apart and matted together, he was wearing what looked like a three year old white t-shirt now brown with a large hole on his chest. He was holding a knife to Mary's neck and was staring right at me. "Don't move or I'll kill her." The guy said as he walked a little closer into the light so I could see his face. He looked like some type of monster he was a disgusting looking creature, his darken face was riddled with scares and blotches. One of his eyes were glassy and slanted from a recent high he was on. I could tell that he was on drugs for some time, and at the time I didn't know what to do. I was in panic and I wanted to get Mary away from this guy as soon as I could. "Give me your shirt, and your shoes." He started telling me, "I'll give them to you if you let my sister go" the hype was a lot smarter than I knew. He had this weird cough that caused him to drop his head and move his hand that was holding the knife.

I took this chance and ran up to him grabbing his hand with the knife away from Mary and broke his wrist. The hype started screaming and tried to punch me with his other hand; I grabbed his arm and flipped him over me to the ground. I put my knee on his back and grabbed his head with both of my hands, and pulled up until I heard his neck snapped. Mary was crying and didn't want me to touch her, I checked on Claxton and noticed that he was still alive but he needed to get to a hospital quick. I grabbed Mary and picked her up and took her to Claxton's car that was outside, once she was in the car I picked up Claxton and put him in the car and drove off to Jamaica hospital. When I got there I was asked what happened and I told them that my sister and her boyfriend were just jumped by some people and I happened to be coming along to help them out. I sat there for a while waiting on the doctors to tell me something, it was getting late and I was getting impatient. Finally this doctor came out and told me that they were going to be ok and that both of them needed to stay in the hospital for the night. My mind was at ease for the moment and I decided to take off to Brooklyn to get myself prepared for tomorrow's hit.

***

The next day, the sun was starting to go down when I realized that I needed to get ready for today's job. I went down stairs and put my holster over my black t-shirt and put a silencer on the 9mm. I put on my large trench coat and walked upstairs and out the door. I took Claxton's car since I still had it with me and drove down to Chinatown. The scene was different at night, to some it's scary but to me, well I felt right at home. I made my way to the movie theater and waited in this corner with a bum who smelled of liquor and mildew. About twenty minutes later J.R. walked inside the theater and went into one of the viewing rooms, I walked in behind him shortly.

The place was a dump and I could see why he came all the way out here, who would suspect to see this type of guy in this place. I ducked my head avoiding the security camera facing the doorway; J.R. went into the third booth to the right and I went into the one next to him. I gave him the satisfaction of watching his smut for a while, but my patience was already running thin after seeing cockroaches ran rapid in the booth I was in. I stood up and cocked back my 9mm and walked out of the booth I was in. I guess he was in such a hurry that he left the door unlocked. I pushed opened the door and the light from the hallway illuminated the room J.R. jumped and looked back at me as I interrupted his perversely activities. I walked inside with the gun in my hand and told him to sit down and continue watching his porn, J.R. started crying and asking me not to kill him. I pointed the gun to the back of his head and pulled the trigger; the round went through his head clean and went into the TV screen. His body slouched down and head went down, blood started dripping as I left the room and closed the door behind me.

Walking out of the store I holstered the pistol and

walked to the car driving off to Brooklyn. On the way there I get a call from Mary asking me to come pick her and Claxton up from the hospital. They weren't too far from where I was so I made the first exit off the expressway towards Queens. I arrived and the two of them were sitting in the lobby of the hospital, Claxton's head was bandaged up and Mary was looking a little healthier. They got in the car and I drove them back to Claxton's house where I left them and walked towards the train station, to ride home.

Chapter 16

GUN'S GALORE

Lele was cooking breakfast when I woke up and my stomach knew it. I was hungry as hell and I could smell the bacon calling my name. I got a text telling to get dressed quick and meet Luther in Long Island for a new assignment. I finished eating and put on my yellow and black Adidas sweat suit and grabbed my .38 just in case. This was the day I started to have funny feelings about life and carried a gun with me at all times. It took about one hour to get there and when I did Luther was standing next to this tiny black chick with a dark purple hoodie dress on and purple Nikes. One of the first things that caught my attention were her thick juicy lips that had black lip stick on them. "What's up" I asked Luther as I stepped out of the cab.

"This is Voodoo child she's going with you on your

next hit not as a partner though, she has some other things to take care of." Luther told me this and automatically I thought that this hit was about guns, Luther gave me the packet and told me that once the hit was done and confirmed I will get paid like the other times. Voodoo walked with me to her car and got in, I opened the packet and before I could begin reading Voodoo told me all about the target. "The target is not the German he is just the key, the target are the guns were going after." Voodoo said in her deep Louisiana accent, she also told me that we had to go to this penthouse where this German guy was holding the key for a large crate of weapons coming off of a boat from Russia tonight.

He was well protected, and didn't go anywhere without five bodyguards and he also carried a snub nose on him as well. Voodoo Child had all the info on this guy. She was a scary looking chick, she had this soft copper type ebony skin with light gray eyes, her hair was done in thick dreadlocks and the tips of them were dyed purple. She had about five earrings in each ear, and this silver Ankh bull ring hanging from her nose. I caught a glimpse of her hands which had this beautiful henna design tattooed on them, which wrapped around her small fingers with these long black and purple nails that came to a sharp point, in another life, she could've been a model. We made it to the Bronx where she told me to pull into this store parking lot, Voodoo got out the car and told me to wait there. About fifteen minutes later she came out with this small case and told me to drive to Manhattan. It was about six in the afternoon and the sun was starting to give off a pretty light show in the sky when we pulled up to this fancy looking apartment. In the car she opened the case and put together this black xp.45 and attached a purple and black camo silencer. Purple must have been her thing I said to myself, I cocked back my .38 and stepped out of the car, she saw that I didn't have a silencer and told me to let her do all the shooting and just watch her back for anybody trying to sneak by.

We walked in the apartment and Voodoo walked up to the security room and knocked on the door. The guard came out and she hit him with the butt of the gun. The guard fell backwards and she let off three shots that sounded like snail whispers into the guard. She started messing with the cameras and noticed that there was a bodyguard on the penthouse floor watching the elevator, and then she stopped the tape from recording. We got on the elevator and made our way up to the top floor. As soon as the doors opened she let off two silent shots into the chest of the guard, there were these double doors in the middle of the hallway. There was loud music playing and lots of laughter inside of the room, "Kick in the door's and move out of the way" Voodoo told me as she cracked her neck and got a tighter grip on the pistol.

I kicked in the door as she said and moved to the right. Like a scripted movie Voodoo came in and let off two shots into this guard standing in front of the doors, one went through the face of another guard looking out the window. This other guard came out of the bath room with his pants half way down and she shot him in the balls, and two in his chest. The last guard tried to go for his gun, that's when I saw him and shot him dropping him to the floor, completely disregarding what she told me back in the car. I had my gun pointed at the German guy who was in a pair of blue underwear and a white robe, he was shocked and getting very angry. Voodoo asked him where the key was at and he kept laughing. There was this chick that came out the back room with this silver snub nose and started shooting at me, she barely missed my head and I let off six shots into her ripping her body apart. The German tried to rush me as I was shooting ole girl but Voodoo shot him in the knee dropping him to the ground hard.

Voodoo looked at the germen and told him to tell her where the key to the box was at; he smiled and told her to fuck off as he quenched in pain. Voodoo had short patience and smacked him with the gun across the face. Voodoo called Luther and told him that she couldn't find the key, now whatever Luther told her made Voodoo smile hard when she got off the phone. She told me to hold on to the German as she reached under her dress and pulled a small knife out from a garter belt. She walked over to the German, and wink right before she drove the knife into the top of his face underneath his cheekbone. The knife went to work making its way deep into his face cutting out his left eyeball. *That was a sight and sound that I would never forget.* As he screamed in pain she just laughed and smiled even harder, as her patience started to get away from her she stabbed him in the neck and watched as he slowly faded away. Voodoo was a sick ruthless bitch, she put his eye in a plastic bag and threw it too me telling me to hold on to it. We walked out to the car and drove off heading towards the gun house; once we arrived it was looking like a mini military base inside. There were armed guards in sexy outfits and lingerie with heavy steel doors, a few more guns were being loaded in through the back. One of the girls was in the kitchen cooking some Spanish food from the smells that were being given off. I sat on the couch and let out a deep sigh. I was about to have a child and I was living a very hectic and confusing life, but I was loving it too much.

My mind was in another world the whole time we were waiting for the shipment to be dropped off. Voodoo was cleaning her gun and I was sitting in a room upstairs closing my eyes trying to find my thoughts after I had a plate of the Spanish rice with these green peas and some roasted chicken. I had an urge to pray from the thoughts of my grandmother but I refused too and cursed GOD some more and focused on my task. Voodoo called me downstairs and said that the shipment was coming in soon and we needed to head that way. I ran into the room with the guns and grabbed a 1911 .45 with a silencer to not bring attention to us like at the apartment. We drove to the pier and waited for the boat to take off after it dropped off the shipment. Voodoo got out the car first and ran up to the gate, it was open to our surprise. I got out of the car and cocked back my pistol. I ran up behind her and went into the gate this place was empty and five large steel cases were by the loading dock. We walked up to one and I scanned the eye on the iris scanner on the front, **"Click"** the locks on the case popped opened and we opened the lid, there were guns all over in this thing. Inside was a sniper rifle broken down to fit, three Ak47's, two SWAT type shotguns, some rocket launchers, pistols, and a shit load of hand grenades and ammo for the weapons. I was surprised and stunned, this was crazy, how did the Kingdom know about this? I didn't have time to ask questions, so we cleaned out the cases and loaded all the weapons in the car. We drove off to the gun house were everything was unloaded; I took a box of ammo for my new .45 and took a cab around Manhattan for a while. The night air felt good as it came into the car from the side window. I loved the way the sky looked with a full moon and the lights from the city made it very relaxing. I made it back to Brooklyn about four hours later and went inside the house, as always I dropped off my work in the basement, took a shower, and fell asleep next to Lele. When I woke up Lele was in the kitchen cooking breakfast again, I stretched and went into the bathroom to wash my face and clean up a bit. Walking downstairs I could smell the food creping closer and closer, there was pancakes, bacon, cheese eggs, and grits on the table, she had two glasses of fresh pineapple juice already set and I was hyped. "Good morning sleepy head" Lele said with a smile on her face, "Good morning sexy" I replied sipping some of the juice from the glass.

I still couldn't believe that I was having a baby with this girl I met two years ago, yea I was living with her, but something was still bugging me about shorty. The food was great and I needed the time to relax with Lele, it felt as if I didn't really know who she was. We chilled on the couch for a bit and watched this one movie with the rappers DMX and Nas in it. That nigga DMX was a wild boy from what I was seeing, right in the middle of the movie there was a knock on the door. Lele answered the door and Elroy walked in and said that he was sent by Luther to come get me and Lele. I grabbed my .9mm and we got dressed, I threw on a pair of black sweats and Lele put on a brown Nike two piece and we drove off with Elroy, we were on our way to Harlem when this dark gray Hummer came swerving up behind us. I felt it coming but I was too slow to react, out of nowhere this guy with a red bandana covering his face popped out of the back side window with a Mac 10. "OH SHIT!!" I yelled out pushing Lele on the floor and covering her up. A few shots came through my window as Elroy attempted to speed off in the opposite direction. I was on high alert and pulled out my 9mm and shot out the shattered window towards the Hummer that was speeding behind us. Elroy came around the corner almost flipping us, but the Hummer was still behind us, and the guy kept shooting knocking out the back window.

A bullet almost hit Elroy and that's when he went into this side alley, I noticed an AK47 in the back of the SUV and I grabbed it and racked back its handle. I told Elroy to stop the car and when he did I jumped out with the AK aiming down the alleyway. The Hummer came around the corner and I unloaded into it. The rounds riddled the windshield hitting the driver causing him to crash into the wall hard. The gunman got out of the car and grabbed his arm, he was hit; I dropped the AK and ran up to the Hummer with my nine in hand. I ran on top of the hood of the Hummer and sent three rounds into him. There was another guy in the car but he was hit in the head from the AK. I ran back to the SUV, we took off to where Luther was at. As soon as we pulled up you can tell that Luther was shocked at what his car looked like. Lele told Luther what happened and he was heated, you could see the steam coming off of his dreads. Luther was staring at his car and told me that we had some work to do and that no one fucks with him like this.

Chapter 17

Revenge

Luther walked inside the house and came out with a large duffle bag full of money and tossed it to me. "That's $150,000 for both jobs" he said to me walking to the gun riddled SUV. "Elroy lets go I need to see some people; Decon stay available." Luther got into the car with Elroy and they drove off down the street. Me and Lele were stuck in Harlem with no ride home, she called a cab and we went back home, Lele was tired from the day's events and went to go lay down. I went downstairs to the basement and put away the money. I was starting to have more money than room and I knew I was going to relocate it somewhere. The day was going by slow and I wanted to go check on Mary, I grabbed my .38 and walked out the house. It was now December and the winter was coming in hard, I had on my blue timberlands and a gray thermal, and a big North face jacket. As I walked out the house snow began to fall and it was peaceful.

I got in the car and drove to Claxton's house, I got there and no one was home. I called Peter to ask him if he knew where they were at. Peter was sounding real jittery and was talking like he was in trouble. "Yo da- D look man I dun fucked up, I fucked up badly mon. Mi no have da money or da drugs mi owe dem!" I tried to keep Peter calm but he was scared and crying, talking about money and drugs. I was so confused on what he was talking about and I asked him where he was at. Peter told me that he locked himself in a room at the projects where I killed Salis. I told him that I was on my way and I checked my .38 to see if I had a full clip, and made sure the nine was equal, I got in the car and sped off to his location. Going back to these projects was weird seeing that I haven't been over here since the hit. I jumped out the car and called Peter to ask him what room and floor he was in, Peter was held up in an apartment on the second floor and he said that some people were outside trying to break in the door to get him.

My heart started racing and I had to act fast I cocked back the .38 and ran into the project gates and up the stairs. I made it to the floor and saw this heavy set

Latino trying to kick in the door, I ran up behind him and smacked him in the back of the head with the pistol. He dropped to his knees and tried to get up, I hit him again this time knocking him out cold. I saw a large Puerto Rican flag on his arm and I thought that this guy was working for the same people Salis was working for. I yelled out to Peter and told him to open the door. He opened the door and I went inside, the place he was in was a mess "You live here kid?" I asked looking around, Peter was scared and started vomiting all on the floor. I walked to him to make sure he was ok "What the hell is going on son?"

"I was sellin some drugs for this cat named Salis but he got dun off a while back. So, I was filling his spot, but mi don fucked up, I fucked up real bad mon."

"But why are they after you, nigga?"

"Mi use dem too much mon, I turned into a bumbaclot fiend, and now mi owe dem wit mi life." Peter was shaking and out of control crying and dry heaving, I shook my head and went off on him saying that this was his fault and he was going to get himself killed. This was my friend and I couldn't just allow him to go out like this he needed my help.

I asked him how much he owed and he told me

$10,000 I told him that I had that and I can help clear this up, and we walked out the apartment together. There were two guys in black ski mask walking up the stairs with guns in their hands, one had a shotgun and the other one had a pistol I pulled out my .38 and put three rounds into the guy with the shotgun causing him to fall backwards. At the same time I was pushing Peter away from the stairs, the guy with the pistol started shooting and running up the stairs. I moved back from the stairs and ran the other way with Peter shooting behind me hoping to hit the guy. We ran down the other stairs and out the back gate, this brown and black sports bike came around the corner speeding towards us. The guy on the back had two Uzi's and we started running the other way to hide behind this car that was on the side but Peter was too slow. The gun let off like firecrackers ripping holes into his chest, I was grazed in the left arm, but was still able to let off four rounds but only one hit the gunman in the leg. The other guy came out of the back gate and was too slow to train his gun on me when I put five rounds into him from my nine.

Peter was on the floor coughing up blood and tears fell from his eyes, there was nothing that I could do at this point but hold onto my friend until I felt his life slip from his body. I tried my best to hold back the tears that were beginning to form in the corners of my eyes but I was losing that battle and once one fell it started a chain reaction for the others. I ran through the projects and grabbed the big Puerto Rican that I knocked out and dragged all the dead weight down to my car, and threw his ass in the trunk. I needed to know more about the men who were sent to kill my friend and he was going to help me one way or the other, next I drove the car around the corner to put Peter in the car.

I peeled off to Nate's house where he and Mark were working on some new songs, I pulled up to the house yelling for Nate to come out and help me. They came out and saw Peter bleeding and motionless with him in my arms. I was holding on to him knowing that our friend was gone and wasn't going to be waking up. Mark and Nate were upset and crying but who could blame them this was our brother, Solomon 7 showed up to chill, instead he made it in time for an unexpected tragedy. Solomon7 saw Peter and was heated, as soon as I stepped out of the house he ran up to me "Yo WHO THE FUCK DID THIS DECON?" I saw the look in his eye's Solomon wanted blood, and who was I to keep it from him? "It was a gang of Puerto Ricans, they worked for or with Salis, but I'm not sure."

"This shit doesn't sit well with me sun, you fuckin with me right?" spat Solomon 7 "Dog I'm telling you all that I-" my words were cut off when Solomon 7 grabbed my shirt and pushed me against my car pulling a .45 out and pointing it to my head. "DON'T LIE TO ME D" Solomon said pulling back on the hammer. I looked into his eyes "Calm down B, I wouldn't lie to you, now get the damn gun out of my face!" I said in a calm but very serious tone, Solomon dropped the gun and walked away from me. I didn't blame him he was upset and I needed to find out who set Peter up to die. "Now that you're willing to listen, I don't have the answers but I know someone who does."

"What? Who?"

"He's in the trunk." Solomon 7 ran over to the car with Nate in step behind him. "Now listen we need this guy alive so we can find out who is responsible for this mess, ya feel me?"

"Yea I got you" Solomon said calmly, I opened the trunk and the guy was still motionless, Solomon shot him anyway and said he deserved it. The guy screamed as he woke up and reached for his foot, we pulled him out and dragged him into Nate's basement and tied him down in a chair. "What's your name nigga" Nate barked as he pointed his little .22 at the guy's head, "It's Angel bitch!" Nate smacked him across the face with the pistol for cursing at him.

"Calm down son" I said to Nate pulling him back, "Why y'all kill Peter?"

"Who?" Angel said with a puzzled look on his face, Solomon 7 slid past me and slapped him across the face with the back of his hand with lighting speed. "My friend motherfucker, the nigga y'all killed" Angel spit out the blood forming in his mouth and looked up at us and smiled. "Oh yea, Peter ha-ha, yea he got what he deserved." Angel gave us a wink and continued with his sinister smile, Solomon 7 cold clocked him across his face and drew his .45 pointing it to the middle of his head "Fuck this rice and bean eating motherfucker, I'ma just kill him and get it over with" Solomon 7 spat. I told everyone to chill out and pushed Solomon's hand away from Angel, "You might as well let him do it kid, I aint saying shit." Angel said lifting his head back up to look me in the eyes. "This guy is a real badass huh?" Solomon 7 said as he pulled out a knife and stabbed Angel in the right thigh. Angel let out a loud scream and barked off "FUCK YOU!" to Solomon 7 as he pulled out the knife and laughed, Angel's phone started going off in his pocket I pulled it out and all it said on the screen was *"El Gato."* "Yo who is this?" I said answering the phone "Who the fuck is this?" the guy on the other end said in a confused tone. "You can call me death, now that you know me, who do I have the pleasure of speaking with?" I asked him being a smart ass. "I'm Felix but you can call me EL GATO, and if you have this phone that means you're the one responsible for killing my men huh?" the guy on the other end said getting real serious, "So... What did you do with Angel?" Felix asked me. "I killed him, like you already assumed, I told you my name was death, Felix or EL GATO whichever one you prefer to use. I like Felix, so that's what I'll be calling you from now on. He started laughing and said that I fucked up big time "When I find you amigo, I'm gonna skin you alive."

"I like that, actually I plan on finding you, but first I need to know why were you callin your man's Angel?" I asked him curious into what he would say. He told me that I didn't need to worry about it and my time was coming soon, and hung up the phone.

"Who the hell is Felix?" I asked Angel who was angry and very upset, "He's going to be the last face you see you black bitch!" Angel was serious and I had to show him that I was too; I walked up to him and slapped him across the face with the back of my gun. He looked at me and started laughing, the strike opened a cut on the side of his face but that didn't stop the fact that he knew we were stuck and we didn't know who was who. So I looked through his phone for some type of clue, he had *My Queen* logged into his phone and I called it, Mark taped Angel's mouth shut so he wouldn't scream while I was on the phone. This sweet voice answered the phone "What's up boo you done with work yet?" "I'm sorry ma'am this is Angel's partner D, he was hurt and I wanted to get in contact with you."

"A dios mio is he okay?" She said franticly, "No not really he is in bad shape"

"Oh no, what can I do to help?" I told her to come to Nate's house and help me get him to a hospital, she agreed and ran out the house on her way to our location.

Nate and Mark took Peter's body to his mother's house, from what they said when they got back was that she broke out into a hysterical wreck, she was heartbroken and I knew exactly how she was feeling. About ten minutes went by and the girl was outside the house, she was this fine Latin chick, short had to be about four, eleven or five feet even. She had on the tightest jeans ever that looked like they were painted on, that struggled to fit over her fat ass. Her jet-black hair seem to flow wildly around her face and danced around her pretty pink lips. "Hey come on hurry I need you to help me get him in the car" she ran up behind me into the house, as soon as she came in Solomon 7 grabbed her and pointed his gun to her head. Angel was watching the whole time but was helpless and still taped up, you could see the fire in his eyes as he shifted violently in the chair, but there was nothing he could do.

"So who is El Gato?" I asked the girl who was now starting to cry, "He... he's Angel's boss." She was scared and shaking "Calm down ma, we won't hurt you as long as you continue to help us out. So where does he live?"

"I don't know I swear."

"Well it looks like we can't use this bitch." Solomon 7 snarled cocking back the .45, the girl's eyes shot open wide and tears began to flow faster, "I don't know where he is, but I do know where his brother is working." The girl sobbed "Now were getting somewhere, ma. So go on, don't keep an asshole in suspense." She sang louder than a caged bird, and mentioned that Felix had a brother who owned a corner store in Corona. Nate came in and grabbed the girl off the floor and walked her outside "What's your name ma?" Nate asked sincerely, "its Cindy"

'Nice to meet you I'm Nate." Nate tried his best to

make her feel comfortable and somewhat safe. Mark grabbed Angel and walked him outside, it was more of a limp for Angel but he was put back in the trunk still taped up. We all squeezed into the old Cadillac, drove to Corona to this corner store that was still a little busy. Cindy pointed out Felix's brother Azúcar, he was a short dark skin hispanic male giving orders to his workers.

Cindy was looking nerves, probably from the gun that Solomon 7 had to her head, it was about eight at night and we decided to wait behind the store trying to figure out a plan on how we were going to find Felix. Mark saw one of the guys standing outside the back smoking a cigarette, Solomon 7 told Nate to come with him as they got out of the car with Cindy still at gun point. I was lost didn't know what to do I just sat there and watched as Solomon 7 gave Cindy to Nate and he ran up and held the gun at the guy's temple who was in the back of the store. My eyes got wide and I knew shit was about to get crazy, I grabbed a full clip from the glove box and put it in my gun cocking it back. "Mark stay here!" I said as I jumped out of the car behind them. Solomon 7 pushed the guy into the store and ran in holding him at gun point "DON'T NOBODY MOVE OR I'LL BLOW HIS HEAD OFF!" Solomon 7 was crazy and a loose cannon, I knew in the back of my mind that I was gonna have to kill him at one point or another.

Nate was right behind him with Cindy and walked with her to lock the doors in the front. I came in and saw two guys standing with their hands in the air; one was this fat Puerto Rican who looked to be 16 or 17, you could tell that he was still in high school by the school football team T' shirt he was wearing. Then there was Azúcar who was looking serious and ready for war "Who the fuck are you guys and what do you want?"

"We want El Gato" Solomon 7 shouted still holding the skinny kid at gun point "Ha-ha do you know who your fuckin with, kid? I can have you all dead within seconds, trust me on that."

"Man you can miss me with all that tough guy bull shit papi, the way I see it, I have the gun and you aint got shit." Solomon 7 explained, I had my gun trained on Azúcar and I noticed that he kept shifting his weight trying to inch towards his foot. Solomon 7 must of saw this too and shot him in the right arm, the blast caught everyone off guard and I spotted the fat kid reaching for something behind the register, I ran up on the counter to make sure the kid didn't grab the large revolver resting on the shelf below. I pointed the gun at the kid and told me to go in the front and lay on the floor, he complied but Solomon 7 was so irate he pistol wiped the kid dropping him to his knees and forcing him on the ground. Azúcar was yelling out profanity and holding on to where the bullet was lodged in his arm. Solomon 7 was so out of control he grabbed the skinny kid that was stuck frozen in fear and threw him on the floor next to the fat kid. "Somebody better give me some answers or I'm a body one of you niggas" he said pointing his gun in Azúcar's face. He was bleeding badly and even more pissed off than before. Nate still had Cindy who was now crying even more and started to get on Solomon 7's nerves "Look bitch if you don't shut the fuck up I'm gonna kill ya" I looked over at Solomon 7 who was serious and grabbed the revolver just for safe measures.

I held both guns out watching over everyone as Solomon 7 walked over to Azúcar and asked him again where his brother was located, Azúcar looked at him and spit in Solomon 7's face. This set him off and he wiped his face and pistol whipped Azúcar making him fall sideways to the floor. Solomon 7 then started stomping Azúcar and pushed me away from trying to stop him, he saw that Azúcar was trying to get up and he shot him in the back of the head. The bullet made a mess of his head or what was left of it, blood went everywhere and Cindy started to scream again "NATE SHUT HER UP!" Solomon 7 yelled wiping the blood from his face. I was helpless and stunned, I'd never seen this side of Solomon 7 before and I didn't like it he told Nate to move and pointed his gun at Cindy **"POW"** her body flew backwards into a stand full of chips as the .45 punched a gaping hole into her chest, "NOOOOOOO!" I yelled out running up and pushing Solomon 7. "See what you made me do, you see what you did?" Solomon 7 started yelling at the corps of Cindy. "Why did you kill her I asked Solomon 7 who was looking at me like I was next, he told me that we didn't need her and she was taking up space. As we were arguing the skinny guy stood up and tried to run out the front door Nate shot him in the leg and caused him to hit the floor screaming, Solomon and I both jumped from the unexpected shot from the .22. Solomon 7 dragged the guy back to the middle of the floor where the fat kid was who had now pissed himself and was starting to pray. Solomon 7 pointed his gun at the guy who tried to run and asked him "Do you know where El Gato lives?" The guy shook his head no and started to cry some more, "You have to the count of three to tell me where he lives" Solomon 7 said putting the gun to his head "one" the kid was praying faster and faster, Nate was looking around and I could tell that he was shocked. "Two" the guy kept shaking his head and snot started running from his nose and mouth; I looked at Cindy's dead body and at Azúcar who looked nothing like a human anymore, it almost fazed me that I had his blood on me. "Three" the guy spit up right before Solomon 7 pulled the trigger "138th and Ozone park the house with the red saint Mary in front of it" Solomon 7 looked at him and smiled "See was that too hard" right after he spoke he shot him in the side of the head painting the side of the store with his blood and brain matter.

The fat kid was still praying and I guessed I found a heart somewhere in my body and told Solomon 7 "That's enough!" Solomon 7 looked at me as I walked towards the backdoor "LET'S GO!" I yelled. Nate walked out and I turned and looked at Solomon 7 knelling down and looking at the kid who was praying, "To live is a privilege, to die by my hands is god's reward!" Was what I heard Solomon 7 yell as he put two rounds through the kid's heart ending his life. My ears were shocked and my eyes couldn't believe what I had just heard and saw him do, this guy was nuts. I could never look at this guy the same ever again and I knew why he was a disciple, he embraced this lifestyle and I knew that it wasn't for me, but I was on the same path. In the car riding to Felix's house we all sat in silence I mean no one said a word, Mark was driving and Nate was in the passenger seat, which left me and Solomon 7 siting alone in the back. I looked over at Solomon 7 who was staring out of the window, "Son what happened in there?"

"What you mean?" Solomon 7 responded still looking out of the window "You know what I mean, you killing everyone in that joint."

"Yea well, no loose ends B" Solomon 7 was a cold dude but was also very knowledgeable and kept quoting some things from the Nation of god's and Earth's that I didn't understand.

We got to the house and the streets were packed with cars and people were piled inside of the house with a few on the outside. It looked like Felix was throwing a party and we knew getting to him wasn't going to be easy. Solomon 7 handed Mark the revolver we took from the store and he reloaded his .45, I had forgot about Angel in the trunk of Cindy's car until he started kicking the trunk. I opened the trunk and pulled him out of the car he was all beat up and his foot was still bleeding, I showed him Felix's house and his eyes got wide. I told Mark and Nate to walk around back and wait for my signal. Solomon 7 held onto Angel and we walked right up to the house, the people that were on the outside looked at us and knew trouble was about to go down. Those few scattered and some ran inside, by this time we had to wing the whole plan. Nate and Mark were already around back and waited for us in the bushes. This random guy stumbled into the front door smiling and dropped his bottle of beer when he saw Angel all taped up and bloody. I hit him in the face with my nine and pushed through the door with Solomon 7 right behind me both guns pointed around the room. "Ok EVERYBODY KEEP CALM!" I shouted waving my gun around. "WHERE IS FELIX?" Solomon 7 yelled out also looking around.

Without any warning this guy came out of the crowd of people with a shotgun and yelled out "FUCK YOU!" I pushed Angel into the way of the guy as he sent hell fire from the gun, the buck shot round made a mess of Angel's chest killing him instantly. **"POW!"** **"POW!"** **"POW!"** Solomon 7 let off three shots into the crowd ripping through two people who were just in the way, he jumped out of the front door ducking outside of the house behind the door frame. I hid behind this couch that was in the room closer to the living room window, out of nowhere we were getting fired at by about seven or eight guys. Nate came through the back shooting one guy in the back of the head and firing two more shoots into the room where we were at; Mark ran in and fired also. There were women screaming and people running everywhere some tried to run out the house and others were getting shot and falling to the floor. Solomon 7 let off three more shot's hitting this guy with an AK in the body I shot this girl who honestly at the wrong place at the wrong time. There was gun fire back and forth from the kitchen in the back, to the front door where Solomon 7 and I were. Mark took out three guys who were hiding on the stairwell before going empty. When everything calmed down and we noticed that everyone downstairs were either dead or injured all four of us walked up stairs, I grabbed one of the AK's that was abandon on the floor and walked up behind everybody, Felix was in the attic yelling that he was the king and some shit in Spanish as he fired from the attic. "Come on Felix we just want to talk."

"Fuck you Puto!" Felix yelled out, I fired the rest of the clip of the AK at Felix causing him to fall through the ceiling crashing to the floor. He was hit four times and was in pain but still moving, Solomon 7 and Nate walked up to him and fired into him blowing off the left side of his face. After Felix was dead we took off running out of the house and noticed that there were bodies everywhere, the party was officially shutdown and the cops were coming around the corner and we all took off through the back of the house into another neighborhood, leaving Cindy's car and went separate ways back to Nate's house. When I made it to the house I noticed that Solomon 7 and Mark were standing out in front, we waited for Nate to show up before we did anything. Nate showed up about thirty minutes later, Mark was frantic and shaking "Dog I never did anything like this before, what do I do?" "You don't do shit, just stay calm and relax" Solomon 7 barked at Mark getting him to calm down. It was at this time I knew Mark wasn't going to take this too well and I was gonna keep him and Nate at a distance with this killing shit. "Mark you gonna be fine kid just don't worry about it" Nate was shaking too but he was calm and had a handle on what just happened. I got into my car shortly after and drove off to Lele's back into Brooklyn.

***

When I got home Lele was upstairs in the bed sleep, her stomach was getting huge. I guess that's what happens at six months, she looked calm as she slept in the bed full of white and purple bed sheets. I took off my bloody clothes and looked at my grazed arm which was still tender and full of dried blood and lent from my shirt.

I jumped in the shower and allowed the hot water to take away all my pain, looking at my feet with my head under the flow of the water I could see the blood from others and myself fall to the drain. I lifted my head and took the water to my face; as my eyes closed I saw fear looking at me in the face and I embraced it trying to become fear, but there was something wrong. I heard my grandmother's voice asking me why? Why was I committing death with my hands? Why was I acting as the shepherd for the devil? I started to talk back to the voice telling it that I was death and that the devil works inside of me and I enjoy it. Then this pain ran across my body dropping me to my knees, the water ran down my body like rain drops and the pain got stronger. I reached up to the handle to help myself up but I couldn't move.

Then this light flashed in my head and I was back in church with just me and my grandmother. We were sitting in the front looking at this statue of Jesus on the cross. I was a little kid again and I could hear her tell me the story of how Jesus died on the cross for our sins. Throughout the vision I could feel the tears in my eyes begin to fall, I wanted to become free but I was too wrapped up in anger and sin that it overpowered the pain and allowed me to stand up and open my eyes. I got out of the shower and saw myself in the mirror, my curly hair didn't fit the way I was feeling so I grabbed a razor and clippers and shaved my head bald. I walked into the bedroom and laid down for the rest of the night.

The next morning I woke up to cold water being splashed in my face, "WHAT THE HELL HAPPENED TO YOUR HAIR?" Lele yelled out obvious in shock. When I got over the cold wake up I started to laugh and said it was a new look I was trying out. She didn't find it so funny and walked downstairs upset, minutes later I heard Luther calling out for me from downstairs. I put on some shorts and a t-shirt and walked downstairs. Luther walked in and sat down in the kitchen, Lele was watching TV on the couch and I grabbed a bottle of water before I sat next to him. "I know you heard about the shootout last night, ha-ha that shit was crazy, I hear it was a couple of young black dudes that ran up in that joint and started blastin. See D it's shit like this that the Kingdom can't have going on without us being brought up to speed ya know?" Luther was animated about the whole ordeal but he spoke like he knew I had something to do with it, or that's how I was feeling at the time; guilty conscience. "Yea we had some dealers at that a party who were ready to merge with us as well as a connected buyer. But let the dead stay dead, we need to move on this play and bring forth a win for both of us. Oh and get this, somebody murdered this other Latin dude who had connections as well named Azúcar I didn't care to much for the cat but non the less he was apart of a power move." I looked at Luther like I didn't know what he was talking about, and tried not to show any fear in my eyes. "But that's not why I came here man I need you to come with me so we can handle this work I got set up." I was confused but knew better then to question Luther so I just went with it, went upstairs to get dressed. As I walked downstairs towards the basement I saw Luther talking to Lele telling her that everything will be ok, I went down and put on my holster and put a full clip into the 9mm. I also took the .38 just for back up.

Luther was waiting by the door when I came upstairs I grabbed my jacket and walked out the door with Luther. It was starting to snow heavy and the streets were painted white, Elroy came out the car and opened the door for Luther and I. we sat in the car across from each other Luther pulled out his silver Magnum .44 and started shinning it and loading it one round at a time. He then looked at me and asked me if I was feeling ok, I looked up into his face and nodded yes.

We pulled into this ghetto neighborhood in Yonkers, there was this greenhouse we were looking at and Luther pointed across the street to these three guys'. One of the guys I recognized as this Blood named Killer T he used to go to school with me until he dropped out, he was with two other guys Luther knew Freddy and Lil man. Freddy was this medium sized dude with a head full of box braids that traveled to his shoulder, he was copper complexion and was talking crazy with his hands, Lil Man was short and a little on the fat side, he wore his hair cut into a light cesar, he was drinking from something concealed in a brown paper bag. "Killer T set me up and tried to kill me but failed, that's the day he almost killed you and Lele." Luther said this as he pulled the hammer back on the revolver and stepped out of the car. I followed beside him as we walked across the street towards the three guys, they were sharing swigs from the brown bag when Lil man saw us coming, and he dropped the bottle and reached for his gun. Luther aimed towards his head and let off a single shot that roared loudly making Lil man about three inches shorter, Freddy grabbed an empty bottle and threw it at me when I reached for my 9mm. The bottle hit me and made me drop the gun, Luther pointed at Freddy and let off two shots that ate up his chest causing him to fly backwards onto the ground.

Killer T was cocking back his gun and before he could point it at Luther I had mine in hand and shot him twice in the right shoulder forcing him to drop his gun. Luther walked up to him and smiled and shook his head "You almost killed my pregnant sister nigga."

When I heard Luther say that I knew this shit was about to get personal; Luther put the gun into Killer T's mouth and right before he pulled the trigger he looked around at all the people gathering around and looking out of their window. Luther pulled the gun out of his mouth and handed it to Elroy who was standing next to him, he kicked Killer T in the ribs and spit on his face "Now crawl to the edge of the steps." Killer T did has he was told and was in obvious pain from the bullets still in his shoulder. "Now bite it"

"What?"

"Did I stutter ma'fucka? Bite the goddamn edge." Luther said this time raising his voice. Killer T tried to resist but Luther got angrier and dragged him to the steps, "Bite it!!" Killer T bit down on the brick edge, you could hear his teeth grinding on the stair case. He started to cry but that only fueled Luther even more, he saw the crowd and turned and addressed them "If any of you motherfuckas ever put my families lives in danger this is what will happened to you." He quickly turned to Killer T and almost in slow motion I saw the snow come off his gray Timberland as he raised it off the ground and forcefully moving down. You could hear the pleas from some of the people in the crowd begging Luther not to do it, but their cries went in vein as he came crashing into the back of Killer T's head into the brick stair case. I stared in aw like this was some type of television show; the screams from the crowd depicted the horror that was just witnessed.

The white snow was now tinted dark red from Killer T's face being split open wide and his face being remodeled, I stood there just watching the monster that did this and thinking of how can a man be so content in such a brutal act of violence. How could any human being just stomp a man's head in two? It started to become more clear that I was in the wrong family and I was definitely in the wrong line of work.

Chapter 18

𝕿HERE WILL BE BLOOD!

Three days went by since Luther killed the three men who were after him, Luther showed me that he wasn't afraid of anything. He had this look in his eye's that showed death, I could feel this dark presence when I'm around him.

Peter's funeral was today and I had to get ready for the event. I picked up Mary and Claxton and we rode down there together, it was a real beautiful day, the sun was out, and my side of the world was riddled with snow. Everyone we knew was at the funeral except Empress and S-Dot who were both doing bids, it was a sad event and what made it worst was the sight of Peter's mother crying and breaking down from the tragic death of her son. I understood her feelings and I had a feeling that I hadn't felt in a long time. I dropped off Claxton and Mary and went inside to see how Mary was doing, she was holding up but still looked bad and strung out. I could tell that she was still on some drugs and inside I felt the anger building, before I allowed myself to get any angrier I sat on the couch next to her, "Hey Mary how you feelin?"

"Huh" Mary was in a trance like state, "I asked you how are you doing, but I see that you aren't in the right state of mind to talk."

"Decon I'm ok, I just need... Need some medicine you know what I mean?"

"Naw I don't know what you mean. You need help and I'm not going to sit around and watch you shoot your life away."

"What do you mean?" Mary asked looking me straight in the eyes "I'm taking you to rehab today, right now." Mary tried to fight me, but I was stronger and I had Claxton come and help me get her in the car. We left the house with Mary and drove her down to Manhattan to this nice building near Central Park. I walked with Mary and checked her in at the front desk where a young looking nurse was getting all of our information. "Mary you know this is for the best." Mary didn't want to hear it and tried to fight me and everyone that was touching her, Claxton caught her hand as she tried to strike him and he spun her around and gave her a loving kiss that calmed her down. After the two of them had a private conversation in a small office she started crying and agreed to stay, the nurse at the front desk pulled her away from Claxton. I gave her three hundred dollars and asked that she looked over her and make sure that she stays until she is clean. Claxton was in love with Mary and ensured me that he will check on her every day; I tapped him on the shoulder and walked out the door to drive back to Brooklyn.

***

As soon as I got back to the house Nate called me and told me that he was throwing a party in memory of Peter, I told Lele about it and she decided to go with me. I was watching the news when a young looking officer came on the screen being interviewed about the recent spike in murders happening in the city. He was a young white guy who was determined to put an end to it all. "Hey babe, how did it go with your sister?" Lele asked me taking a seat next to me, "she's fine, it will take some time but I think she is going to be fine." I said leaning over and giving her a kiss, the night was beginning to creep up on us and we needed to get ready for the party. We got dressed up and wanted to make an impression, I put on these black Calvin Klein slacks with hard bottom Stacy Adams and a black silk shirt, Lele suggested that I top it off with a large platinum cross with a jet-black fedora and dark tinted shades. She put on a black lace romper with pink lace Louboutin knee high boots, and she grabbed her black floor length mink coat. I went downstairs to the basement and opted to go with my .38 since it was smaller than the rest of the guns and it would be easier to conceal under my black overcoat. After I was set I came upstairs to find Lele waiting by the door, we got in the car and took off to the Bronx were the Party was just getting started, the night air was chilled and on this particular night it was beyond cold. Mark let us in through the back since the line was crazy and we were quickly engulfed by the energy from the atmosphere and everyone seemed to be having a good time. Nate and Mark were a major hit on the underground scene and tonight they were going to perform some new hits and try to get signed by this hit label called Diamond Empire. The party was lit, and the dance floor was packed, people were really feeling the music. "Hey y'all I want to say thank you all for coming out this evening in support of my fallen comrade and best

friend, rest easy big dog, we will always remember you."
Nate said while on the stage, Mark walked up to the front
of the stage with a bottle of Hennessey and popped the
top "To Peter!" He shouted out and poured some of the
liquor on the ground and took a long toke from the bottle.

While Nate and Mark were performing on stage Lele
felt sick and wanted to go home, I wanted to stay but she
was six months pregnant I couldn't blame her.

As we walked towards the door there was a fight
that broke out in the middle of the floor. This skinny kid
with glasses was getting punched in the face by this guy
named Kirt Thomas. He was known in Queens as a
troublemaker, known to shoot first asked questions later.
A real hot headed dude who you didn't want to joke
around with, he was a member of the Crips and ran the
streets like he was untouchable. The fight got out of
control and Kirt was dropping security guards left and
right. The music had stopped and three huge security
guards came and wrapped Kirt up and threw him outside;
he was heated and had this crazy look on his face. He
was yelling out at the kid that he was going to see him
outside or something like that. The kid with the glasses
was bleeding and was escorted outside, Lele asked him if
he was ok and asked why Kirt was beating on him. He

told her that he had feel into him when he was dancing with this girl and made Kirt spill his drink; *see I told you real hot head.* I went to get the car and drive it to where Lele was standing waiting for me, I got there and Lele got into the car; the kid with the glasses was walking towards his car holding his face when I saw Kirt jump out of this black truck holding a large hand gun.

"Hey lil nigga" Kirt yelled out, and just as the kid turned around to see Kirt, he was met with three hungry rounds that came screaming down the barrel and making a feast of his lower jaw and chest. The kid was dead before he hit the ground. Kirt saw me looking at him and he smiled, hoped back into his truck and sped off into the darkness. I looked at the kid again and I couldn't believe what was happening to me, before this kind of stuff was normal to me but now I was starting to feel a change of heart, like this kid died over nothing. I got into the car shaking my head and took Lele home. We were silent the whole ride home both of us lost in our own thoughts, I waited till she was passed out to bath. As the hot water hit my cold body a shiver ran up my spine, my mind ran circles over my life and what I was going through. It hit me Peter was gone, "Damn!" I said to myself as I closed my eyes and submerged my head in the water. I tried to get Killer T's mutilated face out of my head, it was so gruesome it was like a bad nightmare that wouldn't go away. I lifted my head out of the water and dried off, and got into the bed with Lele.

The cool night's breeze from the bedroom window felt good on my naked body and allowed me to sleep peacefully. As I stretched my hands behind my head I closed my eyes and feel into a deep sleep.

The sun was barley coming through the window when I felt this sweet feeling of pleasure, I thought it was a wet dream, but as I opened my eyes I could see Lele licking and sucking on me. I let out a shivery sigh of pure delight with each movement from her mouth, I twitched and squeezed my toes began to curl. I gripped the sheets as if I was trying to strangle someone as she stroked it with her soft hands up and down and with the warmth of her mouth it only raised the ecstasy level. I couldn't hold on much longer, I felt the pressure building up getting ready to burst. I sounded like a baby speaking in sounds, I couldn't hold it, as I exploded my eyes clinched tight together and my leg stiffened up I relaxed and laid there paralyzed.

"Good morning baby!" she said running the shower

"Now that's what I call a good morning" I said to her with a smile on my face. I snapped out of my astound state and put on my robe and walked to the kitchen for something to drink. I grabbed my phone and saw that I had a text from Luther telling me to meet him at the gun house around four. My mind was still wrapped around my great morning start I attempted to cook breakfast. I made scrambled eggs, bacon and some toast, Lele came down stairs smelling like a bushel of sweet smelling roses on a bundle of sandalwood and looking great with her baby bump, I gave her a kiss and we sat down and ate breakfast. It was a Saturday and Lele wanted to go shopping in the city, we got dressed after eating and drove to Manhattan to hit a few stores. I looked at my watch and noticed that it was almost time for me to meet up with Luther. As we arrived at the gun house Elroy stepped out of the car and opened the back door grabbing a large bag and an envelope. "Luther had to meet with the boss" Elroy said handing me the items in his hand. I put the bag in the trunk with the other shopping bags, I opened the envelope and saw that my next job was in New Jersey, I had to take out these three guys who were setting up drug trades in North Jersey and they were starting to bleed into New York pissing off the Kingdome.

The instructions on the paper said that I had to take them out today before 11 o'clock, there was a guy named Jazz who everyone in Brooklyn knew. He was a known Crip who used to chill with Keith outside of my old apartments, there was one guy I didn't know named Jump, but the other target was Kirt another Crip but I didn't know why he was in Jersey. The instructions also said that I had to make the hit real nasty. I put the envelope in the trunk and closed it, I walked inside to grab some things for the job. I grabbed three grenades and this remote controlled trigger and some military grade C4; I was going to make this shit epic.

I drove Lele home and told her what I had to do, it was like everything I did didn't bother her, and then again her brother is Luther so I didn't think too much on it, but it still felt like she was in on all my jobs. I opened the large bag that Elroy gave me and looked inside it had to be over $300,000 inside, I put it with the other money I had stashed away and grabbed an empty book bag. For the job I grabbed my sawn off and a box full of shells and my .45 with two extra clips, I also had my .38 that was already in the holster. It was around six and the sun was starting to go down as I came across the bridge into Jersey, on the back of the picture of Jazz it said that he had a corner store in Jersey City as a front to move some of his work. I figured he should be there around this time. I was in luck, by the time I arrived to the store I saw Jazz and this random guy who I noticed was Jump as they get into the black truck Kirt drove off in after he shot the kid with the glasses. Jazz was a dark bronze cat with a deep scare running across his left cheek, he wasn't tall but he wasn't short either, but he was rocking this dark blue hoodie with dark blue jeans and a blue bandana around his bald head. Jump I didn't see too well because he was already in the driver's seat, but from the photo I had of him he was this slim Arab looking cat. He wore his hair in criss crossed box braids. I followed them as they went to these apartments were Kirt was outside talking to some kid at the door, he was dressed in all blue from head to toe and seemed pissed. It looked like he was yelling at him about something, the other guy in the truck, Jump called over this kid who had to be in high school or something from the same building. He walked over and Jump gave the kid a hand gun and pointed at both ends of the street. The kid walked back across the street and stood in the doorway of some other apartments; Kirt took a large brown package from Jazz and walked inside the apartment building. Jazz hopped back into the truck after talking to a few of his lookouts and they drove off. I followed them around the corner about 12 blocks down the street from the apartments. They stopped at a red light and I pulled up next to them. Jump was smoking a cigarette and his window was down, Jazz was searching for something in the back seat, and that's when I got an idea. I grabbed two grenades and stepped out of the car, pulled the pins on them and smiled as Jazz looked over at me from the passenger seat. "Merry Christmas!" I said as I threw the live grenades into the truck one landed on the floor in front of the driver and the other bounced of the head rest and landed in the back of the truck, I didn't stick around to see them panic trying to get the grenades out. I was back into my car as the grenades were making their home in the truck, and took off running the light barley getting hit by another car.

Two seconds later **Boom!!** The explosion was loud and crazy; the truck flew about five feet in the air crashing hard to the ground fully engulfed in flames. I hit the gas and went around the corner back towards the apartments, my heart was racing and I was excited ready to take out Kirt next. I thought about the kid he killed for no reason and I thought to myself karma is a motherfucker. I parked a few blocks from the apartment grabbed the other grenade and put it in my book bag with the .38 in my holster and the .45 in the back of my pants.

I grabbed six shells for the sawn off and put them in the bag with the gun, I was ready for war and I wanted to make this one was a mini Vietnam. I walked around the corner and walked into the building where the high school kid was watching the spot across the street. I started walking up stairs and right before I got to the top of the stairs I yelled out at the kid "Yo! you sellin?" the kid looked at me and told me to keep it movin.

"Fuckin Bitch!" I said trying to get the kid upset, it worked and he was heated and jumped up walking up the stairs to me "What the fuck you say to me nigga!" he said brandishing his gun that was hidden under his hoodie. He was serious, kid had to be about seventeen years old "Oh so you bad my nigga?"

"Nigga is you crazy? Don't make me stretch you out over some bull shit." The kid said standing in arms reach, I threw a right jab at his face, he moved back and stumbled a little down the stairs. He was reaching for his gun, I couldn't let him pop it off, it would bring too much attention from the drug spot across the street. So I kicked him in the chest making him fly down the flight of stairs hitting the floor hard, *before I keep going with this story I must say that was some movie shit, but back to the story.* I ran down towards the kid who was on the floor in pain and trying to figure out what just happened to him, I picked him up and threw him into the wall. I hit him with a few knees to his ribs, one of them gave in and caused him to double over in pain. I hit his face with a fury of punches over and over with both hands, he slid down and I threw my knee into his face breaking his nose and causing him to hit the wall with the back of his head. This kid was fucked up and knocked out but still breathing. I grabbed his gun and put it in my bag; I shook my hand from the contacts to his face and head and walked out the door towards the apartments.

The guy that was getting yelled at by Kirt was this light skin cat with a messy fro, he was talking on the phone when I walked up on him pulling my sawn off out and shaking my head no as he reached for his gun. "Let's take a walk upstairs." I told him as he complied, he was pissed and starred at me with this hard scowl "You know you fucked up right?"

"How so, youngin?"

"This building belongs to Jazz and his crew,"

"Yea I know, I already had a talk with Jazz, but I can ensure you that he won't be a factor. I'm here for Kirt, now if you would be so kind." I said pushing the muzzle of the gun to his head to show that I wasn't playing any games. "Okay...Okay I'll take you there just move that gun away from my face." The young dude walked me to the fifth floor and pointed to a door that looked like it has been changed from the rest of the doors on the floor and had been painted a different color. "He's in there,"

"Okay go on open the door" I said, he walked to the door and did a secret knock, I stood on the side of the door away from the peep hole. The door opened with the door chain still attached and I saw a shot gun in the door man's hand, the guy outside flashed his eyes at me and the doorman cocked back the gun. That's when I kicked the guy into the door and moved out of the way, **Boom!** The gun blast went through the door and the kid killing the poor guy. On the outside, I let off two shots from the sawn off into the door hitting the doorman. I threw my shoulder into the door busting inside, three single shots were let off from the inside followed by a tech 9 that ripped holes into the wall behind me, I ducked back outside and reloaded the sawn off shooting inside the room. There was cocaine and naked women inside and I didn't know how many people had guns in there.

I let off some more shots into the room with the sawn off and dropped it, pulling my .45 and letting off four shots from around the corner blindly. There were screams everywhere and gun fire was getting out of control. "How many of them up there?" Kirt was yelling and shooting at the same time "YOU GONNA DIE MOTHERFUCKAS!" I looked at my bag and grabbed the last hand grenade, pulled the pin and threw it inside the room and hopped outside in the hallway. "Oh shit, get down!" **KABOOM!!** The gun fire was silenced, I walked back into the room that was cloudy and had fire splattered over in random places. There were bodies all over the small apartment, I let off two shots into this chick with a pistol and one in the guy with a Mac 10. This girl tried to run out and I shot her three times allowing the bullets to eat up her back. I looked around and saw Kirt in the corner with his hand holding on to the Tech 9, but his forearm was hanging from the skin and his leg hanging from the nerve. He was laughing and coughing up blood still talking shit, "you dead nigga you hear me you dead!" **Pow!** The blast from my gun split his face wide open.

I looked around at the destruction from the grenade, bodies mutilated and split open a few were even still moving, I put the C4 inside the oven and turned it on. When I ran outside and saw a crowd of people trying to figure out what was going on, it was dark and you could see the police lights coming from up the street. I pushed the button on the remote control and **KABOOM!!!** World War III was in Jersey, the people outside were scared and started running to the other side of the street as fire and debris flooded the ground. I took off down the block towards my car and drove off back to New York. I looked at the time it was almost midnight and what I did in Jersey was already hitting the radio news, *"Jersey City has been hit with unimaginable violence, Police are on the scene responding to two explosions in one night. The New Jersey Mayor has issued a state of emergency for the city calling for all citizens to remain inside and report any information on the crimes committed tonight to the authorities."* Luther called me as I was heading for the Holland Tunnel and he was excited "My Nigga that's what the FUCK I'm talkin bout!" He was ecstatic and told me that he loved how nasty I made that shit look. Luther was watching the news and saw Jersey in a state of death and destruction. There was chaos all over Brooklyn when I got there around five in the morning, NYPD was on fire and were keeping the streets on their toes. There wasn't a corner that wasn't flooded with red and blue lights, I made it home and quickly went inside. Lele was also watching the news and when she saw me she jumped up and ran to give me a hug and kiss. "Babe you did this?"

she said with a huge smile on her face. "Yea that was all me" I said smiling at my work that was being portrayed on the six o' clock news.

Chapter 19

CHILL FOR THE

MOMENT

The next day was worst; the governor of New Jersey came on the news and gave a whole spill about protecting the streets and ending the violence. But as always the streets had their own way of revenge. There was war between the Bloods, the Black Knights, the Crips, the Latin Gangs, and the police. No one was safe anymore, people were afraid to send their children to school, or even walk three blocks to work. New York also caught the virus and was in a state of civil chaos. I got a call from Luther telling me that there was going to be a big party tonight in my honor, the Kingdom was throwing me a party and it was time for them to see the man behind the scenes; the big play maker.

The party was going to be at this strip club in the Bronx and he didn't want me to miss it. I had this feeling that what I did was going to lead to something larger than I thought. Some of New York's major street gangs were going against each other and the Kingdom was becoming the stronghold of crime, the voice of reason if you will. I kept thinking to myself about what I just did and if this was the plan of the Kingdom the whole time, and in the back of my mind I knew once they were done with me I had to be dealt with. There was a shootout in Queens that day that left eleven Blood gang members dead in the streets and another gun fight in Harlem that killed five Crip's. Things were getting out of hand and I knew it was because of me.

I was getting ready for the party when I got a call from Lemon telling me that he heard about what was going on up here in New York and asked me if Mary and I were doing ok. I told him that we were safe and I let him know that I was thinking about going to Florida soon, till some of this madness cooled down. He was happy to hear that and told me that he had a feeling that didn't sit well with him about everything that was going on. We got off the phone and I went back to getting ready for this big party that was going down tonight. Lele and I walked into the packed strip club; every member of the Kingdom was in there, everyone from the ladies of the gun house to the dealers running the streets. The liquor was flowing along with every drug known to man weed, coke, pills everything. As I walked in I noticed that there were eyes wondering who I was and why I was even at the party. With a half full bottle of Gray Goose in his hand that he was drinking from, Luther came up to me smiling and threw his large arm around me and introduced me to a few of the members of the Kingdom.

This guy in an all-white silk suit walked out of the backroom with two beautiful girls on his arm, both were tall slim goddesses one was a beautiful dark bronze and the other was a golden cream, both modeling an all-white see through body suit. He was smiling from ear to ear and was walking towards me and Lele. He reminded me of a deep south pimp, with all gold jewelry, and a white fedora with a golden yellow feather on it. He had on all white gloves, snake skin shoes, he even had this furry vest shit draped over his shoulders. He walked up to T.M.D. who was sporting a skin tight dark red dress, and make-up that gave him slight feminine features, but you could still tell that he was a man. Percy whispered something in his ear, he looked at me and smiled, I was lost and didn't know how to feel about that, after he said his piece to T.M.D. he walked up to me and shook my hand. "Welcome to the Kingdom Decon I am very proud to have you on our team." He looked over at Luther and told him to get some Champaign for a toast. As we lifted our glasses to the sky this guy started to speak, "We are the Kingdom and this is our paradise! I Lord Percy welcome Decon Rice into our family" after he said that everyone in the room said together "FOR THE KINGDOM!" we toasted and drank. Percy walked up to Lele and rubbed her belly saying that babies bring him luck; he wrapped his arm around me and asked me to walk with him. "You've done some good things for the Kingdom Decon, Luther has told me a lot about you." His laid back voice made me feel a little uncomfortable; you could tell he was a pimp by his movements and actions.

"I want you to take a vacation, chill for a moment, your next job will be by me. So when you get back I'll give you a call and we will talk business, but tonight is a night of pleasure." As he sipped the Champaign in his left hand Percy walked over to the rest of the members and talked and laughed with them. Lele was all smiles and so was I, but I kept getting this feeling of trouble. As the night went on Solomon 7 walked up to me and whispered in my ear

"This is not for you kid" he walked towards the front door and walked out. As the night went on I noticed Lele at a table with the twins giving their attention to a big booty stripper, Luther and Skinny Slim had their eyes on another. Black King, and Lord Shabazz were talking in the corner with a few women around them, the rest of the members were huddled around Percy as he kicked jokes and kept the crowd entertained. I was getting tired and wanted to go home, I talked to Luther for a bit on taking a little vacation, and shortly after I took off with Lele off to Brooklyn.

***

While I was in the basement cleaning my weapons the next morning I get a call on my cell phone from Solomon 7, asking me to meet him in the park over by the burned down projects. I grabbed my 9mm and inserted a full mag. I didn't know what he wanted and from the last time we got together he almost put a bullet in my head so I wanted to be ready for anything. I walked out with my black hoodie on and walked the 12 blocks to the park, Solomon 7 was already there and sitting on the bench where we first met. I walked up to him very cautiously and had my hand inside my hoodie pocket on the gun just in case I had to pull it on him.

Solomon 7 looked up and saw me coming towards him "If you want to kill me do it after I finish talking otherwise take your hand off the gun." I pulled my hand off of the pistol and sat down next to him "What's good?" I asked him as I sat down. "You don't belong in this D, this shit isn't for you at all." I could see the concern on his face, it was sincere but I was still alert and on edge. "They're going to kill you after your next job." I looked at him with my eyes wide opened and serious, "How do you know this?" I asked Solomon 7 he turned to me and pulled out this piece of paper with a red seal on the top of it. It looked like an old 1600's seal that they used for professional documents and I was wondering what it said. He handed me the paper and what it said made me furious, Solomon 7 was ordered to kidnap me after my next assigned job and along with the other members of the Kingdom they were going to execute me. I wanted to kill each and every one of them, I looked over at Solomon 7 and asked "Why are you telling me this?"

"Were boys and I have too much respect for you then to kill you in this manner, I've been in the Kingdom for a long time and I can't leave, but I can help prevent your death. Don't come back D take your money and go far away as possible." "When I get back I'm coming after all who threaten me" I told Solomon 7 as I pulled out my 9mm and gripped it. "That's all good D but you don't understand, Percy got federal agents working for him, how do you think they got pictures of all your targets, the locations? Nigga he will have you killed before you even get out of Manhattan." Solomon 7 was serious and was beginning to get upset, "You know, do what you want D, just know I got to do what I got to do." Solomon 7 stood up and walked the other way, my mind was twisted and I was confused on what I was just told "Hey Solomon 7 WAIT!" I yelled out at him getting up and running to go catch him before he got into his car. "So what about Leandra?" I asked him "What about her?" he said "She knew about this the whole time, she has orders to set you up for me to get you, take everything your money, your clothes, the weapons, and leave you with nothing." "So what about the baby?" Solomon 7 looked at me and laughed "You got to be kidding me lord, she picked you out from the day at the park, she just wanted a baby and you were the guy for her, she don't love you kid. You just another nigga, you're in too deep she is set for life, she is one of the founders of the Kingdom." My body felt numb and I was enraged I couldn't believe this shit, just kill me and take my seed. Solomon 7 got into his car "Look fam, the Kingdom wants to control the city and they will stop at nothing to do so, you coming into the picture was just a play on the chess board. You're a pawn and you just made plays for the King to survive. He said his piece and left me standing there in shock.

I walked back home thinking about what I was just told and trying to figure out how I was going to get out of it. I wanted to take them down but I was only one man and I couldn't do it on my own, I needed help from people that I could trust, I wish Empress and S-Dot were still around I know I could count on them two. I made it home and saw Lele in the kitchen cooking, I couldn't look at her the same as I once did, but I couldn't let her know that I knew about the set up. I walked in the kitchen and hugged her and gave her a kiss on the neck she smiled and asked if I wanted something to eat. I told her yea, we ate and talked about going back down to Florida, Lele wanted to come with me and I knew it was because when she gets back the Kingdom will know that I'm back. After we talked I walked down to the basement to count my money, I had about four million dollars in the house and I had to find a place to hide it all for the time being, but that was gonna have to wait.

Three days later me and Lele were in Florida for Christmas, Lemon was driving us around and we went to my grandmother's house where Luke was cooking dinner. Lele went up to where Mary's room was at and took a nap, I brought Lemon into the kitchen with Luke and I told them that we needed to talk. "That girl upstairs is going to have me killed after my next job" as I spoke Luke stopped cooking and pulled out a butcher's knife "WHAT! Let's kill the bitch" I told Luke to calm down and to keep quiet, "I have a plan; it's not just her that's out to kill me it's the people that I work for. I need y'all help; I want to take them all out." Lemon looked at me and told me that he planned for this when I told him what I did for a living. We walked to the basement and inside my old room was an armory of weapons, "Where did you get all this?" I asked Lemon in shock of what I was looking at. There were pistols, automatic machine guns, shotguns, and rifles of different calibers, Lemon had his own stockpile from this security job he was doing in Miami.

We walked back upstairs and I told them that I will let them know when I need their help. Lele woke up a few minutes after we talked and Luke's dinner was ready and we ate Christmas dinner together. It didn't really feel right without Mary, but I knew she needed help and where she was at I knew she was getting it. That night I couldn't really sleep, it might have been the house or that I was sleeping with, the one who was going to kill me. I stood up out of the bed and walked into my grandmother's room; the bible that she left me in her will was sitting on the dresser still in the box that she kept it in. I opened the bible and a folded piece of paper fell out of it.

To Decon Rice my beloved grandson, I understand that if you are reading this, then that means I have passed away to be with the Lord. I prayed for you every day, but I am no longer able to do so, I prayed that the Lord GOD protects you and that he guides you. I saw the pain in your eyes when your mother came back to get you, and I know you wondered why I let you go with her. I knew my time was short Decon and I had faith in my daughter that she would do right by you and your sister Mary.

I know it was hard for you because it was hard for me but New York is where you needed to be. I know you're wondering why I gave you a bible, ha-ha well that is because I know you and I know you're not right with GOD, and this is a tool to help you find him and your peace. I ask that you try and understand him Decon, if not for me for your soul. I've held on to this for a long time, this bible belonged to your father, I know you and Mary don't know him and I promised to keep this secret as long as I lived. Well I'm dead now and I will not hold this from you any longer, your father lives in New York, his name is Kane, he owns a dojo in Brooklyn and is doing much better now than when you were born. If you ever find him he will be able to explain to you why I asked him to leave.

Ps: John 3:16 read it love MAMA D

After I read the letter from Mama D it felt as if my heart warmed up and was no longer cold, my eyes swelled up and I began to cry. For the first time in months I was crying, I heard a voice in my head telling me to pray, I dropped to my knees and I started to pray. Asking GOD to forgive me and help me along the way,

"Lord I'm not perfect by a long shot,

I have caused pain and gave my life to the wrong side, and the death has been non-stop.

I hit rock bottom Lord and I can't find a way out.

Lord, I suffered so much, the pain causes me to shout.

Where is my salvation? Do you hear the voice

of the inflicted?

This is hell's damnation, and the blood on my hand is already depicted.

I'm a product of pain and torture,

A customer for a better deal on life so make me an offer.

I'm a sheep with no shepherd, lost in the pasture of darkness

But Lord I need help and I need a path to follow

The realization of my life is a hard pill to swallow.

The weather is hot, my soul is frozen

I ask that you save me from myself,

But I know I'm not chosen

So show me the light, allow me to feel your glory

But Lord I can't promise you that what I need to do, won't be gory.

Lord I don't know if I will be ever be saved

But give me peace father, at least for today."

After I prayed I stood up and wiped my eyes and went back into the room with Lele and fell asleep.

Chapter 20

LIVING TO DIE

We stayed in Florida till after New Year's; right before I got on the plane I grabbed Lemon as if I was giving him a hug and whispered in his ear, "next time you get a call from me, make your way to New York" I pushed away from him and walked on to the plane. We made it to New York and Elroy was there to pick us up, on the ride home me and Lele talked about the birth of the baby and how excited she was as the dates moved closer and closer to the due date. We made it home and Lele went upstairs to sleep in the bedroom, I walked down to the basement and grabbed my money and put it in the car, seven large duffle bags full of money, I left about $200,000 in the house and the rest I drove around looking for a place to hide it. When I drove past this graveyard in Queens I saw a body going into the ground and got an idea. I parked in the graveyard and waited till the family left and walked out of the gate. I drove up close and put all of my money in air tight bags and placed them back into the duffle bag.

I jumped down into the hole with the coffin and opened it up, the body was this little old black lady named Cynthia Merritt, she was a beautiful lady. I placed the money in the casket with her and closed it up. I was lucky that there was room in there for all seven bags, I climbed out of the hole and walked back to the car and drove off before the people came to cover the casket. I made it back to Brooklyn and as I walked into the house I got a call from Percy telling me that he wanted to see me today. Three days into the New Year and he was ready for business, I walked outside and there was an all-white Limo waiting for me. Getting into the Limo I was surprised to see that Percy was sitting on the far side with the two beautiful girls, from the night at the strip club. "Happy New Year Decon! How was your vacation?" Percy asked me smiling and smoking a cigar, "I'm good just a bit hungry" I responded. Percy laughed and told me that he had lunch waiting for us at his place "You like Greek right?" Percy said tilting his cigar towards me and smiling. "I never had it before but I could eat anything at this point." Percy let out a cloud of smoke and said "Son you're alright with me." Percy ordered his driver to take us to his home in Manhattan, the ride there was awkward but at the same time I couldn't let Percy know that I knew he ordered my death.

The Limo pulled up to this large condominium and we walked inside to go up to his room on the twelfth floor, this place was huge and as I walked inside the first thing I saw was the great view of the city from the outstretched window. "You like that huh" Percy said, he must of seen my eyes get wide from the beautiful view, "See Decon this is my kingdom, I own all of this and its only right that I have a great view of my investment." Percy said as he pointed to the city. Everything he did was smooth; laid back, from the way he walked to the way he talked; I thought I was watching a movie. "Come let's eat then talk business." Percy said walking to this white marble dining room table that was next to an ivory piano, as we sat at the table these girls in their lingerie walked out of the kitchen and placed the food on the table. I gave a quick silent prayer and attacked my food, "Decon... Decon calm down son ha-ha the food isn't going to run from you." Percy said as he slowly ate his food. "Sorry, it's just as I told you I was starving and this is great."

"Well there is plenty" Percy said still taking small

bites from his plate.

We finished eating and I gotta say the food was great I never had anything like that, "So Decon about your next job, we have a huge problem with our new plan" Percy went on to say as he wiped his face, "I asked Luther to put you on this family because you're some type martial arts super star, right?" I smiled and said "well I'm ok" Percy laughed and continued on to say "So modest, I love it ha-ha the Kingdom is about to bring in a profusion of weapons and drugs into New York, its damn near crazy." He stood up and walked towards the large window overlooking the city, I joined him as he went on with the plans for the Kingdom. "I want to gain total control of this city so that I will be untouchable," he had a slight pause to adjust his choice of words "we will be untouchable. You like that huh? Well there is a big problem, and I mean BIG problem, we can't continue until this problem is out of the picture." He snapped his fingers and this female walked into the room with a folded piece of paper with the red seal keeping it closed. It was the same red seal as the one Solomon 7 had on his; I opened it up and saw a picture of this white guy.

I kept flipping through the pictures of the guy and I kept struggling to place where I seen him before. Then I came across one with him wearing a FBI jacket, then in hit me hard, this was the detective from the other night who made his statement to fight all crime in the city. "His name is Bryan Smith he works for the FBI and he covers over the New York sector, I have over 100 federal agents, and internees on my pay roll and this guy isn't one of them. With him in the picture I can't get the drugs or the weapons into New York from South America and I need you to take him out." I was surprised at the target "You want me to kill a FED?" I asked with a confused look on my face, "Yes I want it to be smooth, no evidence, and no witnesses. Can you make this happen for me; for the Kingdom?" he said as he placed his hand on my shoulder. I wasn't too happy about my assignment usually I kill people who I felt did harm to humanity but this agent is simply doing his job, this was going to be a real job that needed a lot of planning. "Yes I'll do it, when do you want it done?" I asked Percy.

"That is solely on you Decon the sooner the better, and the sooner we can move on with our plans. But there's this one thing I need to insure the job is done right, I need his badge." I agreed to his terms and we shook hands, before he let my hand go he said that I will be awarded five million dollars for the completion of the job.

My eyes got wide and I smiled, he released my hands and called for one of his girls to escort me to the limo and drop me off home. On the ride home I sat in the limo and thought about how I wanted to go about this next mission. I didn't want to kill the guy, I wanted to take out the Kingdom but they were so powerful that it was damn near impossible to take them out all at once. When I got home, Elroy was waiting outside in the SUV and looked at me and gave me a head nod. Elroy rarely spoke, he just did as he was told, but I knew he was loyal to Luther, he had been working for him for years. I walked inside and Luther was watching TV in the living room "How was the meeting?" Luther asked me in a serious tone, "It went well, Percy set me up with a new contract." Luther didn't like that and jumped up in front of my face "I told you that you work for me and me only, I don't give a damn who is higher than me; I own you." Luther was so close to my face I could smell the stale cigarette smoke on his breath. I looked him in his eyes and told him that I understood and I walked past him, Luther's hand reached out and hit me in the chest stopping me from moving, he leaned into me and whispered in my ear, "If you want to live long to see that baby of yours grow up, you would do as your told nigga." Luther pushed me to the side and walked out of the house driving off with Elroy. I was upset and I wanted to make sure I never saw him again, so that's when I went to the basement and started planning the Kingdom's downfall.

I needed pictures of every member's movements, where they live, their daily routine, everything. I thought about the letter that Mama D gave to me and I realized that there was another issue I needed to solve, I needed to see my father. I couldn't believe this, he knew me before I knew him, he knew I was his son the whole time. This thought got me angry and I had to speak to him, I grabbed my .38 and took off in the car to the dojo. I sat in the car watching his dojo from the driver seat going over the game plan in my head over and over. It was getting dark and the class he had was letting out, I got out of the car and ran around to the back door of the dojo. The door was opened and I walked inside, I broke into the office with my .38 pulled and ready to unload on Kane. The room was empty and no one was seen or heard, his computer was still on and there was coffee inside that ugly yellow and brown mug sitting on the table to the left was still hot. Flashbacks of my sister ran through my head, I couldn't take it anymore the pain that the memories gave me were becoming too much to hold on to. As soon as I opened my eyes again, I saw the taser coming my way, to slow to dodge it **"zap"** the surge of electricity screamed through my body locking my muscles to a complete halt. I hit the ground with a thump!! As I laid on the ground still and motionless that feeling came over me again, that warm embracing feeling, a flash of yellowish golden light blinded me.

When I finally woke up I tried to move but I was tied up to a chair in the middle of the dojo with Kane standing in front of me with my .38 in his hand. "What are you doing Decon?" Kane asked me once he noticed I was awake, "You knew, you FUCKIN KNEW!" I said coughing and getting back to reality. Kane started laughing at me and pulled up a chair behind him and sat down, "So Mama D finally told you huh? Ha-ha I knew that old women couldn't keep her word" "Watch your mouth nigga my grandmothers' dead" Kane looked at me and stopped laughing "sorry to hear that..." There was a short silence between us two, "So I'm guessing you want to know why I left you and your sister huh?" I sat quietly and looked deep into Kane's eyes. "I came to the states from an extended trip in London, I was working for this organization training young men like yourself, but when I made it to Florida, I met the most beautiful woman I ever laid my eyes on, your mother. She was working as a bank teller and I used to deposit money into my account daily, until one day I mustered up enough balls to finally ask her out. Well a few days of rejection she finally gave in and we were an item ever since. The group I was affiliated with at the time prohibited me from dealing with women and I was going against the rules and their beliefs. Well they sent for me, and at the end of it all I'm still alive and they are no longer walking this Earth. We moved to New York for a fresh start and I found myself addicted to heroin..." Kane's head dropped in disappointment and disgust, "Needless to say your mother tried to get me off of it and we moved back to Florida, and that's when you and your sister were born. Now as hard as your mom worked to get me off, I was putting her on, and she found satisfaction in crack, ha-ha how about that two lovers who were addicted to each other and their vices." Kane laughed but he was deeply saddened by the reality of his words. "Mama D saved us both and she wanted your mother to be a mother and not another hype, and I was still being targeted left and right, so to keep you and your sister safe I decided to leave. Y'all were so little, you were only a few months when I left. I was responsible for your mother getting addicted and I was there when she left you two with your grandmother. I couldn't bear watching you or Mary growing up without me so I left her as well and went down my path of enlightenment; I moved back to New York and This guy named Percy got me involved with some plan of his to control the city and I was down for the cause until he set me up and got me arrested for five years for a weapons charge. I have been trying to get back at him for years but recently I couldn't find him. I promised Mama D that I was going to get my life together if she never told you who I was and where I was, but when I saw you that night, you getting jumped I almost cried at seeing my son all grown up. I knew you didn't know me because you didn't recognize me that night, so I figure I just become a big brother to you and help guide you to the right direction."

I started to get angry at Kane from what he was telling me but I couldn't get over the fact that he was my father. Kane started telling me that he wanted me to be a better man than he was and he wanted nothing but the best for me. "So how is your sister doing?"

"She's not doing too well, I guess addiction to drugs run in the family, but unlike you I didn't leave her, I got her some help and she's in a center downtown."

"I deserve that, but I'm happy to hear that she is doing well, I can't wait to see her again. What about your mother?" he asked with wide eyes of excitement "You remember those projects that burned down a few years ago?"

"Yea"

"Yea, she was in there." As my words left my mouth I could see his eyes fill with water and a single tear dropped from his face. "I'm, I'm sorry to hear that, I truly am." I decided not to tell the whole story, that was going to be something that I take with me to the grave. Kane untied me and gave me back my gun, "Look Kane, there's something you need to know about me, I'm a hit man for the Kingdom. That guy Percy you were talking about, well I work for him and he is going to kill me after my last contract." Kane looked at me and the seriousness in his eyes damn near cut through me like a knife, "so I'm your target huh?" Kane asked with a slight smile on his face. "No, you're not but I need your help to take him down." As I assured Kane that he wasn't my target you could see a sign of relief come off of his body, "So what do you need me to do?" I told Kane my plan to take out the Kingdom one by one and he agreed to help me, but with one condition, he gets to kill Percy. We shook hands and I told him that the next time we talked I'll let him know where we need to meet.

I left the dojo with relief that I got a chance to get

what I needed off of my chest as well as answers to questions that have been eating away at me for years. I got back into the car and drove off to the store and bought a camera. I needed to get locations of all the members and I needed to track their movements; today I start my plan for my last mission.

Chapter 21

A NOT SO PERFECT

PLAN

I woke up the next morning to the sun hitting my face and this voice telling me to pray, I got up and shaved my head to get it smooth just the way I had it for the past two months. I jumped in the shower and washed my body as I prayed to God asking for guidance, I had to get out of this life and I wanted to do it fast. I walked out of the shower and got dressed before Lele woke up, standing there for a moment watching her as she slept peacefully and I wondered why someone as beautiful as her would want to live in this life and be ok with killing the father of her child. I walked downstairs and grabbed my coat, walking outside to the car with my camera in hand. I started to drive around Queens looking for Black King, the West African who was in control of the drugs that flowed through Queens. I saw BG on the corner and stopped the car next to her, "Yo! Come here" BG stepped off the wall she was leaning against and walked towards me. "What up D" I thought I would be used to her raspy ass voice by now, but it was something about it that still got on my nerves. "You seen Black King?" I asked her, "Yea, he was on the south side setting up some new spots, why what's good?"

"Nothing really, just trying link up with him"

"Oh, aight you need me to help you with anything?"

"Naw I'm good, but I will get up with you later" she walked back to the wall and I took off towards South Side Queens and got lucky. Black King was in Ajax Park talking to a few kids and handing out money like he was some type of big shot. I snapped a few shots of him and waited for him to get into his car, he was the only one I knew to drive a purple and gold Lexus, Black King didn't live too far from the park in fact he was just around the corner. I snapped a few pic's of his house as he walked up the stairs. I saw three beautiful little girls walk out and hug him screaming daddy and this African chick standing in the doorway, "wow he has a family" I said to myself in surprise. I took a few more pictures before I decided to drive off to find Solomon 7, I knew where he stayed and I knew how to find him if I needed him, I just wanted information for Lord Shabazz his cousin.

I pulled up to Solomon 7's house and called his phone "Yo cousin we need to talk, I'm outside" Solomon 7 came outside his house after I hung up the phone and got into the car with me. "What up D?" he said looking a little at ease, "I'm going to take down the Kingdom rather you want me to or not, you can either help me, and live or I'll kill you like the rest of them." After I spoke I could see Solomon 7 eyes get wide and he knew I wasn't joking, "What do you need?" Solomon 7 was tense and he looked like he hadn't slept in a few days. I told him that I needed information on where his cousin lived; Solomon 7 turned to me "WHAT!" he screamed "I'm not helping you kill my cousin Decon you're on your own with that one." Solomon 7 went for the door handle and I pulled my .45 and placed it on his temple. "Then this is where you die!" I said as seriously as I could, looking at him and pulling back on the hammer. Solomon 7 started to shake his head "what do you need to know?" Solomon 7 was my friend and I knew he was trying to protect his family, but my life met more to me than his blood.

"Where can I find him?" I asked Solomon 7 still

holding the gun to his head; he told me that his cousin lives in his shop in the Bronx on Sundays. I knew Solomon 7 wouldn't tell his cousin about me because if word got out that I knew about my death he was going to be the one who gets killed. "Get out and don't try anything stupid" Solomon 7 stepped out of the car as I took the gun away from his head. He closed the door and shook his head as he walked towards the stairs of his building, "Yo, kid" I called out "Thank you fam, sorry it came to this.

I drove off to Chinatown to find China who I knew managed this massage parlor in the heart of Chinatown. It was well protected and getting to her was going to be hard. When I got to Manhattan my cell phone started to ring, it was Lele I guess she was calling to find out where I've been all day; answering the phone right away. I was getting yelled at from a pregnant woman wondering where the hell I'm at. "Calm down ma I'll be home soon I'm just out working."

"Well call me when you're on the way home" she yelled "Okay" I said hanging up the phone. Chinatown was busy and I know if I came out with a camera I was going to highlight myself and that would be bad for business. The massage parlor was called "Shēng Qi" and it was the cleanest place in the whole area, I walked inside and saw this chick at the receptions desk there weren't any pictures of China or the place, but I noticed on the desk that she had a website on one of the business cards that were sitting there. I grabbed a card and walked out back to the car and drove off back home to Brooklyn.

When I got home I had to deal with Lele who was upset and cooking in the kitchen, I didn't realize how long I've been away until I looked at the clock on the stove. "Hey boo" I said trying to lighten the mood, Lele didn't respond and kept on cooking. I didn't know what was wrong with her she was upset, I guess it was the mood swings she been having. I walked down to the basement and put the camera with my guns and walked back upstairs to get something to eat. Lele was at the table eating the soup she had just made, and was staring at me like I just killed her dog, I want to asked her why she was all moody, but I had to remember that she was pregnant. I didn't bother sitting down I walked past her and went upstairs and got into the shower.

The next day Lele was up and talking in a hushed tone on the phone in the other room, I overheard her talking about meeting someone later that day in Central Park. She must have felt me eavesdropping because I could hear her voice get a little softer and she got up and walked towards the door. Before she could even see me standing in the doorway I quickly walked back in the bedroom and shaved my head in the bathroom. Today I had to find out about the other members of the Kingdom, but I really wanted to find out about who Lele was meeting today. "I'm going out today boo do you want anything?" Lele asked me as she walked into the bedroom, "No I'm good ma I have to work today though." I responded. "Oh okay, would you be good without the car?"

"Yea, I will be straight," I said giving her a kiss on the cheek.

Lele got dressed in her baby blue PINK sweat suit and clean all white NIKE's, grabbed her purse and keys to the car and took off. I already had it in my plans to spy on her in the park this afternoon at around three, based off the conversation she had on the phone. I grabbed a black T-Shirt, my construction Tim's and some loose-fitting jeans to wear today. I didn't want to highlight myself today while I took more pictures. I was walking towards the stairs when I received a text from Mark asking me to hit him up when I get a chance, I called Mark right away and he was excited and wanted me to come to Harlem later tonight for a party. I wasn't in the mood to party but I couldn't let my friends know that I wasn't the same as I was a month ago. I told Mark that I'll be there and I hung the phone up and walked to the basement. Grabbing the camera and my .38 I inserted a full clip and walked out the door towards the bus stop, I needed to find Kartoon Killa. I've only seen him once and that was at the party, but I heard Luther ask him about his job at Riker's and if he was still pushing shipment up state. *"So, where I was going? Well I had to start somewhere and that was Riker's Island."*

It was a long bus ride there from Brooklyn but when I got there I saw a few police officers wrestling with some guy who was like twice my size. He punched one of the officers and got loose, but before he could go anywhere Kartoon Killa came out of the building and tackled the guy who tried to run. I was standing across the street and pulled out the camera to take a few pictures of his face. After all the excitement one of the officers shouted out to Kartoon Killa "Hey Juan, what we doing for lunch?"

"There's a nice Spanish joint up the way, I was gonna go there." He was a police officer and it was going to be hard to get at him at his work place, "Damn" I was thinking to myself but as I reviewed the photos on the camera I saw that one of his badges on his shirt said "District Director" and you know they have their information on the internet so contacting him wouldn't be an issue.

I caught the next bus to Manhattan to catch Lele at her secret meeting in central park. When I got to the park I didn't see Lele at all, this place was huge but I knew she had to park the car close to where she was going to meet up because she was pregnant and couldn't walk that far. When I spotted the Blue Acura I ran towards that side of the park and saw Lele sitting down on a bench by herself waiting for someone. I pulled out my camera when I was hiding behind this bush, when this heavy set guy walked up looking around and sat down next to her. When I looked through the camera I saw that who she was talking to was King Jaffy Joker the 12th disciple, and by this point I had all the pictures I needed to start planning my attack on the Kingdom. King Jaffy Joker gave Lele a silver briefcase and stood up and walked the same way he came, I wanted Lele to open the briefcase but I knew she was smarter than that and it was true when I saw her stand up and look around before she walked towards the car.

I took off the opposite way and walked into a print store to get the pictures printed out. During the ride back to Brooklyn I was shuffling through all the pictures and just started thinking about how I was going to take down the Kingdom. I knew it wasn't going to be easy and to be honest it was going to be a death trap if I didn't plan this out 100% with no faults. It started getting real gloomy from the huge storm clouds that began to cover up the warm embrace of the sun. I finally made it back to Brooklyn, just in time for the cool embrace of the rain as I walked the three blocks back to my house.

When I arrived at the house I noticed that Lele hasn't made it home yet and that was perfect I didn't need her questioning where I've been all this time. In the basement, I started crafting together this planning board on the plain wall next to the water heater, where I pieced together this collage of the places and people of the Kingdom. Everything that I needed to know and everyone that I was going to target were secretly apart of my master plan. My cell phone started ringing when I noticed that I almost forgot about the damn party tonight, I answered the phone and it was Lemon telling me that he and Luke were in New York and they wanted to meet up with me. This put me in the mood to party real fast and it was the perfect timing because lord knows I'm going to need those two crazies to help with this plan I got going. I covered up the wall and walked upstairs, Lele was just getting in the door "Hey boo you home?" she yelled out "Babe I'm down here" I shouted as I came through the basement door. I ran upstairs to find Lele in the kitchen, searching through the fridge. "What's up boo" she said as I rounded the corner, "Nothing much" I replied taking a piece of turkey she had out on the counter. I told her about the party at the club tonight and I asked her if she wanted to go, she wasn't feeling to well and told me that she was just going to stay home tonight. Before I left the kitchen I kissed Lele and took a bite out of her sandwich, she hates it when I do that and I always smile.

I took a quick shower and through on some fresh clothes, I decided to keep it street seeing that I wasn't really in the mood to get all dressed up. Lele was in the shower when I left the room grabbing the keys and taking off towards Harlem.

On the road there I put in a call to Kane and told him to meet me at the club, he agreed to meet me and told me that he was in Manhattan anyway so he would be there in no time. After arriving at the club I saw Kane standing by the bar drinking a beer, I walked up and stood next to him. We talked for a little bit and that's when I told him about my plans for how I wanted to take out Percy and the Kingdom as a whole. About an hour since arriving Luke and Lemon walked into the club, I called them over and brought them drinks before we talked business. Lemon didn't want to wait much longer "Yo my boy I couldn't sleep knowing that my little cousin was in danger, so what the plan is?" I told Luke and Lemon the same thing I told Kane and they were hyped, "You know ya... ya... you should set up the wa... wa... wall at our hotel, that way no one would fi... find it." Luke said, all I could think to myself is that he still had that stutter. But the whole idea made sense to me and I agreed to move all the pictures over tomorrow. Mark spotted me from across the room and walked up to me, "Yo, what up my nigga, what's good?"

"What up sun, how's everything?"

"All is good, just chillin, I was with the twins but they had to leave, how you been?" He asked me "I'm good yo, just been busy handling business," I said taking a sip of the water I had "Kid, I'm happy you came through, dog I-" his words were cut off by this group of craze fans, "Aren't you Mark from W.I.C?"

"Yea it's me, baby" he said in a soft sensual tone. The girl screamed and beg to take some pictures with him, after some time, he was surrounded by a small group who wanted to take pictures, and trying their best to get him to sing for the group. While all of that was going on I noticed Kane walking off to the bathroom, I wasn't sure but something kept telling me to watch him as he walked, I started getting these bad vibes. There were these Asian girls standing by the bathroom hallway giggling and flirting with the bouncer, it was a set up something wasn't right. I grabbed onto Luke's shoulder and told him to grab Lemon and get out of here and that I would meet them at the hotel. He didn't ask any questions, just shook his head in agreement and went to Lemon, I moved fast through the crowded dance floor towards the bathroom eagerly to catch up to Kane. Mark had started singing by the dj booth and it had people lit up. Kane opened the bathroom door and I caught a glimpse of 3 shadowy figures already inside "SHIT!" I said aloud pushing people out of my way.

Finally making it to the door I bombarded my way through expecting a fight, there was none, the three figures that I saw were just a group of guys talking and smoking a joint. I was starting to calm down when I realized that nothing was going on and everything was normal. Then this giant white guy walked in, something was up because he had to be the only white guy in the building and he didn't look like he wanted to talk. "Are you Kane?" The guy asked looking very irritated, Kane zipped up his pants and smiled "Who wants to know?" Kane asked with a big grin on his face. The white guy took off his jacket exposing his huge arms full of tattoos and a huge scar running diagonal across his chest, "Percy wants to give you a message." I placed my hand on the inside of my jacket going for my gun when Kane stopped me, "I got this." Kane said as he rolled up his sleeves, pulled a rubber band of his wrist and tied back his hair. It was a staring contest at first, the huge white guy had to be about six, nine or greater either way he was huge and looked as if he was built for war. He had blonde hair that was cut low, and his steel gray eyes were cutting daggers into me and Kane. Kane had no fear in his body he was breathing normally, moved swiftly and his eyes didn't leave his opponent at all. Kane raised his hand up to his face and swiped his nose in the same gesture as Bruce Lee which he was famously known for, the guy threw a strong and instantaneous left jab, and Kane must have been a time traveler because his quick response was amazing. He promptly took a step back just enough for Percy's personal hitman to barely graze the tip of his nose, with his right foot Kane sent an unexpected kick to the hitman's shin causing him to stumble a little. That little distraction was enough to allow Kane to jump and do a spinning left kick to the side of his head, throwing the hitman into one of the bathroom stalls. He quickly stood up and shook off the attack, Kane smiled lifted up his hands and cracked his knuckles focused and staring down the hitman as he moved in closer to Kane to attack. Kane threw a quick left jab, the hitman moved his head quick enough to dodge the strike and swiftly countered with a strong left of his own following a head butt that pushed Kane back slightly. Keeping the flow of his momentum the hitman rushed Kane who was stunned from the attack with a right elbow to his forehead that caused him to smack the side of his face into the bathroom mirror. Blood started to trickle from Kane's right eyebrow; he shook his head, touched the open cut and looked at the blood as if it was a different color from other people. "You just fucked up!" Kane said aloud in a very tense and strong voice, the hitman rushed towards Kane trying to tackle him.

Kane thinking fast moved to the side and grabbed the hitman and threw him into the sink and mirror breaking both of them. Water was flowing from the sinks pipe and glass all over the floor. Kane threw a series of kicks and punches at the hitman connecting on all of them. The hitman grabbed a piece of glass of the floor and started swing wildly towards Kane, cutting him in the arm and another minor cut to his right cheek. Seeing that he drew blood the hitman got excited and rushed towards Kane coming with a wide outside swing that Kane blocked and parried with twisting the hitman's arm backwards until he heard a loud crack causing him to wrench in pain and dropping the shard of glass. Kane went on to doing this Judo move putting the hitman on the ground and wrapping his legs around his neck trying to choke him out. The hitman was fighting the hold and started to stand up, "Kane!" I yelled out kicking over a sharp piece of the porcelain sink. Kane grabbed it with his free hand and jammed it deeply into the hitman's temple. There was a slight twitch and then nothing, with a lifeless body wrapped in between his legs Kane released him and stood up. "Thanks for that." Kane said to me with a smile on his face and wiping some blood from his eye. As we walked out of the bathroom I felt like there was more to come I drew my gun and let off a few shots into the air. The crowd erupted into a riot of people scattering, screaming and jumping over each other to get to an exit; we used this as our way out making it to the car and heading for the hotel.

Kane sat in the car laughing at the whole ordeal, this guy was crazy and drunk. Once we made it to the hotel I walked with Kane up to the room, Lemon was sleep, and Luke was up eating a sandwich and watching the news, a report was on about the shooting and a dead victim found in the bathroom. Kane was feeling like he had to throw up and stumbled into the bathroom. "Everything ok?" Luke asked with half a sandwich in his mouth, "Yea were good just a little blood nothing to crazy. How are things over here?" Luke kept eating as I was talking to him, "we... we... we good, just ch... chillin." Kane was so drunk he fell asleep hugging on the toilet, I shook my head told Luke that I was going home to get everything together for tomorrow and walked out the door.

Chapter 22

$\mathfrak{A}$ Miracle is born

As soon as I got back to the car to drive off my phone starts going off,

"Hello?"

"Baby I need you home now, my water just broke"

"What!! Ok I'm on the way" Lele was having this baby now and I needed to be there, I sped off towards Brooklyn to take her to the hospital, the thoughts that were going on in my head were everywhere. I couldn't even focus on driving almost running into two cars on my way there, I was nervous, scared, and happy all at the same time. I was about to be a father any minute now, it was as if I had a second chance at life this feeling was amazing. About twenty minutes later I arrive to the house with Lele sitting on the couch screaming and holding on to her stomach. I snapped out of my little panic and picked her up off the couch and ran to the car. Lele was yelling for me to get her to the hospital now, and by this time I'm asking the lord for a miracle. We sped out of the driveway and off to the emergency room. I pulled right up to the doors and ran to get her out of the car and into the building, "SOMEBODY HELP ME!!!" I shouted out to the room. About four nurses came to my aid to see what was going on, "She's having a baby" I said as they quickly put her on a bed and wheeled her into the emergency room stopping me from going any further. "Sir you can't go past this point, she's going to be fine." One of the male nurses said has he ran to catch up with the moving team. I sat in the lobby for about ten minutes filling out paper work until they allowed me to go back in the room with Lele; I called Luther and told him what was going on, he was excited and told me that he will be there as soon as he can. "Sir" one of the nurses said motioning me to follow her to the room where Lele was in. She was lying in the bed screaming loudly and begging for drugs, I was so in shock I couldn't believe what was going on. After about four hours of labor she gave birth to a screaming little girl, she was beautiful, I couldn't keep my eyes off of her. The nurse handed me the scissors to cut the cord, they cleaned her off and handed her to Lele. They were a beautiful pair, my little princess was born and I was there to witness it, my heart grew with joy, I had the same warm feeling I did with the thoughts of Mama D. "Decon what should we name her?" I sat there and thought hard about the question Lele asked me, naming my daughter was big and I wanted her to have a name that meant something bigger than herself. "Heaven" I said the name as I held her close to me, her voice was so beautiful, she was warm and healthy "Her name is Heaven!"

Shortly after her birth Luther showed up with a giant teddy bear and flowers, "Wow look at my beautiful niece" seeing Luther smile like this was crazy he was a whole different person. We sat in the room for a while talking until the nurse told us that Lele and Heaven needed their rest. Luther and I left walking back to the front of the hospital. "Congratulations once again kid, today is a good day." Luther said has he tapped my back and walked to his car where Elroy was waiting holding his door open. I got back to my car and drove back home. I made it to the house and noticed that this was the perfect opportunity for me to clean up the basement and move the stuff to the hotel where Luke and Lemon where staying. I still couldn't believe that I was a father; I called Luke, Mark and Nate and told them about my night, they were as excited as I was. It was eight in the morning I haven't been to sleep since yesterday, I was tired but it was for a good reason. I stripped down jumped in the shower allowing the hot water to flow down my body, once I got out of the shower I cleaned up my head and went to sleep.

I woke up around two, got dressed and went into the basement seeing the pictures again it put me back into reality. Seeing that the people that I was working for were going to kill me as soon as I was done with my last mission. This put things into a whole new prospective; I got everything from down there and took it to the hotel. Lemon was looking out the window when I got up there and Luke was in the bathroom on the toilet, and Kane was out running some errands. Lemon helped me get the pictures off the board and we placed them on an empty wall of the hotel. By the time we were done, Kane came rushing in rambling about how he just ran into some of Percy's security forces called the H.I.T. Squad, a group of highly trained gunmen from all over. See Percy had a thing for hiring people from different places so that things couldn't get tracked back to him. Well Kane was out of breath and his left arm was bleeding from what looked like a knife wound, "So what happened?" Lemon asked grabbing a towel for his arm. "So I was working out in

Prospect Park, when I got this feeling that I was being watched and not in a good way, this was some weird eerie shit. I stopped and looked around for a bit and saw three guys walking towards me, they looked suspect, one started opening his jacket and exposed a pistol in a shoulder holster. I knew then that I was in some trouble, "Don't think about it Kane" one of them shouted out at me knowing that I was gonna make a run for it. I sat there until the one with the gun exposed got close enough for me to grab him; and that's what I did. I flipped him over my shoulder dropping him on his back onto the bench behind me, throwing a kick at the one coming to grab me hitting him in his stomach. He bent over giving me enough time to grab his neck and lifting up hard enough to break it ending his life. The one on the ground was starting to get up and the one still standing was reaching for his gun. I threw my jacket on his face and flooded him with a combo of punches which stunned him for a minute, I knew I had to move quickly so I grabbed the one on the ground who was now standing and drawing his weapon. As he lifted his arm to point the gun in my face I grabbed on the slide, moved to the side and brought his wrist to his chest, breaking it and causing him to shoot himself. I ripped it away from him and fired two more shots in to his body, the guy with my jacket on his face pulled out a knife and swung it towards my face, I lifted my arm to protect myself and that's when I got cut, I stepped back and fired three rounds into him. Once the situation calmed down I looked around to see if anyone else was coming for me, the sight was clear people were screaming running around and I started to hear sirens coming my way. I searched the guys for ID's to see who was coming for me and I found these." Kane showed use the ID's and two of the guys were from Texas, and one was from Chicago, we were in some shit, guys from out of state were coming after us and we knew we had to start moving fast.

We started our plan to hit up the gun house in Manhattan, really hurt the Kingdom, we needed to bring the heat to Percy and this was going to start it. The gun house had a full security staff of women who knew what they were doing and very skilled at using those weapons, with an updated security system that was linked straight to Percy and now that we know he has his H.I.T Squad out here in full effect this was going to be a bitch of a job. I got so wrapped up in planning this attack I lost track of time and had to go to the hospital to check on Lele and Heaven. Luke and Lemon agreed to go stake out the house and start developing a plan. It was only right since both of them worked for a high profile security firm. Kane was suspicious of Solomon 7 and wanted to find him and know his movements, we all knew each other's plans and went our separate ways.

On the way to the hospital I couldn't help but think about Mary, my mother, and mama D, the feelings I was having were conflicting with my lifestyle. I knew this was going to end badly and I had no control over the outcome, but I did have control over the life of my child and that was the only thing keeping me motivated. Mama D's voice was all in my head, "Decon, you know GOD loves all his creations even that poor little frog you just killed." Death, yea that's been a part of my life since the beginning and ever since then, I've been holding hands with the grim reaper. I knew I was on a flight with a one way ticket straight to hell and I was enjoying it, every fuckin minute of it was a thrill. And it's funny, the bible talks about how GOD works in mysterious ways and how he has a plan for all of us, but what I didn't understand was what was his plan was for me. Like why, I mean how he allowed me to become this monster on a path of destruction. All I can think about was my daughter, Heaven, I couldn't allow her to grow up under the hands of the Kingdom, and I definitely didn't want her to suffer from my sins.

Chapter 23

It has to BANG!

Percy was at the hospital when I arrived holding Heaven and making baby sounds. The sight angered me but I had to keep my cool, he had the twins with him and they were talking and laughing with Lele. "Hey daddy! How are you?" Lele asked smiling as I walked through the door, "How are my girls doing?"

"We are doing great the nurse said that Heaven is healthy and one of the best babies she ever had to deal with." She was happy and I couldn't blame her, we had a beautiful baby girl together and she was now my world. "Decon can we talk?" Percy asked interrupting and handing the baby over to Spanish fly and walking towards me. I nodded my head in agreement and we stepped outside the room to talk. "So first I would like to say congratulations on the beautiful baby girl, you are very blessed" Percy said referring to Heaven with a smile on his face, "We need that last job finished soon, time is not on our side, and it's looking like we are going to move up the time line." He said quickly changing the mood and looking very seriously.

"How long will you need to get this done?"

"I want to wait till Lele and the baby get home, give me another week and I will have that done for you."

"Good, we also have another problem on our hands; I need you to take out another target who has been causing problems for the Kingdom." He reached inside of his suit jacket and handed me a small envelope, I looked inside and pulled out the wallet sized picture of Kane. "You want me to kill my teacher? I said in a low soft tone, "Yes I know this is close to you but remember, we are family and there could be some very bad things done if you don't get this taken care of; if you know what I mean." Percy said looking through the door window at Lele and Heaven, this pissed me off even more. *You want to threaten my daughter now, this snake ass nigga wanted me to kill or he was going to end her life, fuck you, FUCK YOU.*

"Ok I'll get it done." I said putting the envelop in my pocket and walked through the door back into the room, as he walked in behind me. "Leandra I have to go as painful as it is to leave this little jewel, but I need to handle some business." He kissed Lele on the hand and kissed Heaven on the forehead while looking at me with a smile. I watched him walk out of the room, but kept my cool because I knew the twins were watching me very closely. "Let me see my little princess!" I said as I took her from Spanish fly and holding her in my arms, this was my center, she gave me peace. I stayed there with them for about an hour or two and told them that I had to leave. I left the hospital and drove back to the hotel with the guys, Kane was sleep when I walked in and jumped up, ha-ha I must have surprised him or something.

"Dog check this shit out." I yelled out throwing Kane the envelope with the hit information in it, Kane started to laugh and smile while looking at his picture, "So now Percy wants to take me out huh, and he wants you to do it; you know why right? It's because you're the only one who can get close to me. So what do you want to do?" Kane said smiling and ripping up the packet before throwing it away in the trash. I looked at Kane and smiled, "You know what I'm going to do." I called Lemon to see how things were going they told me that there was a lot of movement and that Luther was there bringing in huge crates. The hit had to go down soon and I wanted to do it when Lele was coming home with the baby; that would be the perfect time to get the job done especially with Luther being at the house. I told Lemon the plan and he and Luke agreed.

To set the plan in motion I had to get in touch with detective Bryan Smith, he was the only thing standing between me and death and for the first time in my corrupted life I wanted to live more than ever. I took Kane with me to go find the detective who we followed from the police precinct to a bar out in Queens. He was with a few other officers and me just walking up to him wasn't going to happen. I told Kane to stay in the car while I picked the lock of his 2002 Honda Accord and got into the back seat of his car laid down and waited for him to get in. I waited for about forty-five minutes until he started to walk out of the bar and walked to his car. He sat in and started the car and before he drove off I cocked back my gun and pointed it to his side. "Don't move!"

"Ahh shit, don't kill me please!"

"Shut up, stay calm I'm not going to hurt you, if I wanted to you would be dead by now."

"So what do you want?"

"I was sent here to kill you by a guy named Percy; have you heard of him?"

"Yeah, I know him. I've been trying to take him down for a while now but he even has some inside help from my division, I'm in the process of getting outside help."

"Yeah he knows all of that and that's why he sent me. I don't want to kill you, and if I don't he has a whole team of killers in the city ready to move on his command."

I handed him the three Id's from the men that Kane killed "Those men where the three from Prospect Park, they are a part of this secret organization called the H.I.T. Squad."

"How did you get these?"

'Don't worry about that just know that you, your wife Angela, and your daughters Kate and Nicole need to get out of town and off the grid for a few months while I take care of the problem." Smith was shocked that I knew about his family, his face was cold straight fear ripped through his eyes you could almost taste it. "Look I know you're thinking about a lot, but trust me your family is safe but I can't promise you that for too long, you have to work with me, and I know that's a lot especially coming from a guy who has a gun to your side." I pushed the gun a little harder into his side to show him that I was serious. "So what do you want me to do?"

"I have a plan to take out Percy and the Kingdom,

but I can't move just yet I need to set something's in motion first, and that starts with getting you out of the picture." I placed a burner phone on the passenger seat, "I will call you on this phone later this week with the details, but for now act normal." I removed the gun from his side and opened the door "Look I'm trusting you Bryan don't make me regret this decision, the guy in the car behind us will kill you without thinking twice."

Don't worry I won't do anything stupid, I just don't want my family involved with all this." I placed my hand on his shoulder and ensured him that everything will be fine and to wait for my call, he nodded in agreement and I left his car running back into the one with Kane. We watched as detective Smith drove off and we headed back to the hotel.

"So what do you want to do about him" Kane asked me as we walked into the hotel room, "I'm going to fake a robbery, make it look like an accident but we need some time." Luke and Lemon walked in about twenty minutes later and updated our picture board, "Yo D wha... wha... what's this sh... shit." Luke asked pointing to the huge crates being transported into the gun house, "Those are either guns or explosives, and by the look of it, they have a lot." We planned for the hit and I went off to the house to get some rest.

***

That night I had a dream of my inner demons talking to me, damn near freaked me out. They made me realize how my actions caused all this chaos "It has to Bang, Decon, DECON!

I'm Americas most nightmare, I kill for fun
The thrill of death and destruction, I murder
her daughters and sons
I eat the souls of the living, take their pride
Crooked motherfuckers, I fight to survive
Take no prisoners, no one can live, take their
hopes and dreams
Rape, torture, and pillage, TAKE
EVERYTHING.!
An eye for and eye, my nine against theirs
Crying mothers and babies NOBODY
FUCKIN CARES!
It has to bang, that's right GET EM! Crimes
went cold no witnesses with him.

You want it, I got it it's in the palm of my hand
You thought he would save you, but I took the life of your man.
Deuteronomy 32:41 GOD said it best
Fucked his whole world up, made a mess underneath his vest,
You ready to be with us? You want run with the pack?
I got you backed into a corner with scorpions ready, attached to your nut sack
Come on D it's hot down here send us some cool motherfuckers to refresh the air.
I heard you were ready to leave us, don't want to work no more?
I gave you jewels and C.R.E.A.M. brought you out from being poor.
This is the end the final fight, take one for the team
Go out from a gun fight.
It has to BANG! It has to BANG!

I woke up in a swimming pool of sweat, my mind was stuck on the dream it was crazy. The demon that was speaking looked like me with blood red eyes, and vampire like teeth. His tongue was like a snake, and his hands were stained with blood. Faces of all my victims were pushing out of his chest screaming from the sound of torture. The room was pitch black, but was filled with heat and the smell of sulfur caressed the air, I could fill their pain. This was Hell, my final resting place if I didn't change my ways quick, and just the sight alone made my stomach hurt. If this was GOD's way of waking me up, I'm telling you now my eyes were open.

Chapter 24

Two Weeks Later

It's been two weeks since the birth of my daughter, Lele was home with the baby and the plans to take out the Kingdom were more defined than before. Today was the day of action, we had no time and Percy was growing inpatient. Luther was still moving in large shipments of guns and ammunition into the gun house and there were heavy movements in the streets with the drug trade. It was getting bad, the streets around the ghettos were turning into war torn urban neighborhoods. Things were getting bad if not worst, I had to stop it, and I couldn't keep living like this. I left the house early that morning and headed out to the hotel and picked up Lemon. Luke and Kane went to go play Ricky recon over the gun house. I wanted to hit it soon and once we made our move the Kingdom was definitely gonna make theirs.

I had Lemon driving to detective Smith's house while I sat in the passenger side and made the call "Hey detective, we have to make our move today. Get your family ready don't ask questions, don't make it noticeable, we have to make this look legit and if we want Percy to believe the job is done than you have to do it my way."

"Ok what do you want me to do?"

"Leave everything the way you would normally for a regular day of work, we are going to make it look like a snatch and grab."

"Ok" he said, but before he could hang up I had one more thing I needed him to do, "Hey Smith, don't talk to no one, no one can say or do anything. I need you all to be ghost, and I'm going to need your badge." I didn't wait for a response before hanging up the phone. It took us thirty minutes to get to the detective's home in Long Island. by the time we showed up the home was empty as I ordered, no one was around and the neighborhood was quite for a pretty afternoon like it was. We put on ski mask and ran around the back of the house and stopped by the locked door. "Yo D you ready for this?" I nodded my head and kicked in the door; the kick broke the side frame and made a loud bang. It took us about ten minutes to go through the house and make it look like a robbery, we destroyed things pushed stuff over, basically made the place a mess. I spotted the badge by the front door on a coffee table, I grabbed it and stuffed it in my pocket. I know the neighbors heard what we were doing and the cops might be on their way soon. So we took off quickly speeding off out of the area. I called Percy and told him that the job was done and the detective was no longer a problem, you should have heard the excitement in his voice. He told me that he wanted to link up for a meeting in two days, I knew this was my last mission and I had a feeling that this was gonna be my last meeting with Percy as well. "We hit the house in two days" I told Lemon who was smiling from the thoughts of use bringing this gang down.

I told Lemon to pull up and link up with Nate who was at his mom's house in Queens. We showed up and Nate was waiting for us outside smoking a blunt.

"What up Thun, what's the Science?"

"We have a problem kid, there's a war about to start and you need to be on the right side of it." Nate's eyes got wide as he took in a deep pull from his blunt, "What do you need me to do?" I told Nate the plan and informed him that he was going to be in danger because he was known to be close to me and that they might try to use him against me. He agreed to the plans and I told him that I will call him. As we left Nate's we headed back to the hotel and met up with Kane and Luke and went over the final run down for the attack on the gun house. While at the hotel I started to think about my sister, I hated that she was going down this path in her life, but I was happy that she was getting the help that she needed. "Hey guys I'm gonna go check on the baby, and I might swing by to see Mary, give me a call if y'all need anything." I took off and headed home; the streets of Brooklyn were busy, the twins started to take charge a little bit more and they were coordinating gang attacks in favor of the Kingdom. Black King took over for Keith and he was building a strong team with BG has his top lieutenant and she was ruthless. Just that week she had killed some dude named Al who was working one of her corners with a pack of pit bulls, fucking chewed up by pits in the middle of the streets. New York City was hell and Percy was behind all of it. Lele was in the living room watching some reality show and Heaven was just waking up from her nap. "Daddy's home!" Lele said smiling as I walked into the room going straight for the kitchen, "Hey mama how's my little princess doing?" I asked picking up Heaven who had woke up crying, she was hungry so I grabbed a bottle that was sitting in some warm water on the stove. "I'm going to take her to go see my sister."

"Thank you, finally a break." Lele said smiling looking up at me as I fed the baby, after she ate I grabbed her things and got in the car and drove off to Manhattan. The ride there was smooth; Heaven was quiet for the whole ride. "I'm here to see Mary Rice." I said to the nurse at the front desk, she logged me in and escorted me to her room, "Decon!" Mary shouted out as I walked into the room, she stopped halfway giving me a hug once she saw who I was holding. "Oh my GOD, who is this beautiful little girl." Mary was shocked and her face lit up brighter than a light bulb; "This is your niece Heaven" I handed over Heaven to Mary so she can hold her, "wow she is amazing, look at her eyes. They look just like yours." Seeing Mary hold on to Heaven warmed my heart, this was my first step moving forward to a better life. This feeling was amazing Heaven had light brown hair just like Mary and she was even smiling too.

"So how are things going with you in here?"

'Things are ok, Claxton comes by every day, the food is ok nothing like Mama D's ha-ha"

"Yea Mama D used to get down in the kitchen." I said throwing out a slight smile, "I miss you Decon, and I'm so sorry about all this"

"No need to be sorry, we all make mistakes and just

how grandma would tell me, "GOD still loves you no matter what you do. So keep your head up in here and if you need anything just call." I gave Mary a hug and a kiss on her cheek; we sat and chatted for about an hour before I left with Heaven and brought her back home with Lele.

"I don't give a fuck Leandra the job gets done no matter who it is, you understand!" That's what I heard walking up to the front door coming from Luther; they had to be talking about me. I walked into the front door and both of them stopped talking and looked at me, "What's going on y'all? Something wrong?" They just looked at me in silence, Luther was slightly angry and Elroy was sitting on the bar stool in the kitchen. "Naw babe everything is ok, Come here baby." Lele said grabbing Heaven out of my arms, I had a bad feeling about this little meeting they were having and something just didn't sit well with me in my stomach. "Yo Luther let me holla at you for a minute." Luther walked with me to the other room and we spoke about the hit with the detective, he still felt some type of way about me taking jobs from Percy, *"Now look at this shit, this motherfucker wants me to work for him and him only, but is going to kill me soon, ha-ha this shit is funny, but if you ask me we have the same plan in mind because something in my mind tells me that Luther wants Percy dead to so he can be the head nigga in charge; now back to the story."* Luther told me to stand by for another job here soon and that he would call me with the details. Once Luther and Elroy left, I went upstairs with Lele, put Heaven in her crib jumped in the shower and fell asleep. The next morning Lele woke me up with some bomb ass head, I mean damn this shit was good and I needed it too. All the stress I had, all the anger, I released it all inside of her as we did our dance for about two hours. I was drained, tired and hungry "You want breakfast?" *now what kind of question was that of course a nigga wanted some food ha-ha.* "Yea I can eat." Lele got up and walked downstairs, I put on my underwear and walked into Heavens room to check on her. She was still sleep and so beautiful. I watched her for a bit until the smell of fried bacon made its way to my nose, I couldn't resist the urge any longer so I made my way downstairs to see Lele butt naked at the stove cooking up a storm. After we ate and Heaven woke up and started yelling for food too, that was Lele's queue. I got up and got dressed to work out and practice my katas; about an hour in I got a phone call from Percy telling me that we are going to meet today, he insisted that he provided the ride. I had a weird feeling about this meeting and wondered why he moved up the date, I didn't like this at all, not even for a minute. I grabbed a sweater and a jacket, my .45 was at the hotel and the only thing I had with me was a sawed off, and my nine. I placed the nine in my shoulder holster and grabbed a knife for back up.

Percy's driver pulled up and I got into the back, I was expecting to see Percy but instead King Jaffy Joker and Voodoo were sitting on the far side of the limo with serious looks on their faces. "So what is this about?" I asked looking at the two of them who didn't take their eyes off of me for one second. "Just enjoy the ride." King Jaffy Joker said in a deep groggy tone and grabbing a glass and a bottle of whisky from the mini bar. The ride there was just a serious staring contest between us three; we got out of the limo and went inside the condominium. Percy's personal security was now all around this place, there was four guards down in the stairs, one at the door, two in the lobby, and one by the elevator. We made our way up to the twelfth floor and on the outside of Percy's door there were two guys on watch. Percy was playing on the piano while a few of his girls were cooking, and the others were just moving around. "Greetings everyone! I'm so glad that you all were able to make it, please come join me." Percy said as he got up from the piano and walked towards the table as his girls started to bring out plates from the kitchen.

"So I know you all are wondering why I brought you here, well its simple, our Kingdom is starting to grow and we are coming out on top. Thanks to you Decon we are now able to move in larger shipments without anyone stopping us and for your actions." Percy snapped his fingers and two girls brought over four huge bags full of hundred dollar bills, "That's the money that is owed to you for your hard work, and plenty of food as well." Percy said as he stuck his fork into a piece of broccoli. "Percy I appreciate the jester but not to be rude or anything I have to go handle the other project you asked me to do." Percy wiped his face and placed his fork on the table, "Son, you're not offending me, you don't have to stay for lunch, but I do need you here for what I'm about to say." Percy stood up out of his seat and moved over to the long outstretched window. "For years the three of us as well as a three others not present have been talking about running this city." Percy said talking about Voodoo, King, Kartoon, Luther, Lele, and of course himself, "Now those talks are put into action and we are all eating well, wouldn't you agree?" We all shook our heads in agreement at his question, "So, what I will be saying next is hard for me to bring forth, but it has to be said and this is why your here Decon." Percy looked me dead in the eyes as he spoke, "Luther wants to take my place as

King in this Kingdom, and that type of mutiny cannot be justified or allowed. The smallest bit of cancer within the body can lead to death, so I ask you Decon, are you working for Luther?" Percy snapped his fingers and the armed ladies pointed there weapons towards my face as well as Voodoo child and King Jaffy Joker. My eyes got wide at the sight of all the guns trained on me, "No, I haven't worked for Luther since you took over, and I've been loyal to you from the start." Percy looked me in the eyes for any signs of deception, but all he found were the eyes of a stone-cold killer, "I figured that as much" Percy lifted his hands and everyone put their guns down and continued to listen to him speak. "I need you to keep tabs on him for me Decon. I will have someone take him out soon enough when the time is right, just need to know who's on my side that is all." Percy flashed his smile and in my mind I was relieved that he believed me. "So now that we have that taken care of, may I be excused, sir? Percy acknowledged me and had one of his girls escort me out the door. I walked outside the complex and into the limo waiting for me outside and had the driver take me back home. I arrived and the twins were in the house talking to Lele about a party tonight in the Bronx hosted by Mark and Nate. "Decon you going tonight?" Baby doll asked me eating a pack of skittles, "Yea I might swing by later."

"Come on Boo It's been a minute since I got fucked up" Lele chimed in, "Who's gonna watch the baby?" I asked Lele but getting cut off by Spanish fly "We have Elroy's sister coming over in a few to watch her." She's been over a few times after Lele got out of the hospital she wasn't a problem so I didn't mind her watching my baby. "Aight I'll meet you all there." I said as I gave Heaven a kiss on her forehead who was in the arms of Spanish fly. The way I saw it, this was the perfect alibi for me and the right time to hit the gun house. I went upstairs to get in the shower and I sent a text out to Lemon and told him to get ready, because tonight was the night we start a war. The girls left before I had gotten out of the shower and Elroy's sister was downstairs on the couch feeding Heaven. She was a tall heavy set girl with coco brown skin, she had beautiful facial features and was a very good singer, "Whats up Kelly!" I said as I came around the corner. "Hey Decon, have fun tonight." She responded, I gave her three hundred dollars and walked out the house and drove off to the hotel.

When I walked into the room Luke and Lemon where loading up the pistols and Kane was putting the final touches on his wakizashi. "You got my vest?" I asked Luke, he pointed to the closet which had my guns and the vest laid out. I put on the vest and my shoulder holster, grabbed my .45 with two extra clips and did the same for my nine. "Hey D!" Lemon called out tossing me the sawed-off shotgun, I loaded it and grabbed six extra shells. It was time for war, everyone was vested up and had their arms ready to take down anything or anyone in our path. Kane had two pistols and his sword, Luke had an M4 with two extra clips, Lemon had his tactical shotgun and a pistol for back up. I had one grenade left and took it with us. We got into the car and drove off to the Gun house. On our way there, Luke handed us all these full faced mask that were in the design of a skull, this was needed so we wouldn't be spotted by the cameras.

We saw one male guard standing outside as we came around the corner into the neighborhood. It looked as if they were just conducting normal business as usual which was perfect for us. I parked three blocks away and we split up. Kane and I went towards the front with Luke and Lemon taking the back on our command. We had to move fast especially since we were going to be loud and attract more attention than we needed. There were at least seven girls on the inside running the place and being on guard 24/7, so when I made my move I had to think quick and fast. Kane ran up on the guy at the front door while he was facing the other way, his sword went through his chest with ease. Before his body could drop, I shot open the front door with the Sawn off that had custom armor piercing slugs to rip through the reinforced door, and tossed in the grenade, "Get down!" I yelled out jumping to the side of the house **KABOOM!** The blast shook the whole house. I rushed in to see two of the girls spread across the peppered room, or whatever was left of the two, Kane let off three shots into a girl coming around the corner with a shotgun in hand. Lemon and Luke blasted through the door with Luke going in first checking the corners, and with smooth precision Lemon came in firing his shotty which carved a basketball sized hole into this girl coming up from the basement sending her flying back down.

Shots began to fly from the top of the stairs and the basement, we were at a short standoff for about thirty seconds, "Luke up top!" I yelled out signaling him to fire upstairs from around the corner as I dashed around and let of a shotgun blast into the girl who was shooting down at us with this automatic pistol. Her body came tumbling down the stairs as Kane sent rounds into the basement and silenced the gun fire. I reloaded the shotgun and walked upstairs with Luke at my back. When I got up to the top of the stairs, this guy jumped out from around the corner and grabbed onto my gun and we began to wrestle back and forth for control. Luke didn't have a clear shot, but that didn't matter because he started to take fire from the rear getting hit twice in the back. Good thing he had that vest on or it would have been tragic. He turned quickly and fired back as I continued to wrestle with this guy. I kicked him in the balls and caused him to quench in pain snatching the gun from him and sending two slugs blasting into his chest.

Luke took out the girl who was firing from around the corner clearing the top floor. I grabbed two huge duffle bags from the small closet on the left and went downstairs, Lemon and Kane walked up from the basement saying that it was clear of all the shooters. "Sun, there is an army's worth of weapons and ammo down there." Lemon said, "Aight take these and fill what you can, take as much ammo as possible and get enough guns for this war we just started." I said handing over the duffle bags, I knew there were more guns upstairs and I wanted to grab some of them as well. I had Luke grab the propane tanks from out back and set them up around the house and let the gas flow out slowly, as I ran upstairs and grabbed what I can. We took what we could filling up six large duffle bags and running out through the back door. Luke had this sick idea and poured gasoline all over the house. The place was soaked in it, and the propane was heavy in the air making me a little light headed. The sirens were getting closer and I knew it was time to go but I had one more thing to do. "Go to the car I'll meet you there."

"Nigga let's fucking go!" Lemon yelled trying to talk me out of going back in "Just go" I said as I ran inside, towards the kitchen I pulled the stove out and kicked out the gas line quickly filling the house with natural gas on top of the propane. I grabbed a concussion grenade from downstairs and ran out the back door. The first few cops came screaming around the corner "NYPD, get the fuck down now!" I pulled the pin and tossed in the grenade and took off as fast as I could, while the first hail of rounds ran across my face.

KABOOM! The explosion was massive and tore the whole house apart, with a strong shockwave that sent me flying and knocked me on my back, the first three cops that came in weren't so lucky by the loud horrific screams I heard from the inside, the rest of the house went up in flames but I still needed to get out of the area because the worst was about to happen. All those bullets and explosives were about to go off and it could be bad.

Running on very little time I made it to the car just in time for the secondary explosions. Rounds were being spit everywhere, and time was moving fast. I needed to head to the party before anyone would get suspicious.

Chapter 25

Hell, in Chinatown

We arrived at the club still high off the adrenaline that was flowing through our blood from the gun fight, I managed to get calm just enough to think somewhat clear, we quickly changed our clothes in the parking lot before we walked in the club. "So what's the story D?" Lemon asked me in a low but even tone, I played with the question in my head for a little bit, and it came to me "Ok so it went down like this, Luke was drunk and it took us a bit to get him up and moving, Kane you can't be here, there might be a chance that Percy might show up especially after the shit we just pulled. So Kane you gotta disappear Lemon you gonna drop him off with the shit and get rid of our clothes." Everyone agreed to the plans and went their separate ways, I kept my .45 because you just never know what could happen at these parties and once the word was spread everyone will be on high alert.

Kane and Lemon drove off and me and Luke started heading towards the clubs rear entrance, I texted Mark so he'll meet up with us at the door. The closer we got the louder it became, this sounded like the party of the year. "Hurry up nigga me and Nate bout to preform our latest shit." Mark said waiting for us outside the back door. The party was still live by the time we walked in, the atmosphere reeked of cheap liquor, and sweat. Nate was getting the crowd hype for him and Mark's final performance, the energy surged throughout the building which was helping me calm down a bit from my adrenaline high.

Not even thirty minutes into their performance a heavy disruption broke out by the front door, security was frantically running around trying to see what was going on and then everything stopped like one massive shut down. The music even got quieter or so it seemed. The crowd started to spread open and out came Luther walking out like he was some type of prince or something. "Leandra! Leandra let's fucking go!" Barked Luther as he pushed through the parting crowd. "What's going on?" Lele asked with a confused look painted on her face. Luther was serious and his energy made everyone around him nervous, I couldn't just sit back and do nothing or it would look bad on me. I made my way through the thick sea of bodies until I was arm's length away from Luther and Lele. "Luther what's wrong?" I asked cautiously.

"You need to come too, we have a problem that's gonna get solved tonight." Luther said in a fuming tone. We followed behind Luther as well as the mob, standing outside were King Jaffy Joker, voodoo, Solomon 7, and the Twins. Luther made his way to the middle of the circle and spoke in a serious tone loud enough to get his point across. "While all of you out having a FUCKIN good time, someone decided that it was a good fuckin idea to rob us all." Everyone looked in shock at what Luther was saying and how he was carrying himself. "They, whoever it was blew up our supply and they have to get dealt with ASAP. And I'm only gonna say this shit once, I want the motherfuckaz to suffer by my hands." Luther was bold and it showed by how he was talking with all the witnesses around our little outside meeting. So after hearing what Luther wanted we all went our separate ways. I caught a bad feeling in my gut and I knew better by now then to dismiss my gut feelings.

Luke grabbed a Cab back to the hotel and I jumped in the car with the girls, but before we could even get the car started Luther was moving towards the car yelling at me to open it up. Now in my mind I'm thinking the worst, was he tipped off about us hitting the spot? Did he feel like I was involved? All of these questions hit at once but it was only one way to be sure and if it came down to it I was gonna be ready. I patted myself to ensure I still had my hammer as if it was gonna just get up and walk away.

"Decon get out of the car!" Luther said ferociously, "What up Luther" I said as I stepped out of the cramped Acura. Luther stepped up and grabbed onto my shoulder and pulled me in close. "We have a huge issue and I know these other Ma'fuckaz aren't gonna get shit done without a little push, so that's why I need you to make some moves and get this shit done." Luther's grip tighten to emphasize his words but I can tell he was putting a lot of trust in me. "I'ight say no more my G."

The ride home was silent no one was talking, there was no music being played, no one was even on their phones. The words that Luther put fourth rang true, this was a time for war and all who were a part of it had no clue that their target was sitting right next to them. Their ignorance sparked a burst of confidence in my plan and the fact that Luther still thought I was on his team did nothing but swell my head that much more. We rode in silence all the way to our house, the twins were gonna stay with us tonight and I was plotting my next move. As soon as we walked in Kelly had the twenty-four hour news channel on and the report ran about the explosion that rocked Manhattan. The news anchor spoke about how there was a shootout with the NYPD that was cut short by an explosion that sent the whole house into flames and destroyed the homes around it. They reported about multiple explosions and weapons in the house. On the other side of town a large manhunt has been started for detective Smith and his family has turned up missing today with his house in full disorder. The NYPD has launched a full investigation for both tragedies, there are no suspects at this time. The news was out and the city was in chaos on both sides of the fence, I left the girls downstairs and headed straight for my bed.

I woke up the next morning and Lele was still knocked out from the faint hint of liquor coming out of her body I knew she was in for the meanest headache. I rolled out of bed and checked the text message that was lit up, "Time to make moves!" Was all the message from Kane read, and he was right it was on the streets and money was put up for any knowledge on the Gun House hit and it was long enough to join a few of the gangs around the area. I hoped in and out of the shower and cleaned my head, I was so used to the bald look that anything outta place just didn't feel right. I put on some black jeans and tank top with my vest on top of it. Threw on a black T shirt to hide the vest and made my way to the basement to grab my arms. Spanish Fly was throwing up in the bathroom and Gloria was talking to someone on the phone in Spanish, from the sound of it she wasn't happy at all. I managed to slip past both of them without being seen and went into the basement. Most of the weapons were at the hotel but I still had my .45. Which I screwed on a silencer just for good measure. I holstered the weapon and went back upstairs to find the twins were now talking to Lele in the room. I tried to eavesdrop but the door was closed and Heaven was starting to wake up. Before any more time was wasted I took off to link up with Kane.

Kane was sitting in Prospect Park wearing a dark hoodie and some sweat pants. "What up D" Kane said as he gave me dap, "Death is all I see man, what's good with you?" Kane sat in silence staring at some guys working out on the pull up bars. "Something doesn't feel right" Kane said in a low serious tone, "Something is off today, it's like the air doesn't taste right. You feel it right?" Kane asked me. Just as I nodded my head in agreement we spotted this Asian girl walking up from a distance wearing dark red skin tight pants, with a black top that was covered by a long burgundy colored leather jacket. As she got closer I noticed that this wasn't just sum random Asian girl visiting the park on a warm Saturday afternoon, this chick had death in her eyes and they were fixed on Kane. I slowly adjusted myself to get better access to my gun and she must've felt it coming because almost simultaneously she pulled back her jacket and exposed a set of silver knives. As fast as I was I still didn't see her pull a knife from its sheath, Kane pushed me out of the way just in time for the knife to barley scratch my face. Within the same motion as the push Kane removed a blade he had hidden on his ankle and threw it, lodging it deep into the girl's throat. Kane looked at the young Asian girl as if he knew her. "Yo who is this bitch?" I said aloud in a frantic yet aggregated tone towards Kane.

"This is the work of this queen assassin China, this is one of her assassin's and by the look of it she was coming after me." Kane bent down next to the dead assassin and checked her arm, the girl had a tattoo of some Chinese characters, next to a small red dragon which meant war over peace. If this was an act of war Kane was already winning. We left quickly so that no one noticed us around the dead body and headed out towards

Chinatown.

Traffic was busy but by the time we made it to Chinatown, busy wasn't the word. The blocks were flooded with people in celebration, I don't know what they were celebrating and I could care less. It was the perfect setup to grab China and do some damage to the Kingdom. We had to park about ten blocks away because most of the streets had been blocked off which was good, that way we could scan the area. The massage parlor was in the heart of Chinatown and it would be difficult to get out if shit were to pop off. I gave Kane the big hunting knife under my seat and told him to grab the .38 special from the passenger side compartment, if we were walking into a bee hive we best have some protection. From the looks of it on the outside the massage parlor was basically empty except for the two people who walked inside shortly after we arrived. Kane scanned around the area and caught a glimpse of a few faces with eyes all over us. "She knows we're here." Kane said barley above a whisper. I could feel it too and to be honest I was a bit nervous, I've only been through here a few times and that's when I killed J.R., and did the initial planning. Kane took in a deep breath and walked towards the entrance way of the shop with me on his heels. There was an older Chinese man sitting on the curb reading a newspaper, he didn't say a word or even look up to see who we were or where we were going. That made me feel a little uneasy but I couldn't dwell on that at the time.

Kane pushed the door and to our surprise it was open, the place was a maze, the floors were made of smooth bamboo with red linoleum lining. There were doors all over on each side of the small corridor leading to a backroom. From the outside it didn't look like much but the inside was crazy. One door lead to another and there were cameras all over the place, we walked softly trying our best not to make any strong noises. I moved past an open door and jumped slightly at the sight of a statue. Kane heard a noise coming from one of the rooms to the left and pulled out his knife to make it a silent death. Before I could reach for my gun in my holster I caught a vibe from behind me, just in time to move out the way of the wakizashi coming for my head. The swordsman was swift and agile with their movements of the mini katana, the swordsman lunged forward towards my gut, I side stepped quickly in the cramped hallway giving myself room to grab the little assassin's head and slamming it as hard as I could into the wooded wall. The wood cracked from the force of the hit against it, pushing out a pointed and rugged piece. I grabbed the piece of wood and shoved it deep into the masked assassin's neck from the top down. Blood drained quickly as the splinter managed to sever the jugular on its way in. I removed the mask to see that it was another one of China's female assassin's, she was young but playing an adults game. Kane on the other hand was in a bind, the noise was another assassin who tried to finish Kane with a few six pointed shuriken's that were lodged deep into the wall in the hallway barely missing Kane's face. He was quick closing distance with the killer inside the dark room, I was right behind this time with the sword from the assassin who tried to kill me. When I arrived in the room, Kane had the assassin wrapped in a rear choke driving the twelve inch blade through the chest of the ninja dressed killer. I was so distracted by Kane's work I didn't notice the assassin sneaking up behind me, "Decon watch out!" Kane tried to warn me but it was too late, I was swept on my back by a large swing of a staff, the killer was on his way to smashing my face in, but my senses kicked in just in time to roll out of the way. I was now in full attack mode and with a strong thrust I forced the sword in my hand deep in the posterior of my assailant. The hilt of the blade was stuck between the legs of the killer as he stood straight with his eyes shot open wide, and let out an ungodly squeal. Kane pulled out the blade of the cadaver and silenced the screaming foe.

"That was fucked up" Kane said looking at what I did to the assassin. "Hey it was him or me" I said shaking my head, "Let's go" Kane said has he pulled me out into the hallway, the huge double doors at the end of the hallway were open and sitting in a large blood red chair was China facing away from us looking at the wall with a dragon embroidered on it. As she turned around I noticed her features right off the back, she was beautiful I must say, she was wearing this purple and gold kimono short skirt set and her eyes were highlighted with matching colors as her outfit.

You can tell she was ready for war because on her feet were these thigh high boots with a round flat heel that gave her enough support to fight. "Kane, it's nice to see you again, what has it been six or seven years?"

"It's been six but apparently, it hasn't been long enough, you still want me dead I see." Kane said looking directly in China's direction. "You see Kane, what you did is unforgettable in the eyes of the guild and you out of all people should know that the price for your crime can only be paid in blood." China said as she walked from one side of the room to the next standing directly in front of a wall full of swords. I couldn't just sit there and act as if I didn't want to know the things they were talking about so I got involved. "What guild? Yo Kane what is she talking about?"

"Oh you don't know Decon?" China said grabbing a sword off the wall and examining it, "the almighty Kane was once a god in the assassins' guild called the Red Dragons. He was third in command and I was right behind him and gaining momentum. To make a long story short, Kane was in a very powerful position and took a blood oath to protect his position at all cost. But the stupid son of a bitch wanna run off and get some whore he met in Florida pregnant."

"You better watch your mouth, that whore was my mother!" I said angrily, China's slanted eyes got sharper as she looked at me as if she could see my soul, you could tell she was shocked at the news and she quickly turned angry. "Does Percy know about this little reunion? Well it doesn't matter now, either way both of you will be dead." With a slight flick of her thumb China sent the sword flying out of its scabbard and catching it with her other hand. As she advanced in our direct, Kane spotted a Bo Staff behind us and moved me out the way. China swung swiftly towards Kane's head which he deflected with the staff, the two of them moved with such grace and proficiency it looked as if their fight was choreographed. China would swing and Kane would block, "You know you gotta be faster than that my love." Kane said dodging a fatal swing and smacked the back of her leg with the staff "Oh my dear I'm just getting started" China said seductively as she spent around and cut Kane on his back. Kane let out a slight grunt from the blow but kept his composer. "Nice move sweetie, lets end this game." Kane tossed the staff to the side and looked up at a sword that was in an ivory case sitting in a bed full of red silk. The sword was in a silver scabbard and with gold trimmings, the sword was smooth and shiny as if it was recently tended to. The handle was silver and gold, shaped into the form of a dragon and the way Kane picked it up you can tell that the two of them had history and by removing it from the scabbard I knew he was ready to re-consummate their love. I watched in amazement as Kane lunched his assault, moving with an artistic flow, he looked like water moving through the air as he and China danced with their deadly mistresses. China was getting winded and Kane had just caught his second wind slicing though her left tricep making her drop the sword and driving his directly through thigh.

China let out a loud screech and a hiss once Kane wrapped his free hand in between her hair and yanked her head back so he could see her eyes. "Baby thank you for the dance, until we meet again in this life or the next"..."May the dragon make us gods amongst the living"

China said finishing his quote. Kane leaned in closer and I watched her whisper something in his ear right before they kissed. As China closed her eyes Kane lifted his sword out of her thigh and drove it through her chest down through her spine ending her life.

As we made our way down the hall towards the exit Kane couldn't stop looking at the sword in his hand. We walked out to a group of Asians holding some very strong equipment and they were all surrounding us and blocking any chance of escape. I went to draw my gun when a voice came out of the middle of the crowd, "I wouldn't do that if I was you, given your current position you wouldn't make it to see that gun let off one shot." A baby faced little Asian dude holding an Uzi with a long clip and a silencer that looked like it had a whisper you couldn't hear if you were sitting right next to it. He moved to the front of the mob and smiled "I'm Tommy Gunzz and from the looks of it, I just moved into the top spot in Chinatown."

"Look we don't have any quarrels with you, we just want to get out of here peacefully." Kane said defensively, Tommy Gunzz smiled and looked around at his crew "Look we don't have any issues, yet! Just the fact that you got the drop on that bitch before I could, if anything you took the heat off my back. And if you came after her

I'm pretty sure you know the Kingdom is coming after you. But I'll tell you this, you have twenty minutes to get the fuck out of Chinatown before we have any problems." Almost systematically after Tommy spoke red dots appeared all over me and Kane so if we didn't get the hint from what Tommy was trying to say the red dots all over our body and head made it loud and clear. "Ok were stepping." Kane said and we walked through the sea of eyeballs as we made our way through the gang. We got back to the car and got out of Chinatown quick, in the back of my mind I just knew Tommy Gunzz was serious about his threat.

***

Brooklyn was busy when we got there, the streets were packed and something didn't seem right, I kept getting a call on my cell phone from Lemon, followed by a text message. After the third time he called I picked up, "What's good kid? Everything alright?" I asked, Lemon was short of breath and seemed to be in a little panic when he spoke which was rare. "Dog Luke fucked up and now were on the run."

"Where are y'all?" I asked this time slightly frantic. "Son Luke killed Lord Shabazz and Black King at BBQ's." Lemon was so short of breath and sounded slightly scared, I never heard my cousin sound like this which made me assume the worst. "Son where are you now?" I asked this time swerving in and out of traffic. He told me that they were held up in some housing building on Hoyt St. And there were about five goons after them. Me and Kane were just pulling up to the spot and I hopped out with both of my guns drawn. My mind was lost in the fact that my cousins were in trouble and death was waiting for them right around the corner, but I had to intervene or I would never be able to forgive myself.

I approached the building and noticed there was a guy holding a technical shotgun, the same style as the NYPD, and he was too focused on what was going on inside the building then doing his job and watching the front, so busy he didn't even see me coming from behind him. Before I could let off a shot Kane stepped in sending his sword going through his back and existing his throat. The poor bastard didn't stand a single chance, I looked at Kane and we made eye contact nodded our heads and walked inside to find Luke and Lemon. The task wasn't hard at all from all the yelling coming from the fourth floor and the concussion from something loud and ugly. We crept up the stairs slowly and posted up against the wall to peek around the corner so I could see how they were laid out.

To my surprise they were bunched up and setting

up to shoot down a door, I leaned up against the wall and let out a deep breath and counted aloud "One, Two, Three" peeling off the wall and around the corner I allowed my guns to have a conversation with the four hitmen. It was like a beautiful orchestra of hot lead and blood flooding the hallway. As I came to a stop, we walked up to the bodies and not one was moving or showed signs of life. "Lemon, the cost is clear where you at?" I yelled aloud trying not to catch a surprised bullet from going into the room. The door unlocked and out came Luke with Lemon following behind. "Dog what happened?" I asked Lemon as he came out the door, "Son it was crazy, so we get hungry and stop at BBQ's for dinner. When Luke went to place his order the lady at the counter started laughing at his stutter which pissed both of us off. Sitting in the booth to our right was Shabazz and Black King who also joined in on the laughter. Well the girl was one thing but seeing the two we just so happen to be hunting sitting right in front of us, that was our chance. We were so wrapped up in anger that we didn't even pay attention to our surroundings and the body guards they had with them. Luke hopped out of line and walked up to Lord Shabazz who was eating. Without saying a word Luke pulled out his 357 magnum and with no warning at all he sent three rounds going through the back of the booth right through Black Kings chest. As swift as he was to pull the trigger on Black King the remaining three rounds went screaming through Shabazz's face slumping him over in the booth. The whole place went wild into a frenzy, screams were being heard from all over and people were in panic mode to get out of the place. Next thing you know we have seven guys after us and were out of ammo. Thank God y'all were close or that would've been the end of us both." Lemon told the story with more than enough details.

Once we made it back to the hotel, the shootout was all over the nightly news and best believe the rumors were circulating throughout the hood of who the two unfamiliar faces were that were being circulated around from a botched sketch. If the Kingdom had any doubts about them being targeted, they were all thrown out now especially with three of their active disciples now dead and all ties pointing to me. The news reported the incident as a gang hit, that left two men killed execution style and five more killed in a housing unit building. My phone started to go off and when I checked it, I had about ten missed calls and text messages filling up quickly. One of the messages I opened was from Luther telling me to get down to the house ASAP and that the Kingdom was on lockdown. I left Kane and my cousins at the hotel and told them if they don't hear from me the next day, get out of dodge or carry on with the plan. There was a storm coming and I was in the heart of it.

Chapter 26

Secrets out the bag

.

As I was pulling up to the house the block was packed full of cars, and bodyguards letting people know the Kingdom was in full effect. I parked my car on the corner because Luther had Elroy park his truck in my driveway. I walked up the block and caught every eye from the streets and the guards on them. Walking into my home was a mess, Luther had organized a street meeting with lower level disciples and some of the local street thugs who ran their corners. "I need you motherfuckaz to hear me very clearly, I want anyone with knowledge or who bared witness to the niggaz who laid down Shabazz and King." You could damn near feel the heat coming off of Luther's voice the more he spoke, everyone was on edge that day wondering what was going on and the last thing the Kingdom wanted was to show any signs of weakness. "Yo my nigga this shit is stupid as fuck, I don't need no bodyguards, I don't need anybody tellin me how to move, everybody know how I gets down." Skinny black spit angrily, "Look blood you need to calm the hell down before you piss me off any more than I already am." Luther said removing his dark tented shades. "Look I don't need to tell you all that we've been hit hard, and that's an act of war if you ask me, now Voodoo and Solomon 7 I need you to keep searching for the niggaz who hit the gun house, somebody knows somethin and I need answers. Slim hit the streets and find out what the hoods are saying about the hit-"

"Man why the fuck I never get to do any special missions!" Skinny Slim fired off cutting Luther off, Luther got so mad at the fact that he cut him off he didn't even realize how close he was to Skinny's face "Cause you a live wire nigga and can't control your damn temper now do what your told." I watched how Luther searched for any reason to hit Skinny Slim but Slim just paced back and walked out the door, cursing loudly. "Fuck him!" Luther spat putting his glasses back on to help mask the anger in his eyes. He ordered the twins to head up to Queens and check the streets for any news. He then looked in my direction, "Where have you been while all this shit has been going on?"

"I don't have a target remember I am to stand by

and wait for further tasking" I said with a slight attitude. Luther looked at me suspiciously, "I need you on these streets nigga, you need to head up to Manhattan and find out where the hell China is. I've been calling that bitch and no one seems to be answering." Seconds after Luther had spoken he received a phone call, "What's good Drama? Who? How? Yo WHAT THE FUCK!! I'm on my way, and have that chinky eyed ma'fucka ready for me when I arrive." Luther hung up the phone and exhaled deeply. "Unbelievable, this day couldn't get any better huh? Somebody killed China, once word gets to Percy he is gonna flip. Everybody get to work, I need an update in three hours." After Luther spoke he motioned for Elroy to get to the truck so they could head off to Manhattan, everyone else took off and hit the streets like instructed. I knew once I heard that Luther was talking to TMD and he told him about the death of China he was going to be beyond heated, And to top it off they had somebody hostage and from his brief description I had a strong feeling that it was Tommy Gunzz.

I ran upstairs and walked into Heaven's room where she was soundly sleeping. I wanted the best for my baby girl, she was growing up so fast right before my eyes and to think that she might grow up fatherless and in a world of hell I couldn't allow that to be. She was an innocent soul and deserved better than that, I wanted her to live a life of love and to know that her father did everything in his power to make it happen. I closed my eyes and offered up a prayer for myself and my baby girl, as I opened my eyes it felt as if God showed me a path to follow and his arch angel Michael was guiding my feet every step. I gave Heaven a kiss on her forehead and walked out the door prepared to conduct my war on the Kingdom.

Lele was in the living room watching TV when I came into the room, "Are you going back out boo?"
"Yea I am, gotta take care of that shit for your brother."

"I need you to be safe ok, remember you have a family back here that's going to need you. Whoever it is out there taking us out might be after you too." Lele said with sincerity in her voice. I tried to look for any signs of distrust in her pretty brown eyes but I couldn't find even the slightest hint of it. "I know baby I'm gonna be fine trust me." I said as I leaned in to give her a kiss on the lips, thinking to myself that this might be the last time I get that chance. No matter how angry I was towards Lele I still loved her and nothing was going to change my heart. I walked out those doors got into the car and drove off towards the hotel to fill everyone in on the plan. On the way there I saw Skinny Slim parked at the park posted on his supped up Oldsmobile. I don't know what it was but something told me to go see what he was up to.

I pulled up next to him and got out of the car, Slim was on the phone with someone and he sounded heated, talking about how Luther treated him and how he had plans to move up on the scales or even taking over his position. I walked up and he hung up the phone, "What up Nigga." Skinny Slim said in an irascible tone. "I don't have any quarrels with you son just wanna see where ya head is at." I said trying my best to be submissive, but just as Luther said he was a live wire and ready to pop off at any given moment. "Who sent you nigga? Was it Luther? Because I don't need no damn bodyguard or babysitter."

"No one sent me I came here on my own to check on you and if you got a problem with that then so be it. Man, you know what, I'm out you're not even worth my sympathy." As I turned my back and walked towards my car I could sense a presence getting closer to me and from the slight glance in the cars passenger window my senses were correct. I smartly slid my foot backwards in-between his and stopped a vertical strike with my forearm as he tried to deliver the blow using the butt of his gun. Moving swiftly I grabbed his arm with my free hand and stepped behind him, driving all of his weight backwards, causing him to fall to the ground and dropping the gun. Slim was quick to respond to the fallen gun but I moved faster kicking it out of the way. He got pissed and lunged forward with all his weight knocking me down, this gave him enough time to get on top of me and send three punches towards my face. Two of them connected and split my lip but I was able to block the third and trap his arm with mine. Once stuck I sent a few punches of my own that threw his balance off and giving me the strength to push him off to the side and gain a stronger advantage. I still had his arm locked in between mine and tried my best to break it, but he was able to wiggle free. We both got to our feet and stood facing each other ready to scrap. Skinny threw a few punches that I dodged, one of his punches slipped past my face and went right through his passenger side window splitting open his knuckles and hand. It must have been his adrenaline because despite the torn hand he was still throwing punches as if nothing ever happened.

A wide right came swinging my way and thinking quick I managed to get on the inside of his punch and block it with both of my forearms causing him to cringe in pain. At the same time I was able to wrap it up with my arm locking his elbow straight and punched him twice in the face forcing his nose to break. He struggled to get his trapped arm free, but my hold wouldn't give and my patience only grew thinner the longer we fought. I timed my attack perfectly releasing his trapped arm and at the same time delivering a powerful push kick to his chest that sent him flying into the side of his car denting it with his back. Skinny Slim stood paralyzed letting out a loud growl, with his arms outstretched and a deep arch in his back. Once he was able to gather himself and attempt to breathe, I noticed that he struggled coughing in pain and blood starting to spit from his mouth. Just from observation it looked as if his ribs were broken and it punctured his lungs. I have to admit, Skinny Slim was a real warrior and I knew then why the Kingdom had him in their inner circle, because even through all the pain he was still ready to fight and it was known from his advancement towards me. He lost his speed and power but he wasn't ready to quit, still spiting up blood and taking painful swings towards me and stumbling along the way. I did a spinning back kick to his thigh dropping him to the ground hitting his face. He struggled to get back up to his feet and I mounted his back placing my knee into his spine. I grabbed his chin with both of my hands lifting his head up high. The pain he was going through had to be detrimental and it was proven from the amount of blood gurgling out of his mouth. His punctured lung kept him from screaming out, but with a strong swift motion upward his neck snapped severing his head from his spine killing him instantly.

After I killed Skinny Slim I stood up to finally breathe and clear my head, as I looked around I spotted BG with her cell phone out. She was recording me and I'm pretty sure she was recording the whole thing and if word didn't get out by Tommy Gunzz then it would surely get out now. "Give me the phone!" I demanded, "Nigga fuck you!" BG said flicking me off and taking off in the opposite direction. "Damn!" I shouted aloud to myself, I grabbed the gun that Skinny Slim dropped and I got into my car and took off towards the hotel. I had to call Kane and the others to warn them that we were in danger, but the whole time I was thinking about people who would be able to hold their own and I forgot all about my friends Nate, Mark, Claxton, and even Mary. I called Nate and no one answered, I called Mark and after the third ring he picked up. "What's going on my nigga?" Mark said "Hey fam you and Nate might be in in so serious trouble."

"Why what's going on you alright?" Mark asked hearing the serious concern in my voice

"Dog I'm in a personal war with the Kingdom and you might become a victim if you're not careful."

Mark understood what I was saying and told me

that he would tell Nate to keep him aware. After I got off the phone with Mark I tried to call Claxton but it went straight to voice mail, I left him a message to stay with Mary and watch her for me. I needed to put an end to this shit and the only way I knew how was to bust my guns, and I couldn't do that with a lot on my mind. As soon as I made it to the hotel room my phone went off, it was Luther. "What's good?"

"Not you nigga, I had my suspicions but you are one bold ma'fucka." Luther said with a beastly laugh. "I thought you were better than that blood, but now I see that you're just some stupid kid in a war that you can't win. Now you got lucky with the others, but now that the whole Kingdom knows about your traitorous acts you're a dead man walking..."

"I've been a dead man for a long time now." I said cutting Luther off. "When I got word that you were gonna have Lele kill me after my last job I knew I only had a short amount of time. I'm coming for you Luther, I'm coming for all of you." I hung up the phone and threw it across the bed. "We need to move quickly, I need Mary here as well as my daughter." I didn't think they would use Heaven against me being that Lele was as much in love with her as I was, But I didn't put anything pass them. Percy was a dangerous man who didn't mind going against the street code no women no children. "Dog we will go get Mary, but let's go get a drink." Lemon was talking in code, so to avoid having the weapons stashed in the room and get discovered by a nosey cleaning lady. He hid them at a small bar next to the hotel, they were safe there being that Lemon has been smashing the bar manager. We walked over to the bar which wasn't open yet, the place was a little spot, but was fitting for the normal crowd that would consume the inside and be spilling out on the outside patio which was laid out with four fire pits and a few tables. The inside was fitted with a large bar that took up most of the room and a small walk way to the bathrooms and a back storage room where they kept the alcohol and where we had the guns. I went straight to the backroom behind the bar where they had the security systems to snoop around a bit.

Luke was in the storage room with Kane putting rounds in the guns, Lemon had to go bed down the bar manager while we took care of business, "Yo D!!" Solomon 7 yelled out. "How did he know I was here?" Was all I could think to myself as I cocked back my revolver that I had grabbed from a secret spot in the hotel. Walking up to the front of the bar I see Solomon 7 at the counter looking around still calling my name, "What up dogg, How did you know I was here?" I asked slowly moving the gun to the back of my leg. He looked up at me and his eyes cut to behind me and he slightly shook his head. I don't think he meant to give away her position or maybe it was my intuition, but I moved out the way just in time for a flying knife to come running past me and digging deep into the bar top counter. At the same time I let off two shots in the direction I thought the knife came from. I ran and ducked behind the wooden support beam, when about five or six silent shots whispered in my direction, leaving me in astonishment. What the fuck was I going to do with four rounds left, I peeked around the wall and saw Voodoo Doll aiming in my direction *"FUCK, this crazy bitch!"* She was a well-trained and highly dangerous, a killer, and Solomon 7 led here right to me. Three more silent rounds collided with the partition that I was hiding behind sending splinters and wood parts all around. Kane came out first with my sawed-off shotgun in hand ready to blast when she sent a few rounds towards him. One of the bullets hit the gun making it drop out of his hand and sending him diving for cover. I pointed my gun in her direction to give off some type of counter fire making her duck for cover. She was quick and precise and I was down to one single round and no way out of this situation "Damn!" I knew I was in trouble, this was the end. I had one desperate attempt left in me and I was going to make a mad dash towards her, she must have felt the same way because by the time I stood up I was looking at the business end of a modified. 45 and no way out.   Then I heard the closing end of my sawed-off, **"BOOM!!!"** I tucked my head and dodged away from the blast. To my surprise I saw Voodoo Doll with a massive chunk of her shoulder missing, her gun was on the floor and Solomon 7 was holding her life in his hands. She turned slowly to look him in the eyes and flashed a faint smile "For the Kingdom." Those were the last words out of her mouth before he pulled the trigger taking her head clean off with her lifeless body dropping and hitting the floor.

"How did you find us nigga?" I asked Solomon 7 with my gun pointed to the side of his head. "Calm down, everybody just calm the fuck down!" Solomon 7 closed his eyes and yelled out. "Yo D, out of all people you should know me. If I wanted you dead you think this was my only opportunity? Nigga I had the drop on you plenty of times, but I want them ma'fuckaz as dead as you do."

"If that's the truth why did you bring that crazy bitch in here?" Kane asked "I was instructed to have her as my enforcer. So you of all people should know that she makes her own calls." Solomon 7 said looking at me. I lowered my gun and placed it in the holster "look all that cowboy shit that just happened I'm pretty sure the cops are on their way here. So let's get our shit and head to the hotel." The others did as I said and went to get the rest of our supplies and we all met back up at the hotel room to get more information about the Kingdom. "So start talkin nigga" I said closing the door behind us. Solomon 7 stood with his back against the wall, "Look, we got the word from Luther to take you out, and before you left the meeting he had Voodoo put a tracker on your car. We are the only ones with access to the tracker and it was easy to find you here at the hotel. We just didn't know the room yet, but while we were in the process of getting the info, you all came out and headed to the bar. That's when she wanted to make her move, look I know how it seems, but it's not like that fam." I looked into Solomon 7's eyes looking for any signs of lying or deception but there was none. I knew he was telling the truth but I still didn't understand him. "How you been down with the Kingdom for all these years and now you ready to turn your back on em?" I asked Solomon 7 who now was taking a seat by the window. "Once I saw how they treated my family when y'all killed my cousin. they wrote him off like another business transaction, I knew then and there that something needed to be done."

"So why go after the Kingdom and not us?" Kane

jumped in. "I was angry at y'all yes, but my cousin did some fucked up shit in his life and wore the scar to prove it, but my aunt and baby cousin. They didn't ask to be in this life and Percy said he would take care of them but instead sent the H.I.T Squad after them, killing them both in their sleep." All of us were in shock listening to Solomon's story, "I started a little squad myself, we call ourselves the Nation and we are on the rise. We killed them niggaz, every single one of them got it. And Percy is next." Solomon 7 spat getting angry, I knew Solomon wasn't lying and he was getting too emotional for it to be staged. "So what's next?" I asked Solomon 7 who just looked up to me "We have to save Mark and Nate."

***

Nate was at his mom's house helping her move in, I called him to give a warning about the turn of events. "Son I need you to be on high alert, they are coming after us and I don't want you or your family to get caught up in this shit." Nate agreed and told me that he was going to stay with his mom's until I give him a call. Mark on the other hand was so wrapped up in the twins grips it seem as if it was too late. He had a thing for Spanish Fly, and when I broke the news to him he tried to reason with me that he could fix all of this by going with them to this hotel and talking it over. But that wasn't the case for the Kingdom, Solomon 7 told us that the plan was for them to take him to a hotel out in Queens that was closed for renovations. He also mentioned that Percy put a price of two and a half million dollars on my head. It was a number so large any and everybody would be jumping to get at me. At that time I wasn't worried about me, my mind was on Mark and I needed to reach him ASAP, we weren't close but close enough to reach him but how much time I had wasn't clear. I took off immediately without warning and headed for the hotel to save Mark.

Chapter 27

Mark saves Spanish Fly

The twins were on to me and they knew exactly what to do to get to me. Mark was always with them and he had a thing for Gloria, something crazy. Percy had the twins working out of a hotel that was closed for remodeling out in Elmhurst, I knew they would be there and from all the missed calls Mark was getting I knew he was with them there. I had to hurry I was nowhere near that part of town and traffic was driving me crazy. I was hoping that Mark was smart enough to know what was going on with his friends. They were a part of this as much as Lele was and on a different level of dangerous as well. I could tell from the sound in his voice that he didn't take the news so well when I told him, and he was going to try and save all of us, by reason. But the time for talking was far too gone; Percy put a goddamn price on my head, 2.5 million dollars, hell who could pass on that offer. The overcast started to get worst the closer I got to Elmhurst, and the snow began to fall. At first it was light and by the time I made it outside the hotel complex it was coming down heavy and fast. I stepped out of the car with at least five inches already laid out over the streets.

I pulled out the Taurus Judge with twelve extra shells and my trusted .45. Mark's car was out front the grill was still feeding out warm air and there was very little snow on it. The cold was starting to get to me and I still needed to find a way inside, but there was another problem, Percy's H.I.T Squad was outside in the front and I knew some were already in. I couldn't let them know I was here not just yet, as I looked around there was this steel and wooden scaffold going up to the fifth floor, hey why not. Once I made it up to the floor I got inside and looked around there was no one in sight, just me and this cold hell from the open windows. The wind was screaming at this point and I still didn't have a clue where Mark was or the Twins. Walking down the hall I could hear voices through the elevator that were coming from upstairs, I couldn't risk going up by the stairs in case there was someone guarding them, but since the elevator was down I had the idea to climb up it to the next floor. I breached the door and looked around no one was insight, I heard voices coming from down the hall walking out of the elevator and down the hall I could hear Spanish Fly's voice but couldn't make out what was being said.

I got into the first open door I could find that was close to where they were, it wasn't the Twins that I was worried about, it was mostly the people they were involved with and what will happen to Mark. The room I got into was being remodeled and some of the walls were torn down, which gave me access to the two rooms next to it. I was standing in between a wall and Mark and being this close I could hear every word that was being said, "Why are you doing this? What did I do?" Mark was pleading with one of the Twins and he was getting serious. "Please just let me go I don't have anything to do with all this." Mark was begging for his life and it was as if God sent me as his guardian angel, I took a few steps back and ran straight for the wall. Jumping through I clinched my body before I made contact, crashing through the wall into the other room which created a fog of smoke from the dry wall and debris. I looked up and saw Mark falling to the side of the room; I threw a wide punch to Gloria aka Spanish Fly which she caught to the face dropping her down to the ground. Baby Doll was on the floor from some of the pieces from the wall that hit her, she was reaching for her pistol when I ran up and kicked her in the face sending her neck backwards in a violent manner.

Blood started to run from her nose and mouth, these bitches deserved death and I was gonna give it to them one way or another.

I pulled out the judge and proceeded to do the honors **"Bang"** one .410 slug crashed into Baby Doll's temple splitting her skull wide open, from that close of a range the splatter effect was crazy, painting me, the floor, and the wall red with her blood. Spanish Fly was still knocked out, I walked up to her and pointed my barrel towards her "Come on dog you don't have to do this, she's knocked out we can get away." Mark's thing for Gloria was so bad it had him twisted, he was wrapped around her little fingers. He always liked her the most, a little bit too much if you ask me. He was scared and it showed in his eyes "This little bitch just tried to kill you, and you want to spare her life." I was so angry and hyped up I forgot all about the goons outside, a loud kick hit the door with the paring of the racking of a pump action shotgun, I pushed Mark to the side and sent the remaining rounds in my gun through the door into his now lifeless body.

The gun shots were loud and I knew more of them were coming, I quickly reloaded and got Mark off of the ground and took off down the stairs. We can hear the doors open from below and voices of the men coming up towards us I told Mark to stay behind me and we walked against the wall down the stairs, the first guy up to us looked shocked his eyes got big and he struggled to draw his pistol from its holster I sent two rounds into his chest pushing him backwards down the stairs. This set off the others and you could hear them running up cocking back their guns, we ran into the door of the 4th floor and looked for another way out. "The fire escape in the back!" Mark pointed out and we dashed for the exit and broke through the door Mark went down first and I followed behind making sure no one was following. We dropped down into the snowy streets and ran towards the side where my car was, "FUCK!!" I yelled out loud seeing that there was a group of five goons waiting for us. Mark slipped and fell when we saw them I had my gun drawn and unloaded towards them. Three of them fell from getting hit the other two started spraying their automatics in our direction, we took cover behind the side of the wall "Oh God, Oh God please help me" Mark was getting hysterical and freaking out I had to do something before he gets us both killed " Shut up take this and fire back, just like we did that night at Felix's spot we are gonna survive this shit you hear me?" I gave Mark my .45 and he took in a deep breath, there were two guys left shooting at us. I poked my head out to see where they were, shots whizzed past my head, Mark was counting and I heard him get to three and jumped out from around the corner sending rounds into the men. I went after him and noticed that the men who were shooting at us were down. We walked up to them and finished them off one after the other, the pure white snow was now stained with blood.

By the time we made it to my car the front door opened up and there was Gloria with her pistol shooting at us Mark was hit and fell down dropping his gun I shot back but missed taking cover behind the car, I was out of bullets and this bitch was walking towards me firing by the second. The group of men that were following us inside were rounding the corner unleashing hell as well. Just when I thought it was all over I heard tires screeching and Luke jumped out of the car with his automatic rifle and let loose cutting Spanish Fly down sending hot lead into her face and chest. He ran over to us and noticed the blood coming from Marks right arm "you ok ki... ki... kid?" He asked me as a huge smile came across my face "yea I'm good" Lemon started shooting at the guys coming from the hotel and yelling for us to get in the car. I got Mark up and put him in the front seat Luke ran back to Lemon and got in firing at the hotel so we can drive off. I got in the car with them leaving my

Acura and we took off heading back to Kane in Brooklyn.

***

Mark was still bleeding but from the look of the wound he was going to need a doctor, Kane went right to work on Mark's arm taking out three fragments and stitching him up. I started thinking about my next move and had the idea to relocate where we were resting our head. "Hey Solomon 7 you remember that place up in Hell's Kitchen with the service elevator?"

"Yea god, why what's up?" Solomon 7 said in agreement "I need you and Luke to go get that and we'll move in tomorrow, this place is starting to get too hot." Lemon walked in with pizza and the smell alone made my stomach tumble, all that shooting and running around I forgot I haven't eaten. I devoured two huge slices and fell asleep in a deep food coma, in my sleep.

I went to a place deep inside my head and saw my mother, she was wearing this all white flowing dress and dancing on top of a tall skyscraper in the middle of the city. She was singing her favorite song by Barry White "Secret Garden." She was looking so beautiful, she wasn't the drug addict I knew. But she was her young beautiful self, smiling so bright that it was a match for the sun. I was floating in the air around my mother and I felt the tears in my eyes began to fall. She was beautiful but the sun that she was dancing under began to burn right red as if it was bleeding and clouds began to form, it looked as if New York was on fire and burning. I turned to look at my mother who was no longer dancing but she was bleeding from her eyes, her white dress was now torn and worn. She stumbled towards the edge of the building and fell off "Nooooo!!!!"

I jumped out of my sleep to find myself no longer floating in the air but in the chair I feel asleep in. I looked out the window and scanned around the area. My attention was drawn to my vibrating phone "What's good?" I said answering the phone. "Hello sweetie, it's good to hear your voice this lovely morning, I was expecting your voicemail." The familiar deep voice was doing numbers in my head, but I couldn't figure it out "Yo who is this?" I said catching an attitude "Oh poor Decon, where are my manners-"

"TMD!" I said cutting him off "Yes it's me indeed and I will be joining the company of your lovely sister here shortly and I would love for you to join us."

"You sick motherfucker, if you touch my sister I swear to God ill murder your ass!"

"Ooo, don't threaten me with a good time. Ha-ha see you soon baby." TMD hung up laughing and it sent me into a murderous rage. Fire was in my eyes and I was no longer in the right state of mind to comply with any rules. My mission now was to kill TMD and have Mary closer to me, but I had to make my moves quick. During my rage I woke up everyone, but it was Kane who broke the silence, "What's going on D?"

"That sick fuck TMD is going after Mary." I said as I grabbed my .45 and two extra clips, and my jacket I should have grabbed my vest but I was in such a hurry, that I left before anyone else was ready to go with me. I hopped in the car and took off as quickly as I could. Traffic was light and moving so navigating through the streets wasn't a problem. The snow was still thick on the grounds but from the plow trucks work over night the roads were slightly clear. I feared the worst about my sister and I knew from the stories I've heard about TMD, he was murderous and diabolical when it came to his methods of torture and death. They say he once held this guy hostage who disrespected him at one of his clubs for being a drag, while during his time in bondage he was raped over and over day and night, then beat half to death. You would think that was all and he would let that guy go to learn his lesson, well that wasn't TMD's style he went to work surgically removing body parts while he was still alive. The worst was that he sent the pieces of his body to all of his family members for added pleasure. I was going to enjoy killing this bastard, but first I needed my sister to be in a safe place before I could focus on him.

I arrived to the rehab center about thirty minutes later and found a parking spot by the side emergency exit, I knew we were going to need a fast get away, the sun was starting to rise and the air was thick with cold and frost. I was in such a hurry to the front door I almost slipped on a thin piece of ice. The nurse who normally sat at the front desk was getting coffee when she saw me enter, "Hey Mr. Rice" the young black nurse said walking towards her seat, "I need to get my sister out now, I know you all have rules and shit, but this is urgent and we need to leave asap."

"I'm sorry Mr. Rice I can't just let her leave like that I have to wait until my supervisor comes in at ten and he would be able to release her into your custody."

"Look, I don't have that kind of time-" My words were cut short when a large SUV roared into the parking lot expelling four large men from the back all armed with high powered machine guns. "GET DOWN!" I yelled hoping over the counter bring the nurse down to the floor with me just in time for a barrage of bullets forced through the glass door and the wooden counter desk, sending shards of both everywhere. The screams of the staff and residents were loud but being drowned out by the barks of the machine guns. I pulled out my .45 that was tucked in the back of my waistband "Fuck I knew I should've grabbed my vest." I said aloud to myself, after a long forty five second assault the guns all clicked empty and I knew they were reloading, I stood up just in time to see one of the masked gunmen running through the shot up door. By the time he saw me, my gun was already trained on him and I let off a shot that punched through his head ending his life. My next two shots made their way to the next target, one going through his cheek and the other through his left eye.

The rest of the gun men ran to take cover behind the SUV but one was too slow as three of my rounds ran through his leg, back and head. Two men were left holding up behind the truck and I knew they were reloaded by now, "stay down" I shouted to the nurse as I crept closer to the truck and posting up by the side of the rear door. "You think he's out?" One of the men said to the other shifting around trying to find me, but they were too slow and I was on the other side with my gun on them and unloading into both men killing them before they could get their chance to test their luck.

I grabbed one of their rifles and ran back into the center and found the nurse crying a prayer on the floor, "Hey, look at me, get to a room and call the police I have to go now." I instructed before dashing off to find Mary's room, she was looking franticly around the hallway. "Decon what the hell is going on?" She asked running up to me and giving me a hug, "Look we don't have time, where's Claxton?"

"He was in the bathroom down the hall." Mary said, "Let's go" Claxton rushed out the bathroom ready to kill whoever it was who came to the door but stopped short when he noticed it was me with Mary at my heel. "Dog, I'm so happy to see you, what the fuck was all that about?"

"I don't have time right now to explain, come with me, we have to get the hell out of here before more show up." I said making hurried steps to the side exit door. We had just pulled out of the parking lot as two more SUV's came rushing towards the rehab center, I sped off quickly into traffic. Sirens were making their way towards us and traffic was put into a crazed panic, we were stuck behind an older couple at the light when two large oversized vans stopped in the middle of the street. About seven or eight men jumped out of the back and side of the vans equally armed as the last were. "EVERYONE GET DOWN!" I shouted and almost instantly a hail of bullets ripped through the couple in front of us, and their car. I opened the door and slid down to the ground trying my best not to get hit by a stray bullet, Claxton grabbed the high powered rifle I took off the dead gunman and went out his door while Mary stayed concealed in the back seat. Bullets were screaming past us and a piece of glass kissed the side of my face, but that didn't stop me in my mission to get my sister to safety. When I heard a slight pause in gun fire from in front of me I took advantage of that moment, I popped up and opened fire on the masked man whose gun had jammed all four rounds connected and I clicked empty 'Damn! I GOTTA RELOAD!" I shouted out to Claxton who took his position on the other side of a parked car. All fire was directed at me and Claxton went to work letting the rifle roar out bringing the attention to him. I was reloaded and back into action, Claxton had taken out three of them and I was about to finish the rest when three rounds whizzed past my face from the back. We were taking fire from the front and the rear and they were closing in on us quick. I had the front and Claxton took the rear, I paused for a brief moment when a cold chill hit my body. It wasn't the type of chill from the brisk air but a chill I would get when something was about to go wrong. The same feeling I got when Peter was gunned down, "CLAXTON GET DOWN!!!" I shouted out but I was too late, bullets tore through his body rocking him back and forth before he fell on the parked car he was in-front of. Mary was screaming hysterically from the sight of her boyfriend stretched out and riddled with holes bleeding onto the frozen street.

The shooting was stopped as the trained killers were pacing towards me, guns trained on me "Drop it!" One of the men yelled out, I reluctantly dropped my .45 and slowly put my hands in the air. I closed my eyes and shook my head, I would've went out in a blaze of glory before I would surrender, but with Mary in the mix I was left with little choices to pick from. Something heavy and hard smashed into the back of my head, and I slammed into the ground going cold and everything went black.

Chapter 28

Too Much Drama

"Wake up sweet heart, Deeecon, Waake, upp!" "Decon, GET UP!!" My eyes shot open with a sharp pain shooting through the middle of my thigh. "There you go sweet heart." TMD was inches away from my face licking his lips which were painted in dark red lipstick, his voice was in my head building up the anger which was already present towards him. My head was in pain and I didn't have to feel the large knot that was pulsating, and my thigh was throbbing from whatever was stuck in it. I wanted nothing more than to see him dead by hands, he grabbed my face with his large hands and kissed me on the lips. I was so disgusted, I felt like I was about to throw up; I shook my head away and spit in his face. He smiled wiping the spittle off his face and threw his large head back and lunged it forward crashing into mine splitting my lip. The blow was strong and the metallic taste of blood began to build up in my mouth, as I spit the blood out on the floor he laughed "Sweet lips, taste good too." He said standing up and adjusting his skirt. Look don't get it twisted this fuckin fairy was no punk, he was built like a WWE wrestler standing at around six foot eight or more, and had to be sitting on two hundred and seventy sum. Dark bronze skin with a bold head which he normally kept covered with a wig of his choice, and always kept a fresh beat face.

I looked him in the eyes as he walked back towards me, he smiled and looked at my injured leg. I wrenched in pain as he pulled out the four-inch blade from my leg and licked the blood off of it and swished it around his mouth like it was an expensive sip of wine. "You taste good too." He said with a smile on his face "Fuck you faggot!" I shot back, "Come on sweetie there's no need for such words. Trust me we are gonna be real close before I send you on your way, really close." His deep voice creped me out and I wanted to kill him even more, but my hands were cuffed together by a pair of pink furry hand cuffs and they were suspended above my head by chains attached to a thick iron bar. I couldn't tell what was going on in his psychotic mind, but from the expression on his face I knew it wasn't anything Godly. I followed TMD with my eyes as he walked over to the far side of the room and flipped on a dim light which exposed Mary who was bound down to a steal chair bolted in the ground, her hair was messy, face was red along with her eyes from all the crying she was doing and her hands were tied behind her. She was gaged so she couldn't talk, only make noises which I made out to be screams for help.

"LET HER GO YOU SICK SON OF A BITCH!" I shouted out, but only to get laughter out of him, "calm down sexy, you will get yours soon enough, but first I need a taste of this young pretty thing. Ooo she has your beautiful eyes as well, ha-ha I'm going to really enjoy this, and I want you to watch as I have my way with your sister." He said slowly caressing her cheek, and stroking her hair.

"Please…"

"Please what? Don't do it, oh you should've thought about that before you fucked with the Kingdom, trust me I won't do her like I'm gonna do you sexy, I'll make fucking her quick but the torture will be long and painful, as I have a reputation to maintain. But I will say this to you, I'm going to fuck you over, and over, and over until you bleed. Then we will repeat the cycle until I'm done with your pretty ass, and when I chop you up I will make sure that I take one of your eyes with me and hold on to it for memories." With his voice and how he described the planned assault it sent chills running down my spine and every inch he took closer to Mary caused me to pull harder and harder at the cuffs that had me bound. I was pulling so hard that blood was trickling onto my face from the metal cutting into my flesh, I grew violent yanking and squirming away trying to get free. TMD was now ripping away Mary's clothes and pulled off the red thong he was wearing and exposed his large penis, I couldn't hold the tears back from the anger starting to build inside of me, "Come here bitch, this will be your last dick inside of that sweet mouth of yours." I felt helpless, pulling, and yanking but to no avail all I had to show for it was a cut up wrist and pain. "NOOO!!!!" I bellowed out in pain and anger.

There was a sound of a car crashing into the building, shortly followed by the tattering of rounds from something heavy. The screams of his men froze TMD with his dick in his hand; literally, the door to the room we were in was forced open and a scared guard came in after "Boss we have to---" his words were cut off from three rounds pushing through his chest putting an end to his life. My vision was hazy from the tears in my eyes but I recognized the voice over the heavy gun fire. "DIE YOU DIRTY BASTARD!" Lemon shouted out "Wait..." TMD tried to plead but was expelled from this life as Lemon emptied his clip into TMD's body. My vision began to clear and I saw Lemon free Mary from her bondage, and the two of them headed towards me. Mary was shaking and crying a lot and Lemon found a key on the table next to me and freed me. My wrist was numb from the pain but the anger still remained, I grabbed the knife that was stuck in my leg off of the floor and I moved over to where TMD's body lay, to my surprise he was still twitching. It could have been from the nerves moving through his body, but that didn't matter to me, I begin to stab his body over and over again until I was stopped by Kane who must've slipped in after Lemon. Kane was holding an M16 and wearing a bullet proof vest and a du-rag to hold his hair out of his face, "Calm down son, we got you." Kane said squeezing me trying to get me to regain my composure. "How did y'all find us?" I asked looking back and forth between Kane and Lemon, "We followed the van after they picked you and Mary up. We spotted y'all after the gun fight, and before we could join in you were already knocked out and being dragged to the back of the van." Lemon explained, "If you didn't run off so fast we could have been there with you, but I'm sure we wouldn't have found that piece of shit." Kane said pointing to TMD who was spread out naked on the cold concrete floor. I could see my breath in the cold air, and said a small prayer of thanks to God for giving me yet another chance at life. We walked out of the room where me and Mary were held captive and I could see the destruction brought on by Kane and Lemon, we were in a warehouse somewhere by the Hudson. There were dead henchmen all over and a car stuck in the side wall of the building, "Kane's idea" Lemon said seeing the questioned look on my face, "Where is Solomon 7 and Luke?" I asked, Lemon told me that they went and started moving our things into the apartment we talked about earlier. We got into the car and drove off to Hell's Kitchen and parked in an ally way that had a door on the side that lead to the apartment.

Chapter 29

Unstoppable

After I dropped Mary off at the apartment with Kane, I grabbed Lemon's phone and called Luther. The phone rang three times before he picked up. "Da fuck is this?" Luther said in a hostile tone, "It's me nigga, nice move sending that fag after me and my sister, but he's now resting in hell where he belongs. But I'ma see you real soon nigga believe that." I ended the call before Luther had the chance to respond. My leg was sore and still bleeding, I headed inside of the building and made my way up the service elevator to the top floor. The apartment opened up to a wide living area complimented by a large wall of windows some faded out so you couldn't see through but for the most part it was well lit, the air had a strong stale damp musk from no one living in the place for a few years. There were four bedrooms and two bathrooms, and a patio that had access to the rooftop.

Mary was sitting in a chair by the window when I walked in and I could tell that she was still shaken from the day's events. Kane must have seen the wound on my leg, because he came out of the bathroom with a medical bag and went to work on my wound. Luke and Solomon 7 came in shortly with more bags of our stuff, "Nice to see that y'all niggaz made it." Solomon said giving me dap, "yo kid, y'all got my clothes?" I asked as Luke threw me a large duffel bag full of my things. I gave Mary something to change into and I went into the other bathroom to wash my ass. It took a min for the hot water to kick on but once it came it quickly put my mind at ease, I was so close to death today I could taste it. I had just finished washing up and putting on some fresh cloths when I got a text from Luther telling me to meet him at the underpass in fifteen minutes. I told everyone that I wanted to go around and get some information from the streets and that I didn't need anyone to tag along. Luke followed me down to the car where Lemon was in the passenger side putting rounds into a clip for the .45 "Everything okay kid?" Lemon asked as he inserted the magazine into the pistol, "Yea I'm good just have a feeling that something isn't right." I told Luke to look after Mary while I was gone and I told him that if he didn't hear from me in five hours take the money and go back to Florida.

He didn't feel good about the plan but agreed bumped my knuckles and ran up to the room with Mary. "You know you don't have to come with me right?" I told Lemon he smiled looked up at me in my eyes "I know nigga, but we blood you bang I bang, I didn't come all this way to bury you I'm here to protect you just like old times." Hearing this from Lemon made me smile; I stared the car and drove off to the underpass. Luther was up to something, I know he seen the carnage from the raid of the gun house, all the way down to TMD's death, and he wanted to deal with me personally. The thirty minute drive brought back memories of the time when I started out, the first time I saw blood, my first fight for the kingdom. Arriving there wasn't much better I mean the smell, the sight, all the memories I was having was like a bad nightmare that constantly hunted me. Elroy was sitting in the car alone and knowing him he had that damn 12 gauge loaded and ready sitting right next to him. Lemon went to go sneak up on him and pointed the gun to his head I was on the other side watching making sure he didn't go for his gun. "You know you're making a huge mistake D, you won't get out of this alive." Elroy said to me placing his hands on the steering wheel "That's a bold statement coming from a dead man." I said motioning for Lemon to watch him as I walked around the corner to find

Luther.

He was in the middle of the makeshift ring with his shirt off and his dreads tied into a long pony tail just the way he always had them. "You remember this place boy? This is where I created the monster in you, I built you bitch and you betrayed me, how dare you bite the hand that fed you?" Luther was heated breathing heaver after each sentenced, I was starting to get irritated at what he was saying, how dare he talk about betrayal "Aren't you the one who is plotting to kill me? Wasn't that the plan Luther? You say I betrayed you when you all betrayed me, I did everything y'all asked and this is how you repay me; I trusted you nigga I looked to you as a brother." Luther smiled "Brothers, no we were never brothers, you was just a job, now it's time to retire you." I walked closer and closer to Luther has he spoke until I was about three steps in front of him; we stood there looking into each other's eyes waiting for whoever was ready to make the first move. I saw his fist tighten, he was breathing heavy the tension was sharp and his energy was coming to me as strong as the sun. I slowed down my heart beat, eased my body and closed my eyes.

Any normal person would think that this was a stupid move and that I just lost this battle, but a true master would know that I was finding my center, my chi, the eternal energy that flowed throughout my body. I could feel him coming closer to me, as I opened my eyes and moved to the left dodging a heavy right hook coming for my head. I threw a quick left jab to Luther's ear knocking him off balanced and causing him to stumble a little bit. Luther quickly shook off the hit and charged at me like an angry bull picking me up in the air, I started countering with a strong right elbow to the middle of his head, which made him release me. I feel to my feet and opened him up to a fury of fist and elbow strikes to his face and body, Luther fell to his knees and started to spit up blood. He stood up wiped his mouth and smiled, "that was a nice warm up bitch, my turn" he threw some dirt in my face causing me to drop my guard and catching a spinning kick to my midsection. I bent over in pain as Luther quickly took advantage by grapping onto the back of my head and neck pulling me into his knee. I flipped over to my back; my face was numb from the pain and Luther than proceeded to stomp on my chest with his giant timberlands. I rolled over and kicked him in the front of his knee, it didn't break but he dropped from the pain I hit him with two low kicks to the face giving me a chance to get back up to my feet. His face started to swell and blood was coming from his mouth and nose. As he looked up to me I ran up and kicked him in the face hard enough to knock him over onto his back.

Luther wallowed in the dirt in pain, the great Luther was defeated, or so I thought. He stumbled back up to his feet and put his hand up, "that's all you got nigga? Huh, I'm King Luther I'm unstoppable bitch!" Luther threw a swift right jab that caught me right in the face, my head jerked back and I stumbled backwards, he came up quick and threw another one I dodged it and countered with a straight kick to his stomach. Luther bent over and I came in with a jolting knee to his head knocking him down to the ground again. He stood up slowly looking in the opposite direction of me; this is when I ran towards him jumping up in the air allowing my knee to crash into the back of his skull pushing him forward. Luther was in pain, face was full of blood and dirt. His eyes were glossy and he was now pissed more than before, he got up to his knees trying to make his way to his feet. I couldn't allow that to happen so I moved quickly sending my right leg into his side, I felt about two of his ribs give in causing him to cough up blood. After all this he was still able to stand up to his feet, he was very strong physically and had the will to match. Slowly wiping his face, he spit out the blood gathering in his mouth and flung his hair to his back, "I told you boy I can't be stopped ha-ha, I'm too powerful to be stopped. They didn't tell you, I am a god!" He clinched after each breath he took from the broken ribs, yet he was still able to walk towards me, I swiftly made it around him and started to choke him out but he kept on resisting, it got to the point to where he was going to break free. This guy would not stop, almost made me feel as if he was truly unstoppable. I tightened up my grip, pushed his head forward with my forearm and sat down and backwards, this action caused his spine to crack and separate from his skull killing him instantly. Luther was dead his eyes were rolled to the back of his head with blood coming out of the sockets and his body was limp. I killed the unstoppable one, the one people feared the most, the king of the streets was now dethroned and I did it.

Luther was dead and Elroy was still a problem that needed to be fixed, "Say Lemon what should we do with this nigga?" I asked limping over towards the car, Elroy sat in his seat and smiled. "Little nigga, I've watched you grow into this monster, you saved my life once, and for that I was thankful, but nothing will change the fact that I wanted you dead just as much as Luther did. That baby girl of yours will never know her daddy, and that's fact."

"False, she will know me, just not her mother. Y'all are foul for trying to set me up B, I did everything I was asked and for what? Death? Look it comes a time and a place where we grow and make our own choices and I've grown a lot." I said stopping Elroy from speaking again, he just looked up to me in my eyes and shook his head. "Percy set this war into motion and he will finish it, but I can't just sit here and let you take my life young bull." Just as he spoke Elroy pulled out a snub nose .380 and shot underneath his chin causing the top of his head to erupt. "What the fuck!" Lemon said jumping slightly "Now what?"

"We go get my daughter, then we end this once and for all." I said grabbing Luther's and Elroy's cell phones. The sun was going down and the air was thick with cold, we rode silently as the radio played a throwback of Beanie Sigel "Die" the mood was set and mind was in the moment, the only thing I could think about was having my daughter in my hands and never letting go. It was dark and the street lights were kicked on giving the whole neighborhood a dim lit look. There were four gunmen in front of the house so going in through the front was out of the question.

Chapter 30

Lele's Death

Lele was in the bedroom and Heaven was in the crib in the next room, the tricky part was getting Lele away from Heaven, my mind was spinning and the stab wound from earlier was starting to bleed even more. I grabbed my .45 and checked how many rounds I had left, I was down to four in the clip and one in the chamber, just enough to get the job done. "Wait here, if I'm not walking out of the front, kill everyone and get my daughter." I told Lemon as I exited the car, I snuck around the corner and broke into the basement using the little window trying not to make too much noise. Peaking around the corner towards the kitchen, I saw that it was empty and I felt that something was wrong. Something was up and I knew she wasn't alone; quietly I made my way up the stairs and saw Lele putting a few rounds into a magazine of what looked to be a .38. She knew I was coming for her when she tried calling Luther and there was no answer; Luther always picked up Lele's phone calls.

"Put it down!" I said in a low growl as she inserted the clip into the gun, she was stunned that I was standing right in the doorway with a gun pointed to her head. Fear was in her eyes as she starred at the barrel of my gun, "You don't have to do this Decon, it doesn't have to be this way." Lele tried to persuade me by using those almond shape eyes, those damn eyes they always get me. I couldn't hold back the tears any longer, this was someone I loved, this was a person I trusted, the mother of my child, why did she have to do this. I started to lower my gun, and that's when I heard Heaven starting to cry, that sweet sound of her cries distracted me enough for Lele to cock back her gun and let off two rounds in my direction. From the sound of the round hitting the chamber it gave me enough time to move from the gun blast. I ran into the baby's room to grab heaven; by this time, she was crying even louder from the gun shots. I heard Lele screaming my name and running towards Heavens room. "Stay away from my baby!" Lele rushed into the room and saw that my gun was drawn and so was hers and now we were staring at each other with guns ready to fire. Just like the old westerns this was a showdown, I had Heaven in my right arm crying and squirming around. "Drop the gun Leandra you don't want to do anything stupid now do you?" Lele now had this face of rage, her gun pointed at me and our baby and I could see the tears rolling down her face, her eyes red and puffy she swallowed hard and licked her lips. "Decon I'm sorry in the name of the Kingdom it has to be done, I wasn't supposed to love you, and I damn sure wasn't supposed to have a child." As she spoke I can her the men running in from the sound of gun fire Lele's finger now moving and getting closer to the trigger, she was a better shot than me and I'm sure she could hit me and not the baby at that close of range.

My gun was still up and pointing towards her, I released one round into the middle of her chest at the same time Lele let off a shot as well. This frigid sensation of sorrow caressed my body watching her drop the .38 and fall back against the doorway. She slid down coughing up blood and blinking her eyes at a steady pace. I walked over towards her and stared down at her watching her slowly die taking deep breaths and with each exhale more blood started to flow. At the same time the men who came in the front door were now making their way up the stairway, I was still looking at Leandra taking her final breaths. Something felt wrong; there was a voice in my head telling me to look down at Heaven who had stopped crying for some strange reason. My mind instantly went to death, I thought that she was shot, looking down I seen blood all over the blanket she was wrapped in, "Please GOD!" I pleaded out loud as I dropped down to one knee and slowly removing the blanket to check on her. "Drop the gun!" One of the men yelled coming into the room, still checking on Heaven I began to tone out their voices I heard nothing almost deaf...

Then I heard her voice, the cries from my baby gave me life, she looked at me and just cried it was as if everything came back to reality. She was unharmed, the blood was mine it came from Lele's bullet hitting my right shoulder and going right through it. Still holding on to Heaven I looked up and saw the two men who were yelling at me to put down my gun and my baby. I squeezed onto my .45 that much more; there were four rounds left and I had one gun pointed towards my head. The guy that came in first stopped short of the door way blocking the way and view of the second guy still in the hallway. "Ok I will." I said aloud placing Heaven down towards my knee and I quickly tucked my head forwards towards his left knee and shot him in the leg at the same time. He screamed and let off a shot inches past my ear and I shot again hitting him in the eye, from this close range the round went through the back of his head hitting the other guy in his side. Before he could pull his gun up to shoot, another round was coming his way hitting him in the middle of his head. The other two men were rushing up the stairs but the roar of something evil came shortly after, it was followed by a second blast and then silence.

Lemon came walking in with his shotgun smoking and an evil scrawl on his face "You said kill everything." Lemon said noticing me eye ballin his gun. "Damn son, you ok?" He said looking over to Lele's dead body, "Yea I'm straight, it was her or me." I pointed to the bleeding hole in my shoulder, I was one lucky bastard that day and happy to still be alive. I picked up Heaven who was covered in a bloody blanket and crying loudly, "Grab her clothes and her stuff we gotta get the hell out of here." I said to Lemon as we grabbed some things and made our way to the car and drove off.

Chapter 31

It's time

The whole city was on lock down, the FBI was now involved and they had my picture on every news station. I was a wanted man but I couldn't stop now, there was a job that needed to be done and I wasn't going to stop until I killed Percy. He had called in the remaining members and the rest of his H.I.T. Squad to link up at his apartment. Solomon 7 was thought to be dead and their only link to me was now in my possession. Kartoon Killa and King Jaffy Joker were the biggest members of the Kingdom and they were as much of a threat as Percy was. I had enough money to just fly away and be done with this all but I wouldn't feel comfortable looking over my shoulder for the rest of my life. I wasn't about to come this far to tuck tail and run, I was down to see this to the end but first I needed to call in my favor.

Detective Brian Smith was in hiding somewhere in

the outskirts of Pennsylvania with his family, safe from all the destruction of New York City. Until I called him after seeing that the news had my face and name all over the media outlets. "Hey Smith, I know your surprised that I'm still alive, ha-ha yea me too. Well it's time to bring you back from the dead detective." I started to fill Smith in on all he was missing and details that went beyond what the news had information on. He was shocked but was ready to get back to work and finish what he started with his case against one of his fellow officers and my enemy. "When I get back you do know that I have to turn you in right?" Smith said in a serious tone, "Yea about that..." *What I didn't share with you, was that we had a short meeting before I called the detective, I knew someone was gonna have to take the heat for all the crimes that were committed throughout the city, and in some weird turn of events, Kane stepped forward saying that it would be his pleasure to save the life of his children, and granddaughter. I guess it was his way of making up for not being there for us growing up.* "Yea detective, the man you want is known as Kane, he would be the one to pin all of this on." Detective Smith was shocked when he heard the news, "Does he know what he is signing up for?"

"Yea he's aware." I said looking over at Kane playing with Heaven by the window. "I'll be back in town tomorrow night, well make the arrest then."

"No we wait until I get you more evidence then you can have your man, and your case, until then you come back into town and I'll call you when the time is right." I said hanging up the phone and walking back into the living room where everyone was sitting huddled around the television watching the news. There was a loud buzzing sound to let us know that there was someone downstairs trying to come up to the apartment. I looked at the security monitor to see Nate standing outside moving around trying to stay warm. "Come on up." I said into the speaker buzzing him in. Nate walked in shortly after with a look on his face that said he had knowledge, "Yo thun peep this shit, ever since you niggaz done killed all more than half of the Kingdom and disrupted the flow of power, the big three, King Jaffy Joker, Kartoon Killa, and Percy.... Well they hoisting a meeting for all the gang leaders, and thugs in the Tri-cities, in a place called the Tombs." He was speaking so fast that he was getting out of breath and stumbling over his words. "Where is the Tombs?" Asked Solomon 7 "Its this club out in the Bronx, it was shut down for years before it came under new management, who uses the spot as a secret getaway for the rich and wealthy to get their desires filled."

"How did you come across this information?"

Lemon asked for the group, Well seeing that you niggaz have been laying low in the spot, I'm out there listening, and that bitch BG well since you killed Luther she became the Kingdom's go to for product and muscle, and she can't hold water if it was in a cup. She was going around talking about the secret meeting to this boss I promoted for named Queen Ivy, she runs a murderous gang of females out of Queens and her and BG have been working together on a few moves, so I guess they about to test their hand with the remodeling of the Kingdom." Nate knew a lot and his word was always tight, especially since he didn't have any true involvement with what I had going on the city. He basically had a free pass.

"Ok so we hit them at the meeting."

"Well that's the problem, the place is going to be packed, it's a little more than just a meeting, and it's a party as well. Keeping everything low key." Nate said punching holes in my train of thought. "So who's throwing the party?" I asked Nate who was big in the music scene and him and Mark knew just about everyone who was anyone in the music world. "Well that's why I'm excited, the club owner asked if the West Indy Connection could perform for the whole party, and of course we said yes, but security is going to be tighter than two fat girls in a closet fighting over a bag of Cheetos."

Nate joked, but I knew what he was trying to say to be true, and I had a plan that would work, just needed to know where the meeting was going to be held.

Chapter 32

Flesh of my Flesh and Blood of my Blood

The party was set to go down in two days, and since the day Nate brought the information to our laps I was already in overdrive thinking of any and every way to getting information about the meeting. Percy made sure that the information was locked down tight and that only the need to know, knew about the details. Well what Percy didn't know was that Kartoon Killa had a secret fling with a bottle girl who would be working the party the day of the meeting. Her name was Kendra Perkins, she was a medical student with a strong desire for bosses and an even stronger one for coke. Mark knew about the girl because she was a fan of his voice and tried time after time to get at him, but he decline her jester for the simple fact that she was messing with Kartoon. I asked if Mark could get her alone and find out where the meeting was going to be held on the night, and she agreed, with the help of three thousand dollars, and a date with Mark.

***

The plan was set and going in motion, Me Luke and Lemon, and Kane were going to hind in the back of the equipment van, and Solomon 7 was going to storm the front with his crew. He called in ten solders ready to lay it all down when the time came. We were going to set it off right and I didn't want to risk anything. "Ok guys there's no turning back on this now, we do this we go all the way, there's going to be a lot of guns pointed our way, and I know for a fact that the cards are going to be stacked against us, but no one makes a move until I do. Is that clear?" I watched as everyone nodded their heads in agreement and prepared their minds for the impossible. Mary was watching Heaven sleep in the bedroom when I walked in, "Hey sis."

"What's up D."

"Look I know you..."

"I know you have to do this and I understand the risk of it all, I will be there for my niece no matter what. I just wish it was another way, but I know this has to happen. Just do me a favor." Mary said cutting me off, "What is it?" I said sitting on the bed next to her, "Make sure you kill that son of a bitch!" Mary was serious and her tone didn't hold back at all, "No doubt" I responded kissing her on the cheek and standing up, "Look before I go, if I don't make it out of there alive, go to this cemetery, I wrote the address on a piece of paper and handed it to Mary, its plot 316, find a Mrs. Cynthia Taylor, dig up the grave and inside the coffin with her are a few bags full of money. It's about five million dollars in there, take the money and the fifty in the safe and get as far away as possible and never look back." I gave Mary a strong hug before walking out of the door into the living room.

It was packed with all of Solomon's men who were gearing up and checking their weapons, ready for war. I put on a black tee shirt and a bullet proof vest on top of that, followed by a black hoodie. I made sure to put on my holster and added my trusty 9 mil, and .38 with two extra clips for both. I even grabbed my sawed-off for added protection. I only grabbed six extra shells because I planned on making it messy. The van was outside ready for us to go into action, I kissed my daughter one more time and said a silent prayer, asking the lord to watch over her, and protect her. Kane was in the doorway and came behind me as I was praying to hold her as well, knowing that this might be his last time to do so.

Luke and Lemon were already in the van and me and Kane pilled in next. The ride was tight and you could feel the nerves on everyone running high. But there was no doubt in my mind that we were all ready for this moment. We pulled up to the back of the club where a big buff security guard came walking towards the front of the van, "What up Nate." He said with a smile on his face, "What's good." Nate responded "I was instructed to help you guys set up." The security guard said walking towards the back, "Naw dog its good we got it." Nate tried to explain but it was too late, the guard already opened the back door of the van, his eyes grew wide when he saw me with the shotgun pointed at his head ready to take it off if need be. "Look fam, I know your scared and I'm not here to kill you, I want Percy and if that means I have to kill you to do it, then so be it." The guard just stood there with his hands in the air and his smile was replaced with a hard face trying to look unmoved. "So what's your plan?" The guard asked nervously, "How much are they paying you for this job?"

"Four hundred bucks"

"Not enough to get killed over right? Well look I have a thousand with your name on it, if you act as if you didn't even see us, and when we walk in you walk out, But trust me if you cross me, money will be the last thing you will be worried about." The guard nodded in agreement to my terms and walked back to his post at the backdoor. Mark and Nate went in with their equipment and got all set up, Solomon 7 sent me a text saying that his team was in position waiting on my word. Three hours past and the club was jumping, Music was loud and booming, the time came, as Mark came out to the back and told us that the meeting had started, it was about time because I didn't think Lemon could wait any longer. We filed out of the van one by one and walked into the backdoor, I gave the guard his money and he simply walked towards his motorcycle and drove off.

Once we got into the club the scene was everything but what we expected, there were girls and guys walking around half naked and liquor was flowing freely, the place was huge and without the inside connect, there would be no way to find out where the meeting was being held. Mark's girl came into the back where we were, and walked us to the room in the back of the building where the meeting had taken place. "Who the fuck are they?" One of the two guards said walking up to stop us from advancing further. I pushed the girl out of the way and struck him with the butt of my sawed-off knocking him to the ground and Luke pointed his M16 to the other stopping him from doing anything stupid. I picked the one I hit and forced him to open the door and pushed the both of them inside. "Knock, Knock motherfuckers! Everybody back the fuck up!" I shouted coming into the room. There was an eerie silence in the cramped room filled with smoke, Percy was standing at the end of the long table that was in the middle of the room, and there were people from all over standing around him, Kartoon Killa was off in the corner with King Jaffy Joker standing next to Percy holding a glass of something brown. "Decon what a pleasant surprise, we weren't expecting you this evening." Percy spoke with a smile in his southern accent. Luke stepped up a little closer holding his M16 and his eyes caught Percy's and they stood there staring at each other for a moment, "Wait a minute, is that little Luke I see?" Percy asked tilting his head in closer to get a better look. Luke and Lemon looked at him in aw trying to figure out how he knew his name. "Yes that's you, ha-ha can you believe that Joker, this little nigga is my son." Percy words sent chills down my spine, I knew the twins had a father that left them and moved to New York, but for it to be Percy this was a whole new level of shock. "What are you talking about ma'fucker?" Lemon asked walking a little closer to the table, the whole room was silent, and eyes were wide looking back and forth at the twins and Percy, to see if they can get a glimpse of resemblance. Percy stood there smiling and taking sips from his glass, "You must be Lemon, boy you grew up a lot since I last seen you ha-ha."

"Fuck you nigga!" Lemon said sternly "Now is that anyway to talk to your father boy? You must not know that I will kill you where you stand." Percy said with a devilish grin, Kane just stood there with his gun trained on the crowd waiting for anyone to make a move he didn't agree with. "Why? Why did you leave us?" Luke asked with a mixture of hurt and anger in is voice as if he was going through a ball of emotions. "Well son it was simple, I didn't want that bitch to get pregnant anyway so I left her with two black bastards and two hundred dollars."

"Watch your fuckin mouth!" Lemon yelled out after hearing how Percy was takin about their mother. "Your right, she wasn't my bitch she was my whore, and the nerve of this hoe to threaten me with going to the cops. She got what she deserved." Percy said sucking his teeth. He placed his glass down on the table and quickly drew out a chrome colt.45 with an ivory handle and let off a shot that ripped through Luke. Luke let out a yell and squeezed the trigger of his rifle sending wild bullets into the crowd of men and women hitting three people in front of him before he hit the floor. The sight of Percy's gun caught us off guard but Kane quickly bounced back shooting into the crowd towards Percy only to hit BG who jumped in the way last minute. Gun fire was now filling the room from all sides, I shot the shotgun into the security guard I hit earlier tearing through his back before I took cover behind the metal wall next to me, Lemon shot the other guard with his shotgun and fired another shot in Percy's direction hitting King Jaffy Joker in the chest knocking him on his back. Luke was still on the ground screaming in pain but still firing his automatic rifle cutting down anyone in his path. I reloaded my sawn-off and fired twice hitting some random guy shredding the right side of his face, Kane was right with me firing off his Mac10 until it jammed on him. There were bullets flying everywhere, companied with screams that erupted in the main dance area. People were running out of a side door into the main area, I noticed Percy and Kartoon Killa getting away, I grabbed my phone and went to press the speed dial number for Solomon 7 when I heard "RESPECT THE MOTHERFUCKIN NATION BITCH!!!" Solomon7 was already inside from the front with his army dropping bodies left and right. The meeting room was clearing out with a few shooters ducking our rounds and firing back at us to keep us at bay until they had room to escape, but Lemon made sure that they regretted that choice once they turned to exit out of the door.

Kane emerged with two twin glocks in each hand raining death into the panicked crowd on the main dance floor. I was behind him this time with my two pistols dashing bullets as they flew past my head, one round grazed my head as I slipped on a spilled drink ricocheting off the metal wall behind me. When I was down I spotted Nate and Mark going out the backdoor, knowing that they were out of the way I had nothing to worry about but myself. In the commotion I saw Percy leaving out of a fire escape Kartoon got caught in the mix of bodies trying to go out of the same door. I let off two shoots in his direction, one hit his thigh and the other went through the head of one of the naked strippers who was caught in the wrong place at the wrong time. Lemon kept firing until he was out of bullets in his shotgun, he quickly dropped the empty gun and pulled out a .38 and fired as he went back in the room where Luke was still laying down in.

Kane was now conducting hand to hand combat with a few men, he looked overwhelmed going against seven men by himself, but Kane wasn't the average man, he caught one guy's punch and grabbed his throat pulling out his esophagus with one swift motion, another tried to hit him from behind, but he threw a kick into his balls, and before the guy could drop to his knees he ripped his eyes out with his fingers. After his two victims, he was on to the next putting them down with similar fates. I made it to where Kartoon was trying to escape out of the door. Sliding on the floor bleeding badly from his thigh where the bullet went through and shattered his femur. I shot him again in the middle of his back causing him to let out an ungodly scream. I flipped him over with my foot and shot him in both knees, "This is for the Kingdom." Those were the last words he spoke before I put two holes in his head splitting it open spraying blood and brain matter all over myself and the dance floor.

Police sirens were screaming up towards us with a few helicopters flying in the distance. "WE GOTTA GO!" I yelled out, Solomon 7 and his army took off out the front and I ran towards the backroom to get Lemon and Luke. Kane was bloody and breathing heavy killing his last adversary. "Get the hell out of here!" he yelled out at me making his way to the middle of the dance floor flooded with blood and bodies all stretched out, he took off his shirt and vest as he stood with his arms stretched out as if he was waiting for more people to fight. I ran to the back and found Lemon picking Luke up who was bleeding badly from the right side of his chest. We both walked him out of the back door and into the van with Mark and Nate, and took off leaving Kane to take the fall.

"Yo dog we need to get him to a hospital now." Lemon said putting pressure over Luke's wound, "I can't be...be... believe that nigga sh...sh... shhhhh... SHOT me!" Luke stuttered out wrenching in pain, blood was spewing out everywhere and I knew that Luke's chances were looking very slim. I kept cursing myself for not being on point with Percy as he pulled out his gun so smoothly, and on top of that he escaped with no traces of him. Luke battled the desire to close his eyes, and when he began to slip Lemon slapped him in the face to keep him up.

We made it to a hospital in Midtown and let the twins out with Mark, I couldn't be there given the fact that I was still the most wanted man in New York. Once the three of them were in the hospital Nate peeled off into traffic heading back towards the apartment. Once we arrived I received a text from Solomon 7 telling me that all of his men made it alive and are safe back in the hood, I was happy to have him in my corner and from the looks of everything the Nation was in motion to take over where the Kingdom left off. Nate came with me up into the apartment, Heaven was sleep in the bed and Mary was in the kitchen making tea. "Where's Luke and Lemon?"

Mary asked with a face full of concern "They had to go to the hospital with Mark, Luke got shot by Percy, who we found out was the twins father." The news was new to both Mary and Nate which left them both speechless.

I walked towards the T.V. and turned it on to the nightly news. "Bob, I have to tell ya, this scene is one for the ages, and it is a blood bath out here in front of the newly reopened club called the Tombs. The police have this place sealed off and we don't have much information at this time but what we can tell you from the amount of bodies coming out of there, it's not looking good." The reporter said as she reported from on the scene. "We have just been informed that amongst the dead is detective Juan Ramos, he has been murdered execution style, and this has to be the most tragic event to happen since 9/11." The reporter continued to go in depth of the famous drug dealers, and music artist that died that night, she mentioned that some were still alive and others were wounded badly, but what I was waiting for couldn't come fast enough. The reporter and cameraman turned their attention to the first detective on the scene, detective Brain Smith stepped out in a swarm of reporters as he began to give an update of what was discovered at the crime scene. "What has happened tonight is nothing ever seen before in our great city, we are still conducting our investigation, but what I can say is that we arrested a suspect on the scene and we have brought him in for questioning, that is all." Reporters' fought hard to get more information from Smith, but that was all I needed to hear to know that Kane was ok and he had taken the heat as planned.

About three weeks passed since the shootout at the Tombs, Luke was out of the hospital after two days in a coma, and he was recovering back at the apartment. Solomon 7 searched the streets for days looking for Percy, but he was long gone without any trace. The trial for Kane began last week and he was found guilty of the shootout, and all the crimes that were committed around the city, He was labeled as "New York's notorious terrorist. He was seen as an anti-hero to some and others wanted him to die for the crimes that were committed, detective Smith presented his evidence of Juan "Kartoon Killa" Ramos involvement in the terroristic events and as Kane's accomplice. He even managed to spin his mysterious disappearance on Kartoon Killa, stating that he set up the invasion and kidnapping. The judge despite her personal feelings towards the case saw that Kane spent life without parole in Attica correctional facility. My name was cleared as being the scapegoat for the police department, it was said that I was one of Kartoon's informants who turned him over to detective Smith, and this gave Smith a boost in his career with a first page feature in the New York Times. Mark and Nate "The West Indy Connection" got a record deal that magnified their reputation and sent them on their road to stardom.

The Kingdom was defeated and all of their operations have been stopped, the city went into a "House Cleaning" of the department, locking up corrupted officers, and correctional officers who had been on Percy's payroll. This particular day I felt as if I was free but I was still uneasy about not knowing where Percy was laying his head. I figured by this time he was long gone and on some island laughing at the events as they unfolded from the case. Natural order was restored and life went on but I knew deep in my heart that I wouldn't truly feel free until I left New York and it was at that moment I decided to take a permanent vacation from hell.

Chapter 33

Freedom

The night air was chilly and struck deep into my bones causing me to pull the string on my hoodie even tighter to conceal my body heat. I was with Lemon when we walked the concreate walkway flooded with dead leaves, trees lined against it bare and eerie looking. We made it to plot 316 and found Cynthia Taylor's tombstone, "How you doing old friend? I want to thank you for keeping my money safe in case of a rainy day." I said talking to the tombstone before we went to work, digging up the grave and opening the casket retrieving the duffle bags that were floating in water. I opened them up to find that my airtight bags were safe and they were full of money that totaled around five million. Once we covered the hole and left the cemetery, we headed back to the apartment to go through the bags. I split the money up from the bags and the money that was in the safe which totaled out to be around fifty-five million. I gave five million to Solomon 7 for helping me out, "Now were even." I said jokingly "We've always been even god." He said accepting the money and smiling. I put fifteen million in a bag for myself and Mary for our escape, five million was set aside for Kane's books in case he needed anything. I sent a million to both Empress and S-Dot, and gave the rest to Lemon and Luke, who decided to stay in New York and establish themselves there, sorta like a fresh start for the both of them.

The next day I bordered a private plane with Mary and Heaven and headed off towards Puerto Rico. I bought an apartment complex on the coast line of Carolina and that's where my sister and I decided to call home having adjacent penthouses with a gorgeous view of the ocean. "Wow that sounds like a dream come true." The young man said with wide eyes and a smile just as big. "Yea that was all five years ago, and now hear we are living our quiet lives on this beautiful island. So tell me kid what was your name again?"

"Tariq, Tariq Martin."

"Yea, please forgive me, I tend to forget from time to time." Decon lied; in fact he just wasn't paying attention at first. "So let me ask you something." Decon said to Tariq, who was getting up from the beach chair he was sitting in, "Yea shoot away, ha-ha no pun intended." Decon laughed at the unintentional joke Tariq made, "How did you find me, and how did you know who I was?" Decon asked curiously, "I'm a journalist student at Colombia university, and my cousin put me on to your story and I wanted to know if it was really fact or fiction. I'm doing a paper on the New York street history and I wanted to be different from the rest of my class." Decon smiled at the kid who was standing in front of him and thought back to how he was hungry for knowledge, but this kid was going to make a difference like him but in a positive way. "That's what's up kid, who's your cousin?"

"His name is Isaac, he told me that he was in Rikers, when Kane came through before he was sent up north. He said that your father was a legend and well respected by a lot of the old heads in there. But I found out where you were from your cousin Lemon, I did a story on black business and I featured his security firm. He is a cool dude, scary but very cool once you get him in a good mood."

"Yea, that sounds like him ha-ha." Decon said chuckling to himself.

As Tariq walked off into the distance, A tall beautiful women with soft brown skin, and green and brown eyes came walking up from the beach waters with a little girl with wild curly brown hair that was in a frizzy afro. Her skin color was that of butterscotch and her eyes matched the woman she was skipping next to. The smile she wore was bright and put a similar one on Decon's face. "Hey Sis" Decon said standing up and stretching out his limbs, "Hey baby girl! How was the water?"

"It was warm daddy, you should come in with us, Auntie Mimi can swim really good." Heaven said bouncing right into her father's arms. "How was the interview?" Mary asked looking in the direction Tariq walked off too. "It was good, he said he interviewed Lemon on his business, and he was curious about the stories of the infamous Kingdom."

"Wow he came all this way for a story, that's dedication." The air was filled with a light breeze that carried a strong stench of a roasted pork being made at the hotel restaurant that was buzzing with people. "Y'all hungry?" Decon asked out loud, Heaven was jumping up and down in Decon arms almost falling out, "I am...I am, can we get Piraguas?

"Ha-ha not right now baby later tonight we can get some." Decon said with a smile placing Heaven down on the floor and gathering his things. "Let's go inside and clean up before we go out to dinner."

Epilog

Three weeks later...

Heaven was running around on the beach chasing pigeons and seagulls, when a slender man with a silky gray hair laid back as if he was back in the 70's era. He was wearing a white linen suit with matching snake skin boat shoes that looked too expensive to be worn on the beach. His shirt was half way buttoned showing off his smooth olive skin tone that was darken from his time on the beach. On his face wore a charming smile that complemented his features, he was stunning to say the least and didn't look like he had aged since his late twenties. "Hey pretty girl" The light skinned man said with a smooth silky voice that held a strong southern twang. "Hi!" Heaven said looking up at the man in front of her with a huge smile on her face. "Where are you parents?"

"They are inside." Heaven pointed towards the

apartment complex, "Oh, so you are out here by yourself?"

"Yea, just playing with the birds."

"Okay! Can I play with you?"

"Sure!!!" Heaven said smiling even harder. The two of them chased the birds around and laughed for about ten minutes when the man fell down breathing heavily, Heaven was breathing heavy as well and stopped playing to help the man up. "Hey pretty girl what's your name?"

'My name is Heaven!"

"That is a very pretty name Heaven, my name is Percy." Percy said extending his hand to her. Heaven shook his hand and smiled gleefully, the soft tender touch of her hands in his made Percy get excited and caused his heart to flutter in his chest. His body was tingling all over from the excitement he had built up in his system ready to explode, but he controlled himself and regain his composer. "Say Heaven, would you like to get some piraguas with me?"

"Yes!! I love piraguas, especially the pineapple kind."

"Really? That's my favorite to." Percy said as he got up off of the sandy ground and dusted off his pants.

The two of them walked hand and hand over to the shaved ice kiosk and ordered their treats. The hot weather made it a perfect day for the frozen treats, Heaven smiled playfully sucking off the Pineapple syrup from the compact ice in the little plastic cups. Percy watched her lick the icee with predatory eyes, and couldn't stop himself from thinking about all the lustful things he would do to the beautiful little girl. It was disgusting to think that a grown man with the features and the ability to have any grown woman he wanted, prime himself to desire the young flesh of a child. But Percy had a strong desire for young girls and he planned on acting on his urges. "Hey Heaven it's hot out here, would you like to go to my room and watch cartoons with me?"

"I don't know if I should, my parents would be upset with me if I left the beach." Heaven said licking the syrup off that dripped down her wrist. "It won't be but a second, I promise. I just want to check on my puppy real quick, but if you don't want to I will be back after I check up on her." Percy said with a disappointed look on his face. The temptation to play with a puppy danced circles inside of Heaven's head, "I want to see the puppy!" Heaven said almost dropping her frozen treat on the floor, "Come on, her name is lizzy you'll love her." Percy said extending his hand to Heaven, she took his hand and the two of them made their way to the hotel next to her apartment building.

As the two of them walked away from the piragua seller, he pulled out his cell phone and placed a call, still watching the pair walking off. "Si, they just walked off." The vendor said before hanging up.

As they entered the elevator Percy placed his card key into the slot allowing him to press the button for the penthouse floor. They made it to the top level of the hotel and walked down the large hall way towards Percy's room at the end of the hall. They walked past a maid cleaning some room and as Percy looked over to her, she slowly lowered her head to where he couldn't see her face. Something about the maid gave him a feeling of recognition but the excitement he had from being steps away to fill his desires caused him to wave it off. They stopped in front of the large ebony door and Percy inserted his card key unlocking it, "I don't hear the puppy" Heaven said putting her ear to the door "That's because she's sleeping." Percy said with a wink and a smile.

They walked into the open door that opened up to a large living room fitted with a black leather wrap around couch against the snake skin wall and a full-sized kitchen. There was a full bathroom on the right and a huge entertainment center in the middle of the living room. In the front was a large sliding glass door that led to the balcony overlooking the beach and a beautiful view of the ocean and parts of the city. There were two rooms to the left of the kitchen that were closed; Percy placed the chain lock on the door and walked into the kitchen. "Where is Lizzy?" Heaven asked "Who?"

"Your puppy." Heaven said looking up to Percy who looked confused, "Oh yeaaa, the puppy ha-ha, she is in the bathroom so she didn't make a mess in the room." Percy explained "How about you sit on the couch over there and I will go get her for you." Percy lied, in fact he was going into the bathroom to grab a bottle of sedatives he had, to knock Heaven out. Heaven walked over to the couch and sat down in front of the T.V. and waited for Percy to come out.

Percy walked into the bathroom and stopped short of the doorway when his eyes widen to the sight of a black glock .45 tailored with a silver silencer. "Decon!!!"

"Hello Percy, looking for this" Decon said holding up the glass bottle of liquid horse sedatives Percy was going to get. "Heaven baby are you ok?"

"Yes daddy." Heaven said looking at her father holding Percy at gun point. "Well, well, well isn't this a pleasant surprise we have here. You know for a minute I didn't think I would ever see you again, let alone find you wondering the very streets I call home." Decon said flashing Percy a sinister grin, the sound of someone knocking at the front door caught Percy's attention, he was frantic and knew his life was going to end tonight, and he had only hoped that the hotel security saw Decon break into the room and they were at the door waiting to save him. "Were you expecting company?" Decon asked sarcastically already knowing the answer to his question, "of course you weren't, why would you be right?" Percy just stared into Decon's eyes pleading for mercy on his life.

"Go on, remove the chain and walk into the kitchen." Decon instructed, Percy complied and removed the chain lock, and walked into the kitchen. The front door opened from the outside and in came a house maid, "Housekeeping!" the woman shouted as she walked into the room with her head down low, but Percy was caught by yet another surprise when he saw the woman's face as she lifted her head for him to see. "Judging by the stupid look on your face I'm guessing you two know each other."

"Hello Percy." Mary said as she pulled a chrome .38 special from under her maid uniform. "How did ..."

"We find you?" Decon said cutting Percy off, "Well it was all quite simple sir, as I stated before I didn't think I was gonna ever find your ass, but once you touched down on the island and word got around that an outsider was making major moves out here, I had to find out who. And when I laid my eyes on you walking out of this hotel and getting in the cab with that beautiful call girl, I almost thought I was dreaming. My blood boiled at the sight and I wanted to kill you right then and there, but I figured I get you alone and knowing your perverted ass I used my daughter to draw you in as bait." Decon smiled and chuckled slightly as he explained how they got to this point, "I asked my security friend at the front desk which room you bought out and seeing that he owed me more than a few favors, getting your information was easy. So when you went out to explore the beach I made my move, got a key to your room and set up my high caliber sniper rifle and watched your movements. Decon pointed to the large rifle in the corner of the outside balcony. My daughter well she was well protected, I was up here watching and that cab driver in front of the building, he is a part of my team as well as the piraguas man you paid your money to."

Percy's eyes were starting to glass over and he was searching secretly for something behind his back under the counter. "You're looking for this?" Decon said pulling out Percy's colt .45 from behind his back, "This is the same gun you shot your son Luke with right?"

"Decon look, we can work something out."

"The time for working this out are long past overdue, your life ends today Percy and that's just the way it is." Decon said almost poetically. "Decon it's time." Mary said pointing to the clock on the wall, "Yea so let's do this, Heaven go into the bathroom and close your eyes and cover your ears, daddy has to kill the boogieman." Heaven got up and ran into the bathroom closing the door behind her, Mary stepped forward "This is for killing my boyfriend." Mary closed her eyes and squeezed the trigger, **Click**. The gun didn't go off and she pulled the trigger again, yet nothing happened, "I didn't put any bullets into your clip" Decon started still keeping his focus on Percy "You're too pure to walk this path with me and I intend on keeping it that way, only a monster can kill another." Decon said sending five silent shots whispering into Percy's face and chest releasing him from this world. Percy's body did a little dance as the bullets went through his body, he was down and bleeding from his chest and brain matter all over the kitchen counter top.

Decon walked closer to Percy and sent one more round into the limp corpse "For the Kingdom!"

Made in the USA
Columbia, SC
19 August 2018